# ACCLAIM FOR DEBORAH BEDFORD'S
## *A MORNING LIKE THIS*

"I finished A MORNING LIKE THIS with tears in my eyes and hope in my heart. Deborah Bedford reminds us that nothing is too hard for God, no heartache is beyond the reach of His comforting, healing hand."
**—Deborah Raney, author of *Beneath a Southern Sky***

"Deborah Bedford once again shines light into hidden corners of the human heart and shows us how God wants to heal our hurts—even hurts caused by our own sin."
**—Robin Lee Hatcher, author of *Firstborn***

"Real problems . . . real faith . . . and a God who gives songs in the night. A MORNING LIKE THIS reminds us all that we can do more than just 'grin and bear it.' We can overwhelmingly conquer."
**—Stephanie Grace Whitson, author of *Heart of the Sandhills***

"Gracefully written, compelling and thoughtful, A MORNING LIKE THIS is a true testimony to God's grace and forgiveness. With compassion and insight, Bedford deals with sin and its consequences and gives us another glimpse of God's love and mercy."
**—Lisa Samson, author of *The Church Ladies***

*more . . .*

# ...AND FOR A ROSE BY THE DOOR

"A story of relinquishment, reconciliation, and grace . . . grabs the reader by the heart and doesn't let go."
—**Debbie Macomber, author of _Ready for Love_**

"A compelling page-turner and a surefire winner from Deborah Bedford."
—**Karen Kingsbury, author of _A Time to Dance_**

"If you love having your heart touched and you delight in surprise, A ROSE BY THE DOOR is for you."
—**Gayle Roper, author of _Spring Rain_**

"A poignant novel that is impossible to put down."
—**Carolyn Zane, author of _The Coltons_**

"Heartwarming . . . Bedford's poignant tale will find a home in all collections."    —**_Library Journal_**

"It takes a special kind of author who can pen words such as the ones found within A ROSE BY THE DOOR. . . . You won't be able to put this one down."
—**_Christian Retailing_**

# A MORNING LIKE THIS

## DEBORAH BEDFORD

Warner Faith

**WARNER BOOKS**

An AOL Time Warner Company

Scripture quotations except those noted below are taken from the HOLY BIBLE: NEW INTERNATIONAL VERSION®. Copyright © 1973, 1978, 1984 by International Bible Society. Used by permission of Zondervan Publishing House. All rights reserved.

Scripture quotations on pages ix, 21, and 117 are taken from the *Holy Bible*, New Living Translation, © copyright 1996. Used by permission of Tyndale House Publishers, Inc. Wheaton, Illinois 60189. All rights reserved.

Published in association with the literary agency Alive Communications, Inc., 7680 Goddard Street #200, Colorado Springs, CO 80920

Warner Books, Inc., 1271 Avenue of the Americas, New York, NY 10020
Visit our Web site at *www.twbookmark.com.*

An AOL Time Warner Company

Printed in the United States of America
First Warner Books printing: September 2002
10  9  8  7  6  5  4  3  2  1

**Library of Congress Cataloging-in-Publication Data**

Bedford, Deborah.
    A morning like this / Deborah Bedford.
      p. cm.
    ISBN: 0-446-67788-4
    1. Bone marrow—Transplantation—Fiction.  2. Illegitimate children—Fiction.  3. Sick children—Fiction.  4. Adultery—Fiction.  I. Title.
PS3602.E34 M67 2002
813'.6—dc21                             2002069157

*Book design by Giorgetta Bell McRee*
*Cover design by Frank Accornero*

To all whose marriages have run aground,
who search for treasure amidst the rubble.

To those who search for safety and shelter
but do not know it by name.

# *Acknowledgments*

To Bill Bunting and Amy Bunting Storrie, my two cousins who shared bone marrow and the gift of life. I'm so sorry, Bill, that you are a boy and couldn't be inducted into The Cousin Club. I love you dearly anyway.

To Katharine Conover, Executive Director of the Community Safety Network in Jackson Hole, for all the time you've given, the questions you've been willing to answer, the stories you've been able to share, and your passion for sheltering women who have nowhere else to turn.

To Sherrie Lord and to Barbara Campbell, whose days of fun and escape have become precious gifts from the Lord. This book would never be what it is without your thoughtful editorial comments, your laughter and, above all, your prayers. You have lifted me up as your sister in Christ, and have held me high. I can never repay what I owe you.

To my family at Warner, Rolf Zettersten, Jamie Raab, Leslie Peterson, Elizabeth Marshall, Andrea Davis, Preston Cannon, and Kathie Johnson, for your enthusiasm and your belief in me. Thank you for running the race beside me. I count it all joy! Together, we offer up this work of our hearts and our hands to the Lord.

To Peter and Natalie Stewart, Megan and Eddie, for letting me borrow Brewster.

To Margaruitte and Bob Cornell, for your fiftieth wedding anniversary celebration, even though you *did* threaten to terrorize us on our wedding night.

To Judy Basye, Director of Oncology at St. John's Hospital, for your willing heart and for all the lives you've touched here in Jackson Hole. This book would not be what it is without your research, insight, and advice. This town would not be what it is without your healing touch.

To my beloved family at the Jackson Hole Christian Center, to whom I am accountable and whom I love dearly, with sincere apologies to members of the presbytery committee, who work diligently.

To Kathryn Helmers, Agent 007, who stands beside me and makes me brave. You are proof that good things, when relinquished into the hand of the Master, reappear as rich treasure in our lives. Thank you for helping me cross into safety.

To Pam Micca, friend and counselor, for making me float Flat Creek with you, and for making me walk barefoot across the thistle pasture when my tube got sucked underwater.

To Joyce Bunting, my aunt, who was willing to share her heart.

To Lisa, who first made The Bunnery a wonderful place to write.

Finally, to K. and S., for your unfailing, honest faith in the Father, for standing on truth when everything else wobbled around you. It is because of your lives, because I've seen the miracle, that I can write this story with great boldness.

The LORD is a shelter for the oppressed,
a refuge in times of trouble.
Those who know your name trust in you,
for you, O LORD, have never abandoned
anyone who searches for you.

*Psalm 9:9-10*

We all agree that forgiveness is a beautiful idea until we have to practice it.

—C. S. Lewis

# Chapter One

They sat together at their favorite corner table, two of them alone, absorbed in the candlelight and in each other. He toyed with the dinner knife that lay beside his hand, his eyebrows raised, gazing at her face. She leaned toward him and smiled, her elbow on the table, her chin propped inside the chalice of her palm. Her dainty gold bracelet caught high on her wrist and dangled there.

"I don't know why they won't let Braden pitch," she said. "All he needs is a little confidence. If the coach would just be willing to work with him a little more."

David laughed.

"What? Why are you laughing at me?"

"Abby. Braden can hit, but he's probably never going to be a pitcher. He throws about as straight as a jackrabbit runs."

"He could *do* it."

David Treasure reached across the table and laid his fingers across his wife's wrist, giving her his habitual, half-amused grin. "I thought we agreed that tonight we wouldn't talk about kids."

"I can't help it, David. I'm his mother. What do you

think? I see everything he *ought* to be able to do, and I
don't know why he's not doing it."

"I think you're beautiful when you're all wrapped up
in being a mother. That's what I think."

She laughed at him then, and felt her earrings dancing like two tiny birdcages against her earlobes. She
sighed and shook her arm and her bracelet toppled from
her wrist to her forearm. "Okay. You're right. We *did*
promise each other, didn't we?"

"Yes."

"So we'll talk about something else. Anything else."
She paused. "Something." She cast about to change the
subject. "How about my new little black dress?"

"I like your new little black dress just fine." He shot
her a learing look, raised his eyebrows at her. "I'd like
you even better—"

"David!"

He grinned at her, the expression in his eyes as unguarded and as open as a schoolboy's. "You wanted to
know what I was thinking, didn't you?"

"Okay. You're right. I left myself open for that one."

"You did." He grinned and lifted his water glass,
holding it high so the ice glistened in the candlelight.
"Happy Anniversary. Just think what we were doing
twelve years ago right now."

"Twelve years," Abigail said. "It doesn't seem possible. We were probably walking down the aisle right
about now."

"Well, no." He checked his watch. "It's three hours
past that. I was thinking what happens *after* the wedding."

"David!"

He crossed his arms and laughed and leaned back in

his chair, his blue eyes mischievous. "Well, you said you wanted tonight to be romantic."

"That isn't *romance*. That's . . . that's . . ."

"I'm a man, Abby. That's romance."

"Don't lean so far back in your chair. You'll fall over and the waiter will have to pick you up."

He raised his eyebrows and righted his chair.

"To twelve years as Mrs. David Treasure," she said, lifting her glass. "Hear. Hear."

David raised his goblet, too, clicked it against hers, and set it down. He squared his shoulders and eyed her for a long moment, the sudden stretch of silence an uncommon thing between them. "You're the best thing that has ever happened to me," he said, reaching across the table and, in a sure sign of possession, gripping both of her wrists. "I want you to know that."

After all these years, the shape of his hands could still stir her. His broad fingers. His powerful, square knuckles. The dusting of blond hair on his arm, showing between the cuff of his shirtsleeve and the band of his watch.

She raised her eyes to his, touched her stomach where the warmth began . . . and blushed.

He grinned and leaned back in his chair.

Anyone watching could see by the relaxed way they chatted, by the way their laughter came in short, sharp bursts, that this wasn't the celebration of new romance. They celebrated an old, strong love. Conviction and commitment had been tempered by the test of time.

The waiter brought around a cake with "Happy Anniversary" scripted in pink-sugar icing. When Abigail cut David a piece and licked the knife, he inclined across the table and kissed her.

"No fair. You always figure out ways to get more icing."

Only a few people recognized them as they rose to leave the restaurant; it was summertime and they'd reserved a late table at the Rendezvous Bistro to avoid the tourist crowd. But the friends who did see them here in the newest, classiest eatery in the valley didn't let them pass without hailing them from across the room.

"Heard about your anniversary on KSGT this morning. That radio morning calendar keeps me up to date on everybody in town."

"Hey, Treasures. Congratulations, you two."

"Heard Braden's pitching's getting better this summer. Great kid you've got there."

"Thank you." "Hello." "Good to see you," Abigail and David repeated half a dozen times on their way out the door. David hurried down the front walk of the restaurant to bring around their Suburban while Abigail carried the white box with extra cake.

"Are you tired?" Abigail asked when he yawned on the drive.

"Yeah. Boring, huh? I'm an old married man these days, anxious to get home."

"Just as long as you're going to the same home I'm going to, we don't have anything to worry about."

When they parked in front of their own house twenty minutes later, lamps shone in every window except Braden's. Abigail grabbed her purse from where it lay beside her on the seat.

"I don't know why she can't turn some of the lights off after she gets him into bed."

"She's young. Probably still afraid of the dark herself."

But everything seemed fine when the babysitter let them inside the front foyer. Brewster, their black Labrador, met them with delirious happiness in the hall.

"Everything all right?" Abigail surveyed the living room, making sure all was right in the Treasure territory. "No problems or anything?"

The teenaged sitter examined the scuffed toes of her clogs as if trying to decide whether or not to tell them the whole story. "Not any problems, really. Except Braden wouldn't go to sleep when I told him to and he kept jumping on the bed. He said he was practicing pitching wind-ups."

"I'll have a talk with that young man tomorrow."

"He threw the ball sideways and it hit the shelf and made his lamp fall off. It crunched a big hole in the lampshade. I'm really sorry."

David draped his arm around Abigail's shoulders. "To think that only an hour ago his mother was saying she wanted him to get more practice."

The babysitter picked up her backpack before she turned back to tell them something else. "Oh, and some lady called and left a message on the machine. I didn't answer it. I just listened to make sure it wasn't you needing anything."

David handed her a twenty and a five—hefty pay for four hours of babysitting these days, but Abigail had encouraged it coming home in the car. Crystal was good and they both wanted to keep her. "You ready to? I'll take you home."

"Sure. Thanks."

Abigail waved them off and smiled to herself as she locked the door behind them.

Well.

*Well.*

David had certainly been in a hurry to get rid of the babysitter.

She padded into their bedroom, eased her sandal straps off of her ankles with her opposite feet, kicked her shoes halfway across the room, and wiggled her toes in the carpet. She assessed herself in the mirror for a moment before she peeled the spaghetti straps from her shoulders and laid the new dress over a chair. Once she'd slipped into her fancy nightgown and robe, she prowled, telling herself she ought to wander through the kitchen to turn lights off. Which of course was only an excuse to snitch another bite of cake.

In the kitchen, she licked icing off her fingers and stared at the blinking light on the phone machine.

Hm-mmm. She should listen. She ought to check and see who'd called.

But just then she heard the door, the click of her husband's key in the lock. He'd scarcely made it inside before he drew Abigail against him and kissed her.

"Let's check on Braden," she whispered against his chin. Before she gave herself to her husband, she wanted to make certain all was right within the circle of her heart and her home. She took his hand, leading him up the hallway to their son's room with its fancy lodge-pole pine bed, Ralph Lauren curtains, and Elks baseball cap dangling from the chair. David crossed his arms over his chest and there they stood in the doorway, mother and father shoulder to shoulder, looking at the little blond head on the pillow. Each of them was thinking how this time together had been good for them. Sometimes being busy with children and jobs and everyday life could make a husband and wife forget how to complete a sentence when they were alone. Every time they went out they had the chance to start over.

Braden had fallen asleep with his head cradled in his baseball glove. David released Abigail's hand long enough to slip into the semidarkness and wriggle the battered leather from beneath his son's cheek. "Hey, sport."

The movement roused Braden, who rolled over and squinted his eyes open.

"Dad." Nothing more. Just the name. Just the word that meant everything. *Dad.* Two arms shot out of the blankets and tangled around David's neck, pulling him low against the pillow as Abigail watched with a weight of gratitude growing heavy in her chest. Her two boys, David and Braden. They meant the world to each other . . . and to her.

*Lord, when I trust you, I can trust everything around me. You've given me everything I ever wanted, right here.*

David readjusted the blankets beneath his son's chin and kissed Braden on the forehead. "Love you, Brade."

"Crystal wouldn't let me practice my pitches," Braden mumbled, still half asleep.

"She told us. We're going to have to work out something about your lamp, you know. You'll have to do a few chores and earn money."

"Did you have fun?"

"Yes. It was very romantic. Your mother wore a new dress and made me feel special."

"G'night, Dad."

"Good night, son."

*Lord, thank you for keeping us secure.*

Braden burrowed his face deep into his pillow and his baseball mitt again, his eyelids closed. Abigail said in a hushed tone, "Ah, he's fine, isn't he?" She leaned her head against her husband's shoulder. "I just wanted to make sure. Do you have any idea how much I love seeing you two together?"

"Well, Mrs. Treasure. You've seen everything you need to see, haven't you?" He cupped his fingers around wisps of her hair. "Maybe we ought to finish what we've started."

"Maybe," she echoed, and this time she couldn't help smiling as David took her by the hand and led her where he wanted. As they passed through the kitchen, though, the blinking light on their answering machine distracted him. He stopped for a moment and stared at it.

"That can wait, can't it? With all the things that go on around this place, can't one of them wait until morning?"

"Exactly what I was thinking."

"A girl after my own heart."

"I *am* after your heart. And I think I know just how to get it."

"Hm-m-mm."

Abigail followed her husband into the bedroom that they'd shared since exchanging wedding vows a dozen years ago tonight. Through the open window she could hear the coyotes yipping and the lilting music of Fish Creek and the hiss of night breeze like rain, moving through pine boughs and cottonwood leaves.

"Love you." Abigail nuzzled the words against his ear. "Nothing will ever change that, David. Ever."

"You mean that?"

"Yeah."

"You promise?"

"I *do* promise. That's an easy promise to make."

"You sure?"

"I *am* sure," she answered without hesitating, her voice reflecting all the fervency of her faith in her God and in her husband.

But in the next room, the answering machine waited, the flashing light relentless as it flickered red against the microwave, the dishwasher door, the chrome faucet, against every shiny surface in the kitchen.

Blink. Blink. Pause.

Blink. Blink. Pause.

All through the night.

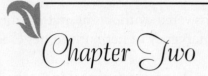

# Chapter Two

Brewster, the Labrador retriever, never let David Treasure sleep in past six-thirty. With dog breath pungent enough to awaken dead things, he would sidle along David's edge of the bed and flop sideways, eighty-five pounds of compact weight jostling the mattress. When that didn't work, the dog would shake his ears. He would pant. He would sink back to the floor with one extended, wretched groan. He would rise on his haunches again. When David rolled over and squinted at the clock, trying to protect his face beneath the covers, the licking would begin.

"Okay, boy. Okay," David objected every morning, although never so loud as to awaken Abigail. "I'm getting up. You win again."

This morning, as every morning, David yanked on a pair of baggy gray sweatpants that had seen better days, tugged on a faded OLD BILL'S FUN RUN T-shirt, turned on the coffee to brew, and, without being completely lucid, started out with the dog for a jog.

Even during the summer months in the mountains, at this altitude they could have a hard freeze during the night. The trail David now followed was crisp with frost, already melting away where the sun hit it, the shape of shadows still encased in ice. He left crushed prints behind him as he ran, a faultless marking of his footfalls where he followed the path along Fish Creek. Above him, early sun from the east had begun to paint the pleats and folds of the mountains, the sheer, chaste light of alpenglow spotlighting the hillsides in an ever-changing wash of gold and pink.

For a little while at least, the morning belonged only to David.

He could hear wind chimes singing from several patios as he passed. Farther along he saw his neighbor doing some early fly-fishing in the stream. The man waved briefly before going back to his casting. The sun glanced off the line with each arc he made, the tiny mayfly landing with precision upon quiet water. "Morning, David!"

"Morning, Joe! Having any luck?"

"I guess I should have stayed in bed. I think the fish are still asleep."

David slowed his long strides and turned toward home; he'd do well to leave time for a shower and a shave. Back he headed along the stream, past patios with cedar hot tubs and pretty wrought-iron gates. His feet pounded a hollow beat in syncopation with the clacking of Brewster's toenails as they crossed the rickety wooden footbridge together. As he trod quietly into his house, reluctant to awaken Abigail or Braden, he spied the cake box waiting on the counter. It made sense, didn't it? After working off those calories, he would eat cake for breakfast.

He'd taken two huge bites when he noticed the

flashing message light. Without thinking much of it, he pushed the play button.

David couldn't explain why the fear came. He knew something was wrong the moment he heard the clicking connection and the empty whirring, someone hesitating on the end of the line. He stopped chewing. For what seemed an eternity, no one spoke. Then, brittle, businesslike, a woman said, "Hello, David. This is Susan Roche."

*Susan Roche.*

For a moment he couldn't place the name. He started chewing again.

Then stopped chewing for the second time.

Oh. *That* Susan Roche.

The message continued. "I'm staying at The Elk Country Inn."

*Elk Country Inn? Susan? In Jackson Hole?*

"Would you return my call as soon as you can?" And then, softly, "It's imperative, David. *Please.*"

Her careful voice went on to dictate a number, but David didn't write it down. He stared at the machine, his anger growing. He turned it off before she even finished the sentence.

*How dare she do something like this?*

The slice of anniversary cake sat abandoned on the counter with two huge chomps taken out of it. Brewster stood over his bowl, panting, waiting to be served from the forty-pound bag that listed to one side in the corner. And David Treasure looked up to see his face reflected in the toaster beside him, his features mirrored and distorted in the dents of stainless steel. It was someone else's face, someone who didn't look at all like him.

*After so many years, how dare she turn up in Jackson and call me at my house?*

He fumbled for the delete button on the answering machine. The motion, which he made several times daily, evaded him now. Which button did he push? That one? *No.* This one?

He hit the wrong button and the message began to repeat. "Hello, David. This is Susan Roche." It sounded louder the second time. In desperation, David found the button marked DELETE and punched it hard.

*"Deleting. Deleting,"* said the liquid crystal display.

The blinking red light stopped just as Braden came barefoot into the room. David reeled away from the phone machine. "Hey, sport," he said and in his own ears his voice sounded too booming, too cheery.

Braden opened the cabinet and pulled out a box of Honeycomb cereal. "Morning, Dad." He stood on tiptoe and rattled the stack of dishes, trying to pull out a bowl.

"Here." David reached over the boy's head and shifted things so Braden could get what he needed. "Let me help you with that."

"You eating breakfast, too?"

"No," David said. "I'm running late. I'd better wake your mother up and get to work."

"Don't forget my baseball game this afternoon."

"I won't forget. It's a big one, huh?"

"If we can beat Food Town, we can beat anybody."

David scrubbed his son's blond hair until it poked from his head like the spines of a porcupine. "Brush your hair before you get to school," he teased, doing his best to be lighthearted. "Your mother will never forgive me if you don't."

*Your mother will never forgive me. Of course she wouldn't. Never.*

*Not if she found out about Susan Roche.*

David walked into the bedroom and stopped beside their bed. He stared down at Abby's face—at her dark, mussed, Meg Ryan hair—his heart tightening. He reached and stopped, his hand poised above her shoulder. He swallowed hard, steeling himself for what the next moment might bring, and the next, and the next. "Ab—" he whispered, jostling her. "Hey. Wake up."

She moaned into her pillow, gave him a sleepy smile and, first thing, before her eyes had barely opened, reached her arms to encircle his neck. "Please don't tell me it's already time."

"Okay, I won't tell you."

"Is the coffee ready?"

"I turned it on before Brewster and I went out."

"Are you leaving?"

A nod. "Braden's up. He's eating breakfast."

"Good." She smiled again as he bent to kiss her and if he seemed subdued about something she didn't act like she noticed. She pulled his head down to hers once more, kissed him again. "Last night was fun. *Real* fun."

He hesitated, a slight moment just long enough for her to narrow her eyes at him. "I've got to shower," he said.

She watched him, her smile gone, and propped herself on one elbow. "David? Is something wrong?"

"Wrong? No? Why would anything be wrong?"

"I don't know. You just seem . . . I don't know. Pre-occupied."

"I'm late." He pulled away from her. "That's all."

He left her and began rattling around in the bathroom. He showered, dropping the soap on the tile with a resounding thud. He shaved and buzzed his battery-powered Crest Spinbrush over his teeth. He dressed without coming out of their huge walk-in closet.

"Honey?" she called past the suit coats and shoes and tailored shirts. "Are you sure nothing's the matter?"

"I'm sure," he lied.

When at last he found the courage to reappear, he grabbed his keys with purpose from the table, managing to depart without so much as a perfunctory kiss for either of his family members. "I'll meet you at Braden's game," he called as he took the porch steps two at a time, feeling like he was running away.

If the minutes before David left for work seemed excruciating, the hours he spent trying to focus on business proved even worse. He helped one confused teller balance her till. He listened to a couple concerned about the time it was taking to process their home loan. He wandered around in the lobby, smiling at customers he knew, shaking hands with colleagues, talking about the bank's newest marketing plan to open two new branches in Wyoming.

But he couldn't focus. The first chance he got, he retreated upstairs to his corner office and leather swivel chair, where he stared at the telephone on his desk as if he faced an enemy.

*Susan Roche. At the Elk Country Inn.*

June had come to western Wyoming with a welcome, harrowing rush of hot weather and RVs and visitors who wanted to stalk bison and bear in Yellowstone. Outside his office window, stores stood with their doors open, the displays behind their polished glass fronts beckoning to sightseers with turquoise and elk-horn jewelry and hand-woven Shoshone rugs. A cavalcade of interstate traffic—campers and motorcycles and cars—inched forward on the street, setting a pace that would make any seasoned rush-hour driver crazy. An apple-red stagecoach trundled slowly past on bright yellow wheels, a group of tourists inside waving to passersby.

David stared past the busy scene without seeing it. Of course he wouldn't call her. He hadn't written down the number.

*Any fool could look it up in the phone directory, you idiot. Right there under* Motels *in the Yellow Pages.*

David grabbed the phone book, flipped open to the motel page, and ran his forefinger down the listings. *The Elk Country Inn.* He picked up a ballpoint pen and scribbled the familiar prefix, then traced over the number a second time, thinking about it, his apprehension rising.

*Abby always thought she could be so sure of me.*

Finally he steeled himself, picked up the receiver, and dialed. A front-desk clerk answered in a singsong voice.

"Elk Country Inn. How may I direct your call?"

"Yes. I . . . uh." David stared at the thick gold wedding band that encircled his ring finger. "Susan Roche, please. One of your guests."

Before he could say anything more, before he could ask "Is she there? Will you connect me?," another series of clicks came, followed by a beeping and then a distant ring. Only one, which he didn't expect her to answer.

"Hello?" came a breathless voice.

Anyone who'd braved the crowds in Jackson this time of year ought to be out driving through the parks or hiking some backcountry trail. Nobody should be sitting in a motel room, waiting beside the telephone.

"Susan Roche? Is this Susan?"

"Yes," she said. "David." And nothing more.

David lifted his gaze from his wedding ring and saw the photograph of Abigail and Braden propped where he could always see it, framed in silver beside his lamp. In it, Abby squinted at the camera and leaned against a log wall, her Sunday shoes sunk to the hilt in springtime mud. She cradled Braden, wrapped in a fuzzy blue blanket, in her arms. The picture had been taken on the sunny spring day he and Abigail had walked forward at their little nondenominational church to dedicate their son to the Lord.

"You phoned my house," he said to Susan. "You asked me to get in touch."

"I did."

One beat passed. Two. "So—" Nothing more. His throat ached for her to say something, anything that might help him know where to go with this or to let him off the hook. "You've come back to visit."

"I have."

"It's been a long time, Susan."

"It has."

Heartrending silence while he waited, she waited, to see who might speak next.

"A lot has changed since I saw you last," he said finally.

"Yes," she agreed, her voice gone soft with what sounded like relief. "With me, too."

The pen in David's hand, the one he'd used to write the number, read *The Jackson State Bank.* He clicked the ballpoint shut with his thumb, then clicked it open again. "This trip . . ." And then he stopped clicking. "Is it business or pleasure?"

He heard her draw a deep breath.

"I came to see you."

David stared at the picture on his desk. Abby beaming at the camera. Braden, so innocent and tiny, nestled in her arms. "I don't think that's possible."

"What I have to say can't be done over the phone. I want to meet you somewhere. For lunch, maybe."

David turned to his Palm Pilot for escape—to a calendar unmarked for the afternoon. He didn't have to be anywhere until Braden's baseball game late in the day. "I don't see how I can fit you in," he lied.

*I've worked so hard to put this behind me. It's been so many years since I made this mistake.*

"Don't push me away, David."

"It isn't the best idea. Getting together."

"There's a café down the street from my motel. Betty Rock, or something like that."

"I can't. That won't work."

"David," she interrupted him. "This is important. Believe me, I wouldn't put either of us through this if I didn't have to."

"I won't meet you at Betty Rock. Not there." He hated himself for not standing firm against her and saying no to the whole thing. But Susan sounded desperate, and she'd come from so far away. "I will meet you for a few minutes," he told her. "Let me think of a better place."

Batting practice for the Jackson Hole All-Star Little League Team kept Braden just busy enough that Abigail Treasure didn't need to worry. Besides, there was always another mother around willing to take the boys out after the drills—to Dairy Queen for a milkshake or floating down Flat Creek on lumpy inner tubes during the heat of the day or biking along the potholes of the Snow King trail.

"You going to be okay this afternoon?" Abigail asked as Braden reached into the backseat to grab his mitt.

He nodded and grinned. "I'm going to Jake's."

"Well, call me if you need me. Tell Jake's mom I'll take you guys to the Alpine Slide tomorrow, if I can."

"I'll tell her."

"Tell her I said thanks."

"I will."

They both hesitated, waiting for each other. "Don't I get a kiss good-bye or something?" she asked.

He looked mortified. "Mom, not here."

Abby let out a deep sigh. "Later then," she said. "Not in front of these guys."

"Yeah."

"Have a good practice."

"I will."

Braden slammed the door. As Abigail eased the SUV out of the parking lot, she couldn't help checking her rearview mirror and watching her son high-five one of his friends. He was surrounded in an instant by a pack of boys, all bouncing up and down like puppies.

For a moment, as she glanced back, she let herself wonder what could have happened to her husband this morning.

As David had showered in the bathroom, he'd made

more noise opening and shutting the medicine cabinet, thumping the soap into the sink, and slamming the toilet lid down than the entire percussion section of the Grand Teton Music Festival Orchestra. As he'd dressed in their closet, he'd remained ominously silent, never breaking into the warbling whistle she'd grown accustomed to. He didn't step out to double-check the weather through the window. He didn't stand before the mirror with his chest to the fore, confidently taking stock of his day.

Most telling of all, when David had emerged and made a beeline toward the door, he hadn't embraced her. He'd grabbed his keys like he was capturing the flag in a cavalry charge. He'd raced out the door and down the steps, pounding his soles against the pavement with such purpose she hadn't dared call him back.

He had forgotten to kiss her good-bye. He always kissed her on his way out the door. This morning of all mornings she'd been expecting a last, lingering reassurance from last night.

But he hadn't even stopped to tell the dog to have a nice day.

To squelch her worry, Abby cranked the song on her CD player. If David was concerned about something, he would tell her soon enough. She prided herself on how he shared everything with her.

Above her, broad sweeps of meadow spilled downhill between dense walls of pine along the Snow King ski runs. The chairlift, empty and still, dangled over the green like a charm bracelet, swaying every so often in the breeze and portending a different season. The winter that seemed just ended would begin again too soon—the days of woolen caps and snowflakes and skiing that made these baseball summers all the more precious and rare.

Abby looked back and saw Braden running into the field beside first base, the brim of his cap tilted skyward. The coach waited for him there, probably to share some intricacy of the game.

Her shoulders lifted and fell with her sigh.

She glanced at the flock of stay-at-home moms. They sat perched above the field on bleachers, bare knees tucked beneath the hem of their sweaters, their faces fresh and rested from sleep, their fingers entwined around steaming thermal mugs.

Abby hated leaving. No matter how much she loved her job at the shelter, she found it difficult turning away from this and dealing with women whose lives weren't nearly as straightforward as her own.

As she did every day at this time, she faced resolutely forward and drove away. She headed the several blocks into town, bypassed the town square, and parked in front of the shelter on Hall Street. For another moment she listened to the music, remembering what the song was meant to be: a love letter to God, something she was supposed to sanction in the very depths of her soul.

*I am overcome with joy*
*Because of your unfailing love,*
*For you have seen my troubles,*
*And you care about the anguish of my soul.*
*You have not handed me over to my enemy*
*But have set me in a safe place.*

*Yes*, she thought. *Yes*.
Above all things, Abby loved trusting in the Father

and in her husband. She loved how comfortable and protected her *believing* made her feel.

⌒

When David stepped inside the turnstile at Ripley's Believe It Or Not, he found Susan Roche waiting. He recognized her from behind as she stood gazing at a life-sized replica of a horse covered with buttons and shards of multicolored glass. A HORSE OF A DIFFERENT COLOR, the sign beside her read.

David stood rigidly for a moment, noting the slope of Susan's shoulders and the perfect length of blonde hair, while she stared up at the gigantic statue.

"Hey," he said at last. "You got here early."

Susan started, as if she hadn't expected him to arrive so soon. She kept her purse raised against her like a shield as she came forward to greet him. She walked the way she'd always walked—with calm resolve, as if she knew exactly where she was going and what she had to do.

For one instant, David was tempted to hold out his hand to her. But only for an instant. The gesture seemed much too businesslike, too grandiose. So he stood before her with his wrists dangling at his sides, feeling the half grimace on his mouth and remembering how once, long ago, he would have touched her.

"How strange it is," she said, a sad smile on her face, "seeing you like this."

She had aged. That surprised him. In his mind he would always picture Susan as the confident college TA, come to spend a summer of freedom in the mountains.

She'd been young enough to wait tables at Jedediah's and crazy enough to try parasailing.

Susan said, "I'll bet you thought you'd never have to hear my name again."

"Of course I—" David stopped. *No.* He wouldn't reduce himself to platitudes. There wasn't anything he could say to save this situation or make it less complicated, so he didn't try. "No. I didn't want to ever see you again."

"That's what I thought."

Silence stood between them like a wall. He struggled to find something else to say. "What have you been doing these past years?"

"Acting grown up," she said, reminding him of how young she'd once been. "Living my life."

A group of youngsters jostled in through the door and shoved one another out of the way to buy tickets. One by one, they pushed through the stile. Who were these kids? Someone who might know Braden? Out of desperation, David did touch Susan this time. He grazed her arm with his hand, fully aware of the contact.

"Come back here." He paid for two admission tickets, slipped ahead, and guided her into the shadows of the museum. "Let's walk."

She let herself be led. And, as if she could read his mind, she asked, "How is your family?"

He didn't dare answer that question for her. He steered her past the exhibits of a buck that had died with its antler impaled on a hornet's nest and the skull of a cow with two heads. "Tell me about your life instead," he said. "Where are you living?"

"I'm in Oregon. On Siletz Bay. Teaching in a private school there."

"Sounds like you're doing well."

"It's a good place to dig up clams." The laugh she made sounded strident, as if it had erupted from her. "You know I've always been good at digging things up."

"Yes, I know."

She stopped behind him and leaned on the railing. "How is Abigail?"

"Abigail is fine. Just fine."

"And the baby?"

Braden, a baby. David almost smiled, thinking how odd that seemed. It had been years since he'd thought of his son that way. "The baby is nine years old. Not a baby anymore."

"They grow up fast, don't they?"

"He's going into fourth grade this year."

"Your son is smart, isn't he? I've always known any child of yours would be smart."

David laughed outright. "Well, he could use some help in reading. We have a hard time getting him to sit down and read a book."

"Really."

"He's okay in math, though."

"You're proud of him."

"He's an easy kid to be proud of."

For some reason, Susan wouldn't look at him. Her eyes had focused someplace in the distance over his left shoulder. She asked, "You never had any other children, then? Just the one?"

"No. No more. Just Braden."

He furrowed his brow at her. This seemed an odd line of questioning. He'd started answering her because Braden, at least, seemed a safe topic to discuss. But she had gone on and on with it. On and on about Braden. On and on about nothing.

"Who does he look like? You? Or your wife?"

David strode ahead of her again, past a sign that read IS IT THE WORLD'S SMALLEST MAN? NO! IT'S THE WORLD'S LARGEST CIGAR! He didn't stop to look at the huge roll of tobacco looming high above his head. Let her catch up with him. He never should have agreed to this. Never. *Ever.*

"Things are happy in my family now. Our lives are good. Better than most." He added pointedly, "Better than they were before."

Susan leaned over the railing, her palms flat on the round metal, her shoulders bearing her weight, saying nothing.

"Susan, do you mind telling me why you've come?"

She gazed somewhere past him, somewhere into something he couldn't see. "I swear to you, David. If there had been any other way, I wouldn't have done this."

"It's been nine years. What could possibly have happened that would—"

"It hasn't just happened now." She met his eyes. "It's been going on for a long time."

A sense of danger rose within him. Whatever Susan's words would be, there would be no escaping them. He felt sure of it. She'd trapped him with something; he already knew this truth. And he'd given her the means to do it. He, too, ran his hand along the rail, as if establishing contact.

"I have a daughter," she said. "An eight-year-old named Samantha."

Oh.

*Oh.*

"You do?"

How pathetic—how inadequate and unsteady—his question sounded.

"Yes."

His heart scudded forward while he figured the math in his head. "She's eight?"

"She'll be nine in two months."

"Oh."

Susan began to fumble around in her purse. "Do you want to see a picture of her? I have one in my billfold."

"No," he said, sounding frantic. "No. I don't want to see her."

She glanced up, and it horrified him even more to see that she wasn't surprised by his reaction. She had expected him to respond this way. And that meant . . . That meant . . .

"You don't have to see her, David. But you have to hear me out."

"I don't want to."

"We've gotten this far. We can't turn back from it now."

All the questions he had never asked her. All those inquiries about her own life, her own children, her relationships with other men. The uncertainty of them loomed like a hammerlock, ready to wrestle him down. He couldn't speak for a moment.

"We've gotten along well, Samantha and me."

He found his voice. "There isn't anyone else, then? Just the two of you?"

"Just the two of us."

His heart pummeled. "Did you ever marry?"

She met his gaze head on. "She has never known her real father."

Another beat. "You've raised a child alone?"

"There have been good things about that. I've liked being in control of Sam's life. I've liked sheltering her. I've liked it that no one else has tried to interfere."

"Susan."

"Things are different than they once were. A child without both parents isn't asked many questions. Employers are willing to work around a single parent's schedule." She fumbled in her purse again and held her wallet open. Even in the shadows beyond the Ripley's exhibits, he could see a photograph in a plastic sleeve, lined up neatly among Susan's other essentials—her Oregon drivers' license, her credit cards. "Look at this picture, David. Please." She held it out to him, cupping it in her hand. "I want you to see her face."

He reached to take it and hated himself all the more because his hands shook. "I don't—"

"You have to," she said. "You don't have any other choice."

He stared at it.

A wrinkled school photo, taken the way all school photos are taken, with the color slightly off hue and the mouth of the subject too broad as if the photographer had used some ridiculous joke to make this little girl laugh. Long brown hair flew all over her shoulders as though she'd just come running in from the playground. Dark eyes a lot like Susan's and a gap-toothed grin that reminded David so very much of his own son's.

*No.*

Susan took the billfold between her fingers so they both held it together, balanced between their two hands. She too gazed down at the picture. For a moment they said nothing.

"She's a pretty girl."

"Do you think she resembles Braden?"

He didn't mince words. "Yes."

"I'd thought perhaps she would."

David raised his eyes from the photo and met Susan's gaze. Their fingers touched over the plastic sheath of the wallet. He felt as if he'd been slugged, sucker punched by something come to pillage him. It took every ounce of his courage even to say it; his tongue almost wouldn't go around the words. "She's mine."

Susan nodded. "Yes."

For the moment, the ramifications upon David's own life were overshadowed by the magnitude of this one truth. For all these past moments, he'd feared Susan's answer. Now the impact of finally *knowing* was profound.

This girl, a part of him.

*Flesh of my flesh. Bone of my bone.*

Around her neck Samantha Roche wore a delicate necklace of pink stones, one tiny spangled heart resting sideways in the camber of her throat. Her denim collar hung open in a lopsided V, perfectly matching the happy jut of her chin. Through all those strands of cottony, uncombed hair, he could see one ear peeping through, the shape of a seashell. She smiled at him, at all the world, revealing teeth that her mouth hadn't quite gotten the chance to grow into yet.

David found it impossible to examine this little girl's face and not be moved by her. A human instinct, as old as Creation, surged within him: fathership. With this daughter he shared lineage, the same stock and strain.

The blood of a dozen Treasure ancestors coursed through this child's veins.

Bemused, David followed Susan as she wandered on past a collection of bedpans, a display of assassination comparisons between Abraham Lincoln and John F. Kennedy, a rolled ball of rusty barbed wire that must have been six feet wide. "Why didn't you tell me?" he asked, keeping his voice low and noncommittal. She could very well have phoned him after she'd moved to Seattle to give him this news. By the sin of omission, she'd stolen something remarkable from him. "Why wait until now?"

"It didn't make any difference, did it? From the beginning with you, I knew where I stood."

"You didn't have much faith in me," he said.

"I had plenty of faith in you. I had faith in your faith. I knew how religious you always claimed to be. I had faith you would never leave your wife."

Her words hit him hard. Because she was right. Because he had told her once that he knew what he was doing was wrong, that he struggled with it—that underneath it all, no matter what he believed about God, he was human. Human like everybody else.

# Chapter Three

"What is it you want from me, Susan? Why this, now? Why, after all these years?"

She didn't answer right off. She kept walking, away from him.

David panicked. Apprehension charged the length of his spine. "I'm not telling Abby about this, if that's what you're here for. Things are good between us now."

"I can't promise she won't find out," Susan said. "I'm sorry."

"That can't happen. It would kill Abby if she found out what happened between us . . . and when."

Susan wheeled toward him. "That's all you think about, isn't it? Yourself. How to cover your mistakes."

"No. There's more to it than that and you know it."

"Oh, yes, David. There's more to both of our stories. So you can forget thinking only of yourself."

He waited.

"Sam got the flu on Memorial Day and she wouldn't get over it. I had it, too, but mine ended in three days. And Sam just kept feeling so . . . tired."

David closed her billfold, which he'd been holding open all this time. He handed it back to her.

"They did some blood work and then they called me. They said she needed to come back in. So we went back. And back. And back. We've seen three different doctors since then—one in Portland, two in Corvallis. They're all telling us the same thing."

"What? What are they telling you?"

For the first time, when he looked at Susan, he noticed her red-rimmed eyes. For the first time she didn't seem like such a predator to him, but instead only a mother, as trapped by her indiscretion as he was by his. For the first time he noticed she looked bad.

"Do you know what it's like to tell a little girl she has leukemia, David? First I just said, 'They've found something in your blood they want to check. There's something that doesn't look right. Your blood's sick.' Then the doctor walked in and said, 'Well, Samantha, you have leukemia.' Without even preparing her. She didn't say anything. She sat looking at him with a straight face like he'd walked in and said, 'You have strep throat.'"

His reply came out empty, frightened, helpless. *"Susan."*

"She didn't cry until she got out into the hall. She took my hand and looked at me and she said, 'Leukemia, Mama? But people die from leukemia.' And I said, 'Well, you won't. I won't let you. You're going to be all right.'"

"I don't know what to say."

"It isn't what you can say, David. It's what you can do. She's a good candidate for a bone-marrow transplant. Only we haven't been able to find the right donor."

The awful truth sank like weighty stones in his stomach. So this was it, then. This was the reason she had come.

"Are you thinking it might be me?"

Susan nodded. "Possibly." At Ripley's Believe It Or Not, he stared at a replica of a woman with brass rings around a neck that must have been stretched to fourteen inches long. EXPERIENCE THE ODDITY, the placard read. Susan touched his sleeve. "You might be the only chance Sam has of staying alive."

⌒

Along the far wall at the Community Safety Network hung an oil painting of five distinguished ladies, known since the 1920s as The Petticoat Rulers of Jackson Hole. Five women who'd grown disgruntled with the way men governed this town and so took matters into their own hands.

In a spirited contest, running upon—among other things—a platform of fencing the town cemetery so cows couldn't graze over the final resting places of beloved townsfolk, these women had defeated their male opponents by a three-to-one margin and since then been lauded as the first fully woman government in the United States.

Mrs. Grace G. Miller, Miss Pearl Williams, Mrs. Genevieve Van Vleck, Mrs. Faustine Haight, and even Rose Crabtree, the proprietor of the Crabtree Inn, gazed down from their cameos with solemn countenances and deep-set, sepia-toned eyes. *You can do this, too!* they seemed to be saying. *You can be in charge just like we were!*

Abby checked the pink message slips strewn across

her desk. She dropped one onto the pile, then picked it up and read it again:

Sophie H. has decided to leave today. You'll want to talk to her.

Kate Carparelli

In a shelter meant for battered women, there were only two reasons a person would decide to leave. One, she had decided to launch out on her own and begin a new life. Or two, she had decided to go back to someone who had hurt her. It happened all the time. Some women came here seven or eight times before they made the choice to give up on their marriages and refuse to live in a dangerous place.

Sophie Henderson could go either way.

Abby found Sophie in an upstairs room stuffing meager belongings into a bag that read *Friends of the Teton County Library*. On it, a cowboy sat atop a horse, burying his nose inside the pages of a book.

"Hey." The sight of this woman packing made Abby's heart clench. She couldn't help feeling close to the women who passed through this place. She couldn't help feeling bound to them. Over the past weeks, Sophie had become a special friend.

"You heard?"

"I did."

"I figured everybody around here would be talking about it."

"They are."

"I've decided to go back to him."

"You have? Sophie—"

Abby stopped herself. She was not allowed to offer advice. Leaving or staying should be each woman's choice to make. She'd trained her shelter staff to offer support, never outright opinion.

"You know what my sister Elaine said the last time I showed up on her doorstep with a bloody nose? 'Mike's a good man, Sophie. He would never do all those things you say he does.'"

Sophie stuffed a threadbare sundress into her Friends-of-the-Library bag. A frayed towel. A lime-green windbreaker. All of these either donated or hand-me-downs purchased for nothing at Browse and Buy, the official rummage shop of the Episcopal Church.

"So, you're going back because of your sister?" Abby asked.

"No. I guess I'm going back for myself. Maybe she's right. Maybe it's good enough that we can make it work this time."

"Maybe so."

"He said he's willing to go to counseling and to try. He's capable of changing, Abby. I just know it."

Abby leaned against the doorjamb, her arms interlaced, a confidante's pose. She fought to remain neutral, even though she cared bone-deep for Sophie. "We'll miss you around this place."

Sophie laughed. "It's been like a slumber party or something here. My sister and I used to share a room when we were little, in a double-sized bed. Have you noticed how easy it is to laugh when you're laying down? In the dark? With someone close beside you like a sister?"

"I remember those days." Abby smiled.

"I don't know. Maybe it's because you aren't folded

over, trying to sit up. And there're no faces to look at except the faces in the ceiling. There's nothing to make you stop laughing. It just comes *out*."

A ragged khaki visor sat beside the bed on the nightstand, its bill shaped to form a perfect eyeshade over Sophie's face. Abby walked over to pick it up and hand it to her. "Don't forget this."

Sophie hesitated, then shook her head. "I don't know if I want that or not. I don't think I'll need it."

Abby turned the frayed brim in her hand and examined it straight on. "I've seldom seen you without it."

Sophie stopped stuffing items into the overloaded bag. "Mike gave it to me for my birthday. I was wearing that the night I left. I don't want to do anything to him that will remind him of anything bad." She glanced out the front window, then aligned her hands as if in prayer, touching fingers to a disjointed nose that had been broken too many times. Her eyes glimmered with precaution—or tears. Abby couldn't be sure which. "I have to go. His truck's out there."

A heartbeat passed between them. Then another. And then they were rocking in each other's arms.

"Thank you for everything," Sophie said into Abby's hair.

"If you need us again, you know where we are."

"Yeah, I know where you are."

"Oh, Sophie. Good luck." The two women swayed to and fro in their embrace. Abby said again, with great emphasis, "We're going to miss you," because those were the only emotional words she was allowed to say.

"Will you get the test done *today?*" Susan had called to David from halfway across the crosswalk as they parted. "You don't have to make an appointment. You just go."

"Today?" he'd called back.

"Every hour matters." She'd pulled up short in the middle of the street and turned back to him, ignoring a huge motor home from Minnesota that bore down on her in the oncoming lane. "Every hour."

"Get out of the middle of the highway," he had called to her. "Everything will be okay."

It took David hours to get to the hospital to have the test.

Although his schedule had seemed light this morning, an impromptu meeting, a hundred small details, filled the afternoon. Every so often, he'd leave his upstairs workplace, thinking he could slip out to St. John's. But every time he tried, someone stopped him in the stairwell.

Finally, he stepped into the cramped laboratory waiting room late that day, knowing he didn't have much leeway if he wanted to make Braden's game. He took a seat in one of the three plastic chairs and shot a covert glance around the office. What if someone recognized him here? "I'm David Treasure," he said to the woman who approached. "I'm here for a blood test."

A stainless steel clock on the wall read 4:47. The woman, who wore scrubs with Snoopy dancing across the sleeves, held out a hand for doctor's orders.

"I don't have anything from a physician," he said. And found himself struggling just to voice Susan's name. "A . . . a friend told me the test had been sent from Oregon. That you would already know about it."

From the next room he could hear the sound of a child whimpering, and a mother's consoling reply: "It'll hurt for a minute, and then it will be over."

"It won't be over," said the child. "It will hurt for a long time."

The lab tech leafed through a pile of manila folders on her desk. David sat down. He couldn't help himself. He had always been one to ask stupid questions when he was uneasy. He bounced his knee up and down, striking up a conversation out of nervousness, as if he could use any friend he could get.

"So, you like Snoopy?" He gestured toward her sleeves.

She either ignored his question or didn't hear him. Probably the first. "Oh, here you are. You're the test kit we're sending back to Good Samaritan in Corvallis."

His knee stopped bouncing. *No, I'm not a test kit,* he wanted to say. *I am a man. You aren't sending me anywhere.*

She gave him papers to fill out, assigned him a confidential number, and told him the doctor in Corvallis should have results in five days. Then, to his chagrin, she ushered him through the doorway to a reclinerlike padded chair. A metal stool gleamed beside it and a nearby cart stood laden with stainless steel utensils that looked as if they could inflict a wide variety of bodily harm.

"Oh, look," said the owner of the voice he'd heard earlier, sounding relieved. "Here's Braden's dad come to have a blood draw, too."

David's heart plummeted. He recognized them. He

couldn't remember the little girl's name, but he knew her well enough. She and Braden had dressed up as pirates together and had given a fourth-grade class report on the migration of whales.

She made him think of another little girl, too. The reason for his being here. A child of his own, who might be dying. A child whom he'd never known.

The mingling smells of rubber and rubbing alcohol set his stomach roiling. He sat on the chair and lifted his arm so the Snoopy-shirt lady could lower the tray where he would lay his arm. "So they do blood tests in groups now, do they?" He winked across the way at the little girl, trying to make light of knowing her. His throat constricted with dread.

The mother gave her daughter encouragement. "See," she said. "If Braden's dad is brave enough to do this, I'm sure you can be brave enough, too. If you don't cry, I'm sure Mr. Treasure will tell Braden how brave you were and what a good job you did."

David hesitated three seconds too long before he agreed with them. "Sure. I'll do that." *I don't even know their names and I'm lying.*

"You'll need to roll up your sleeve, sir."

"Oh, sorry."

The tech at his side began to lay out a row of vials, their lids coded with primary colors. He did as she said, unfastening his cuff with the opposite hand, fumbling with the buttons.

"Make a fist for me now."

He did it. "How's this?"

"Hm-m-mm." She strapped the tourniquet around his left biceps with more enthusiasm than he thought necessary. On the inside of his arm, she swabbed a spot the size of a nickel with cold, brown liquid. "They certainly sent a lot of vials. What do they need so much blood for?"

"Take whatever it is they want," he said, evading the question. "It doesn't matter. Drain me until I'm dry."

The tech raised one penciled-in brow at him before she snapped on a pair of rubber gloves and turned her attention to the blue, bulging lines in the crook of his elbow. She touched one vein with her gloved finger, rolled it around beneath the layer of his skin. "This looks like a good one." She pursed her lips and touched another. "This one would work, too. You've got good veins."

"Either one." He shrugged. "I don't care." *Just get this over with. Please. I have other places to go.*

"Do you get woozy?" She tapped his wrist. "You look pale."

"No. I'm not pale," he answered, although he had absolutely no idea if he was or not. He had handled Braden being born, for heaven's sake, and that hadn't been easy. He remembered it now—Abby moaning and the monitors shrilling, his body revolting as he tried to dab her forehead with a cloth. Every time Abby'd pushed, he'd strained, too. He'd almost hyperventilated and fallen off the stool. He'd gasped for breath as the baby came, until the doctor turned toward him, ignoring Abigail and the crowning infant for a moment, and sat him down so he wouldn't pass out.

The moments after his son's arrival—the delicate orchestry of it—would remain with David forever. The staggering pattern of those tiny brows, the curl of a miniature finger, the faint scribble of blue vein beneath translucent skin, the smell of baby.

But that one instant—that one moment when Dr. Sugden had turned away from Abigail to help him instead. It hadn't been the blood or the baby birthing that had rendered David queasy and ill.

It had made him sick seeing Abby in pain.

As the tech fussed about with vials and needles, other remembrances came unbidden—other memories of Abby in times of hurt and pain.

The time she'd found out a high-school friend had died and he'd held her in his lap while she cried . . . The week of an abscessed tooth when he'd nursed her after an awful bout with the dentist and her face had swollen to the same shape as an otter's . . . Every year when her father's birthday came and went unannounced and she silently grieved . . .

How he loved Abby these days, even if he'd doubted their chances at the beginning.

*If I could only have known then what I know about our lives now.*

Snoopy-scrubs readied her long needle. David watched it pierce his skin and welcomed the twinge. She inserted it the rest of the way into his arm almost effortlessly and must have hit exactly what she'd been aiming for because deep red began to well into the syringe. She focused on pulling the plunger out of the syringe while he stared at the dark blonde roots in her hair.

"You can let go the fist now."

He did as told.

She loosened the tourniquet and David watched with miserable fascination as his blood inched up the tube, the dark red pooling inside the glass.

# Chapter Four

The best thing about living in Jackson Hole, Wyoming, was that even the busiest working fathers tried to make it to Little League baseball games.

David didn't miss a game unless he had good reason.

His absence this afternoon, with no explanation, worried Abby. For a long while after the cell phone had failed to ring through, Abby stood beneath the bleachers where to her right she had a view of cars pulling into the parking lot and to her left a view of bare, sunburned legs, wide-pocketed shorts, and an assortment of tennis shoes, dusty sandals, and mothers' toenails painted *Fishnet Stocking* red.

Every time a cheer went out above her, she knew she'd missed something exciting on the field.

Every time a car pulled up, she stood on tiptoe and searched it out, hoping to see David.

Finally, during the middle of the third inning, she gave up, hefted her stadium blanket high beneath her armpit, hiked her skirt to her knees, and climbed the bleachers. "About time you got here," somebody said as the other parents scooted over to make room. "Braden's on deck."

"I've been here." She unfolded the blanket and made a place for David to sit, too, just in case. "I've been watching from down below."

"Where's your husband?"

Abby shrugged and roosted in her regular seat beside them. "I guess he'll get here," she said. "He's never late like this."

Braden donned a batter's helmet, stepped to the plate, and took a practice swing outside the box. On the stands, Abigail fretted. *Oh, David's going to miss Braden at bat.*

Braden stepped into the plate. "Come on, Brade." Abby clapped her hands. "Take it for a ride!"

The scoreboard at Mateosky Park hadn't been painted in so many years that spectators could scarcely make out the faded words announcing WESTERN BOY'S BASEBALL, JACKSON HOLE. Banners advertising everything from Corral West Ranchwear to the Strutting Grouse Restaurant sagged against the outfield fence. In the dugout, boys teased each other and clamped mitts over each other's heads. They tipped their mouths to drink from the spigot of the orange Gatorade cooler.

With clarity, Abby knew. *Something isn't right. David wouldn't miss this without calling.* Misgiving grew, tightening in her chest. These games meant everything to David. He loved talking with the parents and helping with the coaching and—above all things—rooting for these nine- and ten-year-old boys.

The pitcher hitched up his knee over the mound, positioned the ball, and played out his windup like a major leaguer. With patient, withdrawn concentration, he launched a fastball and Braden swung over the plate. *Thwack.*

Dust flew in graceful whorls as the ball hit the catcher's mitt.

The umpire strong-armed the signal. "Stree-ike."

"Good cut." Abby clapped even harder. "Keep your head down, Brade. You'll get it."

Braden stepped backward out of the box. He turned, his eyes searching the seats as he looked for his family. "Where's Dad?" he mouthed.

Abby held out her hands, palms up, and mouthed back, "I don't know."

"Speaking of David," Cindy Hubner offered Abby some M&M's from an open bag, "how was your anniversary last night?"

Abby shook her head no thanks and hugged her skirt over her knees. "We had a good time. We always do."

"Everybody in town talks about you two, you know. You and David are so lucky, having the sort of marriage you do. I give you both a lot of credit."

Abby hated to admit this, but it always pleased her when someone noticed. "You know, we trust God for a lot of it," she said, grasping for some way to appear humble and divert attention. "We couldn't do it on our own."

High above, the Wedgwood-blue sky was calm as a beaver pond and wisps of evening clouds clung to the summit of the mountain. On the Snow King trail people hiked, looking distant and small. At the extolling of their marriage, at David's strange absence, Abby felt like one of those faraway, upward-bound people: breathless, slightly lost.

Braden moved back into the box and positioned himself in readiness, his elbow angling toward the sky. Out on first base the runner got ready, dancing sideways on muscular little-boy legs, batting-glove fingers flapping from a rear pocket.

The pitcher cocked his knee. The throw came—high and inside. Braden watched it zing past as the runner on first sidled out and then back to safety.

"Good eye!" everybody shouted. "Good eye, Brade. Way to see it!"

"Ball," the ump said, holding up a finger on each hand to indicate the count. "1-1."

"Come on, pitch! You can get him," a parent yelled from the opposite bleachers. "Give him the chair."

"Protect the plate, Braden," Cindy shouted beside Abby. "Don't let this one get by you."

Braden pounded his bat on the plate. He took a practice swing. As the windup started, the spectators grew quiet.

On the mound, the pitcher shifted his weight, readjusted, reared his elbow, and let the ball fly. Braden began a full-armed swing, stepping in to protect the plate.

Braden's bat sliced through empty air. The ball sailed in and smashed his cheekbone with a hollow thud. Blood splattered on his baseball cleats.

The little boy buckled to the ground. The black batting helmet went flying. The bat lay at an awful detached angle in the dirt. Abby rose in the stands. *"Braden!"*

When Abby recollected it later, she would not remember leaving the bleachers or skirting the fence. She would not remember shoving coaches away or kneeling in the dust. She would only remember the sight of Braden's confused expression and tear-streaked face, his bangs matted with dirt and sweat.

Blood saturated Ken Hubner's hankie. "He's got a bloody nose, Abby. Don't panic. I think he's going to be okay."

But when Ken moved his hand away, Braden's nose was already swollen to the same size and shape as an eggplant. Half-moon bruises already shadowed his eyes. Cindy handed an emergency bag of frozen peas from the snack cooler over the fence. "Get these on him, Abby. They'll help with the swelling."

"Where is David?" Ken asked as he reapplied the handkerchief.

Abby couldn't think over the loud buzz in her head. "I don't know."

"You're going to want to take this guy to the emergency room. His nose could be broken."

*This is ridiculous. He's a little boy who's gotten hit by a ball. A minute ago, everything was fine.*

"Do you want me to drive you, Abby?"

"No. No. I'll be okay."

Everyone crowded around, asking Braden questions. "Can you breathe through your nose?"

"Can you see? How many fingers am I holding up?"

"Do you feel like you need to throw up?"

The power of suggestion. Braden's face went ashen. "Ken," Abby said. "Don't ask him any more questions. Just carry him to my car."

"Are you sure you don't want me to go to St. John's with you?"

"I'll be fine. We handle things like this at the shelter every day."

But as Abby started up the car and steered them toward Broadway, her hands were shaking. Because even though Abby was experienced with confrontations and emergencies, with her own son it felt like a different thing.

"Keep your head forward, Brade. Don't swallow." She grabbed a box of tissues from the floorboard and tossed them across to him while he held the ice bag against his nose. Within minutes, blood-soaked Kleenexes littered the seat.

"I can't help it, Mama."

"Are you dizzy, honey? Do you feel like you might faint?"

"No . . . Yes . . . I . . . I want Dad. Where is *Dad?*"

"You know your dad," Abby said with more confidence than she felt. "He'll get here as soon as he can."

At the hospital the minutes passed in a slow march as Abby waited with Braden in the admittance area and Braden fought against tears, struggling to breathe through his swollen nose. The peas in the bag had melted to mush and his foot jiggled with pain as Abby answered a barrage of unnecessary questions. Name. Address. Place of employment. Insurance company. To make matters worse, the admittance clerk kept stopping to answer the phone.

"Look. Don't you have these things on record? My son is in pain." Abby could scarcely bear this, seeing Braden hurting without any help. *I'd like to take that stupid computer screen and hit you over the head with it.*

"I'm sorry. I cannot admit him until we have this complete."

Then, to add insult to injury, they wouldn't give Braden a drink of water. "Sorry, kiddo," the nurse told them. "No drinking and driving. Dr. Meno says we've got to get X rays first. You can't drink until we know what's going on inside that head of yours."

"He can't even have a sip?" Abby said as a nurse pushed him in a wheelchair. "He's thirsty." *If David were here, he'd make them give Braden a drink of water.*

They rounded a corner and, as if this very thought of David had conjured him up, here came her husband, stepping out of a side door, rolling down his sleeve.

"Dad!"

"Braden!" One odd, awkward pause. David's eyes shone with fear. Abby decided he must be worried sick about his son.

"Oh, you're here." She raced forward. "Thank heavens."

"What are you—"

She grabbed his forearm. "I knew they'd tell you at the ball field to find us here."

"The ball field? Oh." For one moment, it almost seemed as if he was struggling to understand. "Oh. Oh, yes. Braden's game."

"He got hit in the nose. Did they tell you that? We're getting X rays. They won't let him drink anything until they know if it's broken."

David began to follow his family, leaning low as a nurse wheeled his son along the corridor. "Braden. Buddy. Let me see."

Braden removed the latest tissue. "It hurts."

"Oh, my." A regretful laugh. "It doesn't look very good, either."

"Where were you, Dad? Where *were* you? You almost missed the whole thing. I was batting."

At David's pause, Abby turned toward him again. A flush had risen on his neck. She had an odd sensation that David felt guilty about something. The sad, set expression in his eyes made him look rigid and bereaved, almost old. Strong frown lines etched the outline of his mouth. He kept staring at the bloody cleats in Abby's hand as if he'd never seen them before.

He answered his son cryptically. "Some days are harder than others. This one has been harder than most."

"David, what's wrong?"

He turned defensively toward Abby. "I never said anything was wrong. I just said it was a hard day."

"It started out lousy. I could tell. Something was wrong this morning."

"Look, Ab. We've got Braden to take care of. I'm not prepared to go into it right now."

"Did you have a late meeting or something?"

He hesitated again. "Yeah. Something . . . came up." He scrubbed his son's grimy hair. "How about you, sport? Wow, I'm sorry. Did you lose a lot of blood?"

"Yes. Lots."

David grasped Abby by the arm, taking charge, and she relaxed against him. "Did *you* do okay?" he asked her, drawing her shoulders close.

"No," she said, her voice finally calming. "I didn't. I needed you."

Lies. Lies.

One led to another, the falsehoods growing around him like snarled vines.

David sat on their sofa with the huge mass of Brewster curled into knotwork at his feet, alternately holding ice against Braden's swollen nose and reading aloud *The BFG*, Braden's favorite library book from school.

He'd promised Braden he wouldn't miss this game. Beside's being late, David had avoided the ballpark because he couldn't bear playing the part. The part that had been his own life yesterday. The part that would have left him faking it, rooting for his son with his arm draped across Abby's shoulders while beneath it all he counted the cost of infidelity.

The telephone rang constantly tonight. At first, each time, David swayed forward on his feet, desperate to answer the calls himself. He was certain it would be Susan Roche inquiring about the test. But the questions all came from people concerned about Braden: team parents, friends from church who had heard about the accident, Ken and Cindy Hubner, and even the little girl named Josey who had a horrible fourth-grade crush on Braden and made Braden's ears turn red each time anybody mentioned her name.

Word of Braden's calamity had traveled around town in less than two hours.

"Thank goodness it wasn't fractured," he heard Abby saying over and over again to everybody who phoned. "He got walloped in the nose, I'll tell you that much. It scared us to death. But nothing's broken. Of course it was terrifying, but he'll be okay."

David squirmed on the sofa, his voice droning on with the Roald Dahl story, his heart lurching within his chest every time he heard his wife speak the words.

*I don't know, Abby, if he'll be okay or not. I don't know if you'll be okay. Maybe, after today, our family won't ever be okay again.*

"Dad," Braden said. "When you read aloud, you have

to read like you're interested in the story. You're making it boring."

David read another two paragraphs before he gave up trying. "Sorry. Guess I'm not much in the mood to read tonight." He lay the book, upside down and open, beside them on the couch. Once again, he replaced the ice bag on his son's septum. "How's the nose feeling, sport?"

"I still can't breathe through it."

"You ought to get some rest now. I'll bring down your sleeping bag."

Dr. Meno had suggested they keep a close watch on Braden tonight, letting him bunk on the floor, waking him up every twenty minutes to make certain he hadn't suffered a concussion. David knew that by morning Brewster would have edged Braden so far to one side that the dog would have a better part of the sleeping bag than the boy.

Once David had spread out the gigantic down bag and Brewster had indeed claimed a spot on it, father and son voyaged to Braden's bedroom and lugged out armfuls of extra pillows.

"There you go. How's that?"

"Good."

David punched one last pillow into shape as Braden climbed in. "Good night. Sleep tight. Don't let the bedbugs bite."

"How can they be bedbugs?" Braden said. "This isn't a bed."

"Okay. Sleeping bag bugs, then." With a light kiss on his son's misshapen, bruised nose, David zipped the bag up to his chin so Braden would feel like he'd been tucked in.

"Dad?"

David bent low over him, worried that Braden might be woozy. He kept looking at things like Abby's old pink cardboard jewelry box and David's stack of *Money* magazines on the floor as if he'd never seen any of it before. "What?"

"I like sleeping in your room."

"You do?"

"I like the way it smells. The smell of Mom."

A melancholy grin. "I don't see how you can smell anything through that nose."

"I just can."

"I see."

"G' night, Dad."

"Good night."

David had just climbed up from all fours and was heading to turn out the lamp when Braden's unsteady voice stopped him again. "Dad?"

"Yes."

"Are you going to wake me up every twenty minutes all night long?"

"Yes."

"To make sure my head's okay?"

"Yes."

"That means you'll have to wake up every twenty minutes, too."

"That's right."

"All night long?"

David switched off the reading light and stopped with his hand on the doorjamb, staring back at the opalescent length of boy spread out on the floor. "I don't mind doing it, you know. It's worth it to make sure you're safe."

No answer came in the stillness, only the arrhythmic breathing of the child and the panting of the dog.

"Maybe I'll stay awake all night," David said. "That way I can be waiting every time the next twenty minutes goes by. How would that be?"

"Good. Dad?"

"Yes?"

"What would happen to me if I didn't wake up?"

"Well, we don't—" David paused. He had to think about that one. What did happen? What exactly would they do if something happened to Braden? "We don't *know.*"

"I'm scared to go to sleep."

David went back and crouched beside his son on the floor. "Here." He unzipped the bag. "Roll over." He shoved Brewster, damp warm breath and all, aside and lifted Braden's pajama top. With an immense hand, he tenderly touched skin as treasured and newfound to him as the day this child had been born. "I don't want you to be afraid."

He worked his callused fingers in circles on Braden's back, stopping just beneath small shoulder blades that jutted like bony wings. As he etched shapes with his fingers—figure eights and stripes and big Ws—David captured all the love he knew for this one child and held it within himself. His devotion to his son at that moment felt almost too delicious to absorb or grasp. It was so familiar that he'd almost been missing it, as if a wall had come between them because he saw his son every day and so never really saw him at all.

It hurt, just wanting to not miss things he knew he was missing. Just wanting to see things that he saw, yet didn't see.

*Go figure*, he thought. *Go figure feeling that way about your kid.*

The misery that had been waiting in the recesses of David's heart came full upon him, powerful, all encompassing. He couldn't help imagining Susan's Samantha, wraithlike and happy, the child in the school picture he'd looked at for the first time today. He envisioned her expectant wide grin, the strand of stray hair blown across her face as if she'd been running in the wind.

"I love you, Dad," Braden whispered again.

"Hey. Come up here a minute. I know you're almost asleep. Let me give you a hug."

David gathered his son in his arms and held him there, so close and hard he could feel Braden's heart beating. He kissed him on the top of his head, in the midst of the wheat-yellow cowlick that would never lie down no matter how Abby tried to slick it. He buried his face into the dusty sweet scent of boy as if he could bury himself away from the world and from the bad moves he'd made.

"Will you bring me my baseball glove, Dad? I can't sleep without my glove."

"Sure. I'll go get it. Hang on."

David rose to his feet, his knees cracking, and passed through the hallway where moonlight sifted onto the floor through thin curtains. He went quietly through the kitchen where Abby bent to load the dishwasher, her silhouette an arabesque over rows of white, dripping dishes. He went to her and wrapped his arms around her from behind, treating their relationship suddenly as a priceless, breakable thing.

"Hey," she whispered, leaning into him, the smell of dish detergent wafting from her arms.

"Love you," he said, kissing her neck.

"I'm not turning around," she said, laughing. "If I do, I'll get your neck all soapy."

*Abby, there's something I need to tell you. Abby, honey, I've made a horrible mistake.*

Once she found out, he would never be able to take back the truth.

David left her and went to find Braden's baseball mitt. He delivered it to his son, who was already snoring through swollen nostrils. Then David circled the living room, moved soundlessly beside the wall, invisible, like a character in a Thornton Wilder play. And saw rooms in his house as if he hadn't seen them before. As if they weren't real to him anymore. As if they were already slipping away.

# Chapter Five

*E*verywhere David went that week, he noticed little girls.

When he strode out for his morning jog, treading along with the burden of his heavy heart, he happened past a little girl who was digging her heels in and hanging on to a dog leash for dear life, pulled along by a golden retriever at least twice her size.

When he spelled one of the tellers in the window at the bank, a little girl rode into the drive-thru with her family, smashed her nose against the glass, and stared at David with huge dark eyes while her father scribbled out a check. He whisked her a Dum-Dum lollipop along with her father's cash.

While traveling on the Village Road, he glanced into a cow pasture and saw three girls in inner tubes bobbing along an irrigation ditch, their bare toes flinging up bead-strings of water. They grasped hands whenever they came within reach of one another, shrieking and throwing or ducking clumps of wet weeds.

At last, David could stand it no longer. During a rare lull in his office, he dialed Information on his phone and gave the mechanical voice on the other end all the information he could remember. A listing in Siletz Bay. On the coast of Oregon, near Lincoln City.

There could be so many reasons not to find it. A single woman alone could very well be unlisted, or indexed under a different initial. He wouldn't put it past Susan to be carefully hiding herself away.

"Please hold for the number," the dehumanized voice said.

David scuttled his desktop for a pen.

Moments later, he was punching in the Oregon number with great boldness, thinking how pleasant it felt to be the one who chose to do right, the one taking the upper hand. But the instant he heard the childlike, sunshiny voice on Susan's answering machine, his bravado failed him.

"Hey! You've reached the house of Samantha and Susan Roche. Don't hang up, just leave us a message at the—"

*Beep.*

And that was all.

He sat incapable of response, shocked to have heard Samantha's voice. She sounded so young. So *guiltless*. A hollow opened inside of him that later, when he took time to think, would draw him down and drown him. After hearing the machine hang up, David dialed the number again. And waited, trying not to listen during the short message he knew would come, before he stammered, "Susan. Listen. It's David Treasure calling from Wyoming. I . . . just hadn't *heard* anything, and I wanted to check in." He took precious seconds during the recording, measuring his words in case someone might be listening. "Please, Susan." Another long, desperate pause. "I need to know what's happening. Get me at my office," he said. "Don't call me at home."

After that, whenever a message or a phone call came in at the bank for him, David leapt at it like a pouncing cat. "Hello? Yes. Oh, yes." And every time, when it wasn't Susan, a pendulum swung in his chest, knocking the air out of him with disappointment and frustration and fear.

When a knock came on his office door just after noon, David rose to meet it, his arm outstretched, adrenaline stinging his skin. But it was only Nelson Hull, David's best friend and pastor of the church, with auburn hair ragged around the edges and, no matter how he tried to tame it, poking in every direction from his head. Everywhere he went, Nelson always looked a bit electrified.

"I'm in the mood for mountain climbing," Nelson said after they'd shaken hands. "How about partnering with me. Let's have a go at the Grand this afternoon."

David opened one drawer, then another, looking for his Palm Pilot. "I'll have to check my schedule. I don't know if I can get away."

"What are you looking for?"

"My PDA."

"It's right there," Nelson said, pointing. "Lying on your desk in front of you."

"Oh." They both stared at it for a moment before David asked, "Isn't it too late to start up? There's no way we'd make it to the top."

"Come on, buddy. Save me. The copy machine's gone out and they can't finish the bulletin for Sunday. There's the mission's conference next week and the elders meeting tomorrow morning and Theresa March can't find enough toilet paper rolls to build the walls of Jericho for children's church. It is nuts over there."

David was warming to the idea. "I guess we don't have to go all the way, if we don't want to."

"Maybe only to Upper Saddle. Let's go far enough to use the ropes, if we can." Nelson grinned. "I snuck into your garage on the way over. I grabbed your stuff, too."

During their five years of friendship, David had learned that Nelson didn't often have time for casual relationships. They were both forty and busy, and they'd grown accustomed to grabbing time together whenever they could. A chance to make their old climb together seemed too big an adventure to turn down—a retaliation against a day of waiting for Susan Roche and a phone call that hadn't come. "Okay. You've convinced me. I'm in."

And so they were off. They drove into the national park and, after changing into sturdy climbing boots and loading two bags of climbing gear with cams and rope, abandoned the car at the Lupine Meadow parking lot. They chatted about unimportant things while Nelson Hull led the way along the distinct footpath, their feet dislodging pebbles and razor-sharp chunks of stone.

"Sarah's having a garage sale next Saturday and she wants to sell my flannel shirts. She says I never wear them anymore and they're taking up room in the closet. How about that? I've had those since before we got married. They're my camp shirts."

"Garage sales are bad. All that great stuff a guy manages to hoard, gone in a day."

They entered a fragrant tunnel of pine, stringing out along an eastern slope, breathing hard, taking long switchbacks around shaded fronds of fern and pale strands of bearberry.

Chickadees flew in scallops from bough to bough. Above them, in shades of gray and shadow, spires of schist, granite, and Precambrian gneiss jutted into the sky.

For the first time in weeks, the landscape surrounding David loomed larger than the impenetrable self-reproach he carried. "It's *extraordinary* here. I had forgotten."

Nelson stopped to catch his breath. "No one should ever stay away so long that he forgets."

"I didn't mean to do that. It's been years since I've done this. Time just . . . gets away."

"You ought not to let that happen."

A prominent rib of granite divided the gully they climbed and the first stone tower loomed above them. The Needle. David returned his attention to the rocky terrain at their feet. For several hundred feet he climbed in silence again, to where a granite face rose to the east.

"Abby put my turntable in a garage sale and I had to grab it out of someone's hands. All those people wandering the front yard, and I put it back inside the house. Imagine. I wouldn't have any way to play my old albums from college."

"Do you play your old albums from college?"

"No. But that doesn't matter. It matters that I wouldn't have any *way* to."

A narrow vertical crack split the tower of rock, suitable for climbing, but Nelson continued plodding uphill. He didn't stop until they'd traversed a high ledge onto one large, conspicuous boulder. "Nelson, every other preacher I know goes to The Pines to relax with a round of golf. You're the only one I know who has to climb."

"Sarah sold my clubs at a garage sale."

Below them the valley sprawled like a gathered skirt, the Snake River rickracking a border beside the straight seam of highway. To the northeast glistened Jackson Lake, sunk into sage flats and gleaming like a mirror. To the southeast lay the Lockhart hayfields, already green from a first cutting. David grasped his pack and sprinted on ahead of Nelson. He knelt on all fours and crawled through a narrow tunnel formed by the angle of one huge boulder.

Nelson scrabbled through behind him. "The Eye Of The Needle," he said.

"Appropriate name."

After that, they climbed for a while without talking. David's thigh muscles began to burn. He welcomed the pounding of his pulse, the rich aching in his obliques.

*If everything goes the right way . . .*

As each step became harder, he embraced the fierce physical exercise.

*. . . Abby won't find out what I've done.*

He leaned into the slope, climbed higher, earning both his progress and his pain.

*If everything goes the right way . . .*

With each step, he did penance, made restitution to himself and to the mountain.

*. . . I can hide this.*

"Hey," Nelson said between breaths when they finally stopped to rest. "Got . . . a question . . . to ask you."

"What's that?"

"You like that Husquvarna chainsaw you bought?"

"It's a good one. Six-point-one horsepower engine. Best chainsaw I've ever had."

"Next time you go out to cut firewood for the church with your chainsaw, can I go with you? I'd love to get my hands on that piece of equipment."

"Sure."

"One of the occupational hazards of being a pastor. Having men serve the church so well that I never get out to do the fun stuff myself."

"You're too important," David said. "Think what it would do to the congregation if a tree fell on you."

They started up again. The landscape opened into tundra, continuing north, following a faint track in the loose scree and crossing hard-frozen patches of snow. Long ago they'd discovered that from here they could see all the way to Gannett Peak on a clear day. David shaded his eyes and searched for it now, some sixty miles away against the southeast horizon, the crowning height along the purple line of the Wind Rivers.

"Probably the same thing it would do to them if I fell off a mountain," Nelson said.

The air was growing thin, making it harder for them to breathe as they climbed.

"It's hazy, isn't it?" David said between gasps. "I don't know what happened to the sun." For a long time, he stood on the edge of a precipice, looking out, staring off into the distance. Nelson stood on the outcropping beside him, eyes raised to the sky and to the heavenly Father beyond the sky. If anyone had been watching them with binoculars from the valley below, they would have seen two human figures jutting beyond the silhouette of the mountain, their statures confident, their feet braced wide, as if by gaining height there, they'd gained perspective on the world.

A deep bass-note of thunder rumbled at them, so close they could feel it resonate beneath their feet. Seconds later, the sound ricocheted off the far side of the valley and a streak of lightning doglegged across the sky.

"All those things the Bible says a man is supposed to be." When David's voice came at last, it came gruff and hard. "I don't think I can live up to those anymore."

Nelson searched the sky, his hair lifting in the wind. "What brought this up?"

David gestured wildly toward the lightning. "I don't know. Life. The mountains." *What I've done to my wife.*

"Don't get confused. Living the right life in God's eyes has never been about trying, David."

"Oh, no?"

"It's about the things you're willing to do each time you blow it."

The bluster bore down upon them from the Upper Saddle, blindsiding them because it came—as all Teton weather does—from the west. David hadn't noticed when the warmth left and the wind became changeable and the far reaches of clouds became mottled by gray streaks of rain.

Nelson paused long enough to survey Mount Owen and Teewinot below them. "Even up here, there's no getting away from the storms."

"Storms in your life, Nelson?"

The pastor nodded. "That's why you're a good friend. It's nice, spending time with someone who doesn't have such a messed-up life and who doesn't expect me to know the answers to fix it."

David said nothing.

"Guess we won't get high enough to use the ropes."

"I never called Abby."

"Well, you aren't going to do it now."

Wind sluiced over the mountain, threshing David's hair and the tops of the trees below them, making it difficult to descend the trail. He started toward the steep ice gullies and crags rising above the mouth of Cascade Canyon. When the thunderbolt came, he didn't have to count before he heard the rumble.

Two seconds, at best. Hardly any time at all.

"Nelson, let's get out of here."

Stones came tumbling downhill as Nelson followed. David lost his footing once and slid several yards. A lightning flash underscored each crevice and outcropping of granite. David felt the roots of his hair begin to stand, negative ions attracting positive ones. *"Hurry."*

Together they lurched downhill. The rain began in sparse, wet pelts before the sky opened. The wind caught the downpour and slammed it sideways against them. Rain needled their skin. They squinted against it but that didn't help.

The hail came all at once, hitting the ground and bouncing like popcorn around their feet, striking and stinging their ears. Water began to rush in little rivers past them, pursuing the way of least resistance. Rivulets joined in the gaps to become streams, racing downward, filling furrows and troughs.

"We ought to find a rock to duck under," Nelson bellowed as he scrabbled past his friend.

"With this much water? I think we ought to keep heading down."

But then Nelson stopped so abruptly that David

slammed into him. "Look over there!" Nelson hollered over the wind. He pointed. "Can you believe that?"

David's shirt was plastered against him. He pried it loose so it didn't cling to his chest and squinted into the cold rain. "What are you talking about?"

"Over there."

"I don't—"

"There."

Sure enough, as David squinted through the weather, he saw what Nelson had seen: two little girls crouched beneath the brow of a narrow ledge. Two coats—a pink one and a yellow one—flew like banners from where they'd been hung on the crooks of a stunted blue spruce. Two little girls, alone.

For one instant David allowed himself to indulge his anger. Tourists visiting these mountains could do idiotic things. He had a saying for whenever the weekly *Guide* came out with an article about a sightseer. Every week in the summer, someone got lost in the mountains or burned in a hot pool or stranded in the Snake River or gored by a bison in Yellowstone. *Your brain, don't leave home without it.*

More often than one could believe, visitors camping in the Tetons allowed their children to wander farther afield than those same children would be allowed to wander at home. Now David and Nelson hurried toward these two little girls. Though they were protected from the hail, a mad gush of water had entered the gulch of their hiding place, threatening their feet. They huddled among a vast assortment of accessories: two dolls dressed in sweaters and mountain gear, a trunk, and a table with a plastic birthday cake, all arranged upon one dry strip of earth.

Nelson bent down and peered in at them, noting

their somber, serious faces. "What are you girls doing up here?"

One tucked her knees tighter beneath her chin. "We climbed up this far with her brother and her uncle. But when we got tired, they said we should stay down low and wait."

The other clutched a pair of tiny doll crutches and a yellow plastic foot cast made to open and shut on tiny hinges. "We had to bring them someplace dangerous," she said. "Our dolls wanted to break their legs so they could use their crutches."

"We didn't pass anybody climbing this route." David surveyed what he could see of the mountain's summit. "They must have tried the Exum Ridge instead."

The hail tapered off even as the rain came harder. Tiny pellets of ice covered the ground. Lightning cracked in the trees below them, sending up sparks and the splintering crash of breaking wood. Thunder boomed against the rocks.

"How good are you two at piggy-backing? Bring your Barbie stuff and let's go."

Indignant, one of them said, "This isn't Barbie stuff. They're American Girl dolls. Don't you *know?*" She began loading the dolls and the little birthday cake into a sodden paper sack. A minute later, they were fording the washout and getting soaked to their bones. Nelson lifted the child in the yellow raincoat. David took the one in the pink. She grabbed on and hung there, a dangling weight just like the pack beside her on his back. Slippery legs wrapped around David's ribcage, ankles plaited in front of his midsection. He hitched up her knees and locked them against his hipbones with his elbows.

A wet little girl felt contradictory to everything he'd ever known on his shoulders—light and willowy, like driftwood or a sparrow, so opposite from Braden's robust, square weight. She held on to him for dear life, her doll's sharp plastic fingers jabbing David in the ear. The two of them together, doll and girl, smelled like dust and vanilla and toothpaste.

Down they went, flapping pink and yellow coats behind them like flags. David wondered who on earth could have been stupid enough to climb a mountain and leave two little girls waiting behind with no one to make sure they were out of danger.

"We're in a tent in the campground," the girl atop David said. When she spoke he could feel the jut of her chin working against his scalp.

"Try this way." Nelson edged over to one side of the path. "It might be easier."

But there wasn't an easier way. David's feet slid and his ankles buckled every time he broke through into a hole in the scree. His knees ached from going downhill. His calves burned.

Just when he'd managed a steady gait, the little girl atop him began to sing, the cadence a jarring rhythm to each of David's steps.

"The een-sy, ween-sy spi-der went up the wa-ter spout . . ."

Her innocent, clear voice resounded all through David. On one side of his head, doll fingers poked holes in his scalp. On the other side, two small, real fingers walked up his temple and into his hair, sending goose bumps the length of his neck.

"Can you not sing, please?" he asked, feeling her fingers meddling with his hair.

"How come you don't have very much hair on the back of your head?" she asked back.

Mercifully, the thunder began to echo again, far enough away that they could hear it bouncing back from across the far mountain. A forest-service campground came into view; soggy dome tents sat like gumdrops in spaces among the trees. Everywhere lay the signs of fleeing in haste from the rain—tablecloths left in rumpled puddles on tables, aluminum coffee pots and grills hastily thrown into boxes, firewood brought up under cars and covered with tarpaulin.

"Grandma. Grandma!"

"Oh, my word! Mandy. Kendra," said the breathless woman who met them, screwing her grimy shirttail in her two hands. "Oh, you're *here*."

"We found them up the mountainside," Nelson said. "We thought maybe we'd better lug them down to civilization."

The distraught woman cupped each of the girls' faces in her hands. "We didn't know where you were. The boys got back hours ago."

The girls slid off and fled into their grandma's arms. She embraced them in a tight hug. And another. "Oh, you're all right. Thank heaven you're all right." She rocked back on her heels and they all saw her face become stern. "You should be punished, you know that? Both of you. They've gone down to the ranger station to see if people could help find you." She gave them both a swat that didn't reach home. And then hug, hug, hug. "You had us worried sick."

"You ought not to punish them," David said. "Someone just left them there. Someone deserted them."

"Thank you so much," the overwrought woman said

in the direction of her left shoulder, without ever even asking David or Nelson their names. And then, to the girls, as she herded them inside the tent, "Get on in there and change if you can find anything that's still dry."

The only sounds as the disappointed rescuers made their way to the car were chickadees lilting in the trees, the chatter of hikers along the trail, and the slop of their boots in the mud. David called Abby to let her know where they'd been.

"Yes, there's a storm here." He took the phone from his mouth. "Nelson, it's clear as a bell over at the house. Can you believe it?"

They didn't speak again as they strung out along the trail and broke into the open of Lupine Meadow the same time as the sun. Nelson dug out the keys to his Subaru, jostled them to unlock the door. They pitched ropes and cams into the backseat and loaded up with a slam of car doors.

Side by side the two friends sat staring at the front windshield. They sat for so long that the Subaru filled with the smell of their sweat, the windows fogged from damp clothes and hot breath.

In that moment, David thought about saying something about Samantha. He thought about bringing her up, only he didn't know how to begin.

*Nelson, I wanted to talk to you—*

*I made a bad move and I don't know what to do—*

*Nelson, you'll never guess who called the other day—*

But Nelson must have decided it was time to pull out. The Subaru sprang to life on the first twist of the key. He shifted the car into reverse and slung his elbow across the car seat. The moment was gone.

# Chapter Six

Saturday evening. All quiet except for the neighbors eating outside two doors down, leaning in toward their conversation, their plates mounded with exotic barbecued shish kebabs. The food smelled so good for two square miles that there ought to be a law.

When the telephone rang, David didn't think to be concerned. He and Braden—his nose bandaged and still slightly swollen—were outside playing catch, doing their best to ignore the fragrance of marinated teriyaki beef wafting down the street. The rhythmic *slap slap slap* of the baseball as it exchanged hands, the long-awaited cool as the sun wallowed atop the western ridge of hills, had lulled David. That, and the sight of Abby standing on their back deck in black pants and a sleeveless chambray blouse. She was sans makeup, fresh-faced and young, and David thought her the most beautiful woman in the world.

"I couldn't stand it." She saluted him with a tray of dismembered chicken that she'd arranged drumsticks parallel, thighs aligned, breasts together. "Whenever the neighbors grill out, it makes me want to do it, too."

"Let's find something that smells better than theirs. Do we have any barbecue sauce?"

"Yeah." She pulled a plastic jug from beneath her arm. "The old Treasure family recipe. Stuff in a bottle."

That's when the telephone rang. Right then.

David mindlessly caught Braden's throw and side-armed it back. "You want me to get that?" he asked Abby.

"No, I will. The grill has to warm up before I put on the meat."

"I'll cook if you want me to."

"Nope. I'm in the mood. Just don't let Brewster get into this chicken." Two decks down, the diners began to scoot back their chairs. Two little girls began to joust with shish-kebab skewers. David heard Abby's faint voice answer the phone indoors: "Hello?"

Brewster loped onto the deck and began nosing around the table. "Hey, you dog. Get away from that chicken."

With a sidelong, disappointed glance, the dog sauntered away and, heaving a sigh from the very depths of his soul, slumped into the grass.

"Dad." Braden opened and shut his glove like a clamshell. "Throw it back to me. I want to show you how I changed my knuckle ball."

The screen door slid open. Abby stood framed in the dark rectangle, her bewilderment illuminated by the backyard sun. "David? The phone's for you." Her voice sounded uncertain and confused. "It's a woman. I can't imagine who."

The moment she said it, David knew. When Braden threw the ball, David missed it. It nicked the edge of his mitt and bounced onto the grass out of reach. He ignored the ball completely and laid his glove with precise care on the patio table.

"Well. Guess I'd better go find out what this is."

He squeezed past Abby where she stood scraping the grill with a wire brush. He tried to take his time, tried to pretend it didn't matter, tried to pretend he wasn't in a rush. Once inside, though, he seized the receiver off the counter. As an afterthought, before he answered, he searched for Abby again, outside the window.

"Hello?"

"I'm sorry." Susan's voice, no surprise. "I know you wanted me to phone you at the office."

The snare of guilt clamped tightly around him. He said cryptically, "I certainly did."

"I couldn't get you there. First you were gone yesterday afternoon. And then I didn't think you'd want to wait over the weekend to hear."

"Why not, Susan?" He wouldn't give himself away. He wouldn't let her know how disconcerted he'd been, thinking of them. "I've waited all these years. Why not a little longer?"

To Susan's credit, she floundered a bit at that. "I thought you *wanted* me to hurry. On the phone, you sounded odd. Anxious. You said you needed to know."

"Of course I sounded odd." He stalked around the kitchen stool, yanked it up to the counter with one hand, and straddled it like he would a saddle. "I thought this chapter of my life was over." He said one thing, and was thinking another: *I heard her, Susan. This little girl is for real.* "I've been trying to put an end to this for nine years."

"Well," Susan said quietly. "I see you haven't

changed a bit. You never were one to let your heart get in the way of what was really important."

Back to the measured words—unresponsive and impenetrable. "You have news."

"I do."

"And?"

"It didn't work, David. You're only a marginal match."

"What?"

"It isn't good enough."

The barstool creaked beneath him. He leaned forward, as if changing his posture could change her answer. For a long moment, he stared at himself in the reflection of the stainless steel over the stove, seeing nothing. "You want to explain that to me?"

"There could be better matches. With you, we'd run the risk of graft versus host. That she'd reject. That it could be fatal."

The constriction in his heart pressed clear through into his spine. None of the emotions he'd expected came to liberate him. Not anger. Not blame. Certainly not relief.

His ears rang. He tried to cope with her words, but couldn't. All of his running away, and now this. "Oh, Susan. I'm so sorry."

"If one more person tells me how sorry they are, I'm going to break something."

The screen door scraped open and in came his wife. Brewster followed, his toenails clicking on the linoleum. Abby rummaged through the utensil drawer, her back toward the counter where he sat. When David spoke now, he was deliberately vague. "But you said it was close. Would that make any difference at all?"

Abby fished a long, two-pronged barbecue fork out of

the drawer. Something to stab meat with. When she started scrabbling again, he figured she was searching for a knife. He could tell from the angle of her back that she was listening.

"Please say there's something else you can do."

"We keep searching is what we do. But that takes time."

Without Susan explaining further, David knew the dire implications: Samantha doesn't have that much time. He eyed the camber of Abby's spine, hating how still she was, hating how he encrypted his words. He cupped his hand over the mouthpiece and whispered a lame explanation to her. "This is somebody from the bank." Well, Susan used to be from the bank. She'd walked in the front door one day, hadn't she? Maybe a half-truth now was better than no truth at all.

He spoke into the receiver again. "There isn't anything else?"

A pause. Then, "Well, yes. There is. But, how badly do you want to hear it?"

Abby found the knife. "Braden!" she said. "Can you bring the chicken back in? I decided to cut those breasts apart."

"Abby's there," Susan said. "I can hear her."

"Yes."

"You can't say much then, can you?"

"No."

"Then listen," she said. "Only listen."

"Yes."

"We have one hope."

"What?"

Susan waited what seemed like forever, while Abby struggled to hacksaw through chicken bones with a knife he'd mail-ordered from TV because it claimed to cut baling wire and pennies. "I want you to think about it. If you do, you'll know."

He did think. And knew. The truth dawned on him, unspeakable and preposterous, the very impossible thing he'd feared. "No."

"They say that siblings are the ones, David. The chances are very high."

"No."

Piece by piece, Abby hacked through the chicken. When she finished, she arrayed the pieces on the cutting board and situated them to her liking. They sat largest to smallest, perfectly ordered, the way she liked to keep their lives. "Braden? Can you open the back door again? I'm ready to put these on."

David waited, the receiver held slightly away from his mouth, until his wife and his son had gone. "I can't let that happen, Susan. You know that." Only Brewster remained in the room, lying on the floor and peering up at David, his eyes pools of melancholy amber. "Don't you understand? I was willing to do this myself, but there's too much at stake if we get Braden involved."

"I thought you cared about Sam. When you called, I heard it in your voice."

"You're asking me to risk everything that's good in my life for a mistake I made nine years ago."

"You can't call Samantha a mistake."

"No, Susan. I didn't mean Samantha. It was us that was the mistake." *After all this time not telling me, living her life out according to her own plan.*

"I can have another test sent for him. We could find out. We could just *try*."

"Susan, do you realize what you're asking me to do?"

"I'm asking you to involve your son so we can save our daughter's life. She's your daughter, too."

"You're asking a lot."

"Yes," she said. "I know."

*You already know what's going to happen here, don't you? You're going to lose your family. The harder you seek forgiveness, the farther it will slip away.*

"Susan," he said. "I want to do something to help you. Financially, with the medical bills. Anything." But to do anything would take David deeper and deeper away from Abby, and he knew it. "Anything but telling my wife and involving Braden. Anything that doesn't come at a cost this high."

⌒

Braden dug through the junk drawer, making way too much noise for this early in the morning. "Mom?" he asked in a loud stage whisper. "Where's the Scotch tape?"

"It's in there."

"No, it isn't."

"Keep digging. You'll find it."

"Mom, it isn't *here*."

"Sh-hhh. If you talk so loud, you're going to wake up your father. If you want to surprise him in bed, you've got to be quiet. You know when he wakes up, he always sets out for a run."

"Oh, here's the tape."

"I told you it was in there."

"Where's the wrapping paper?"

"In the closet. Do you still need to sign your dad's card?"

"Yeah."

"I'll get it."

When Abby returned minutes later with the Father's Day greeting cards she'd stashed away, she found Braden with an entire roll of blue foil paper slung across the floor. Brewster was sprawled out on top of it, punching holes with his toenails while Braden kept trying to shove him off. "Mom, get the dog, would you? He's messing up my paper."

"Sh-hhh. Don't wake your dad."

"Will you cut this so it's straight, Mom? I never can do that."

So there they sat, mother and son on the floor, brandishing the scissors and the tape and tying bows with the dog edging in close beside them. What David's gifts lacked in originality, they made up for in enormous love. A pair of fuzzy camping socks. A ratchet set that Braden had picked out himself at Sunrise Lumber (tools were always a sure winner with David). A pair of plaid pajamas from Coldwater Creek.

Abby showed Braden once more how to miter the corners on a package. While she folded each paper triangle over each box end, her head welled with gratitude. So many years had passed since she'd wrapped Father's Day gifts for her own dad. So many years since she'd been innocent and had thought every man who was a father ought to be revered and admired.

*I don't know how my mother did it, staying with that man all those years.*

But no, this morning wasn't the time for remembering her past with remorse. It was a time for celebrating. David was different from the man her mother had married. David was everything Abby had ever prayed for. A loving dad. A man who revered the Lord. Someone she could trust with the deepest needs and hurts of her heart.

"Mom," Braden whispered. "Can I go wake him up yet?"

"Have you signed his card? Don't get so involved in his presents that you forget to sign his card!"

"Oh, nope. I'd better write it."

For the next ten minutes, one little boy and one ball-point pen made lines and drawings and ink smudges all over the envelope. Then came the laborious words and the signing of his name, which couldn't be done without the tongue stuck between his teeth in concentration.

Abby stood behind him for a moment, watching his effort with pride, her fingers curled over the back of the chair. She wanted to squeeze him, as mothers do, but she knew she'd only annoy him.

*Oh, Braden. You're so lucky, having this life you have. Everything we've been able to set up for you.*

Braden licked the envelope flap so thoroughly Abby didn't see how it would ever stick. He pounded it shut with the heel of his hand. "There we go. Completely ready."

Abby couldn't resist the urge. She leaned over and gave him a huge kiss right on the cowlick, right on the top of his head.

"Mom!"

"I had to do it, Braden. I had to."

"Can I wake him up now?"

"Oh." A deep, happy, frustrated sigh. "Go ahead."

Braden gathered the presents in his arms and started

away. Halfway to their bedroom door, he turned back to grin at his mom.

"It's going to be really good, isn't it? Dad is going to like this."

"Yes," Abby agreed. "Your dad is going to like this a lot."

~

"Happy Father's Day, Dad." Braden's voice feathered, wet and tickly, into David's ear. "You awake?"

"What? Hm-mmm?" For a moment, David basked in the comfort of the thick, weightless blankets around him and the sweetness of his son's small arms encircling him. And then the dog jumped on the bed. "Ah . . ." David shoved Brewster aside as his son's words sank in.

Happy Father's Day.

*No, not Father's Day. Please, I can't do Father's Day.*

"Open your card. And I got you presents."

"Braden." Abby's voice. "Give your dad a chance to open his eyes."

"Here, sport." David used his elbows to prop himself up out of a dead sleep. "I'll open something." He scrubbed his nose and sniffed. Rumpled his own hair.

"This one. Open this card first."

David tore open the envelope and began to read. The card said "A Dad Like You Deserves To Have A GREAT DAY."

*Oh no, I don't. I don't deserve a great day at all.*

"So have a big sundae, drink plenty of pop, sit in the sun or fish till you drop. Have a picnic with your kids or go to the zoo . . . but whatever you do, DO IT FOR YOU!!!'"

"To the greatist dad in the world," Braden had written in elaborate cursive. "Anybody to have you is lucky, which means I am lucky!!! From the boy in your life. Braden."

David almost couldn't hold the card. A lump of emotion wedged itself behind his sternum and stayed there.

"Hurry, David, and open your presents," Abby said. "Church starts in an hour."

"It's Father's Day," Braden reminded her. "Maybe Dad doesn't want to go to church. Maybe the rest of us don't have to go, either."

"Oh, yes, we do," David said, even though that was the last thing he wanted. How important it was, he thought, keeping up appearances. How important, making sure no one around him knew anything was wrong.

With resolute determination, David opened his gifts. With each personal item he uncovered from the layers of frothy tissue paper—the socks, the pajamas, the amazing set of gleaming ratchets all in a row according to size—his self-contempt and his survival instinct dug itself deeper.

"Hey, Brade." David smashed the paper into a ball and sank a swish shot into the trashcan beside the dresser. "You're a good kid, you know that?"

"Yeah."

Without looking at his wife, David grabbed their boy and rolled him over onto his belly on the bed. Fiercely, maybe not quite gently enough, David set out to win a war of tickling. Braden shrieked and wrestled and giggled and tickled right back.

When the Treasures arrived at the Jackson Hole Christian Center later that morning, the spaces were full and latecomers had already begun to park off the pavement in the hayfield. Praise and worship had started inside; they could hear music through the windows and across the meadow. They took their bulletins from Harold Maddox at the door, Abby gave Harold a hug, and they wove in and out along the crowded aisle to their usual pew. Abby laid her Bible and her purse in her seat and began the thing that David knew made her the happiest of all: she lifted her hands outspread to the Lord, swaying lightly with her eyes closed, and began to sing. David sat down. Braden roosted between them and did his best to poke his hand into David's pocket for a pen.

"Wait a few minutes, sport. You aren't bored enough to start drawing yet." David moved away, standing up beside Abby in self-defense.

And immediately wished he hadn't.

The sight of Abby trusting the way she did, with uplifted hands and lilting voice, evoked the full turmoil in David's heart. *Look at me, Abby,* he wanted to say. *Look at me and see who I am.*

Everyone tended to trust David in this place. Because he worked as an officer at the bank, they'd signed him on to the church financial board. He served on the presbytery committee and on the groundskeeper advisory group, and just about every other place people would let him put his name on a list and volunteer.

He tithed regularly, rotated-in whenever they were short-handed on sixth-grade Sunday school teachers and, yes, as Nelson had mentioned, he often drove up Mosquito Creek to cut firewood with his new Husqvarna for the wood-burning furnace in the church basement.

*Ab, look at me.*

Nelson took the microphone at the altar, led his congregation in one last song, and challenged them to hug one another and greet visitors and welcome others around them in their seats. For long moments, everyone's arms became a web of proffered handshakes, hugs, and God-Be-with-You greetings. Several friends sitting nearby congratulated David. "Happy Father's Day! Happy Anniversary!"

And just as Nelson Hull began to signal that it was time to return to their seats and quiet down, here came Viola Uptergrove shuffling toward them with her walker. She was at least eighty-five years old, hunched and darling in a pink dress with pink blush powder caught in the wrinkles along her cheeks, pink lipstick staining her lips, and a pink silk butterfly bobby-pinned behind one ear. The butterfly sparkled and flickered on tiny, spring-balanced wings, as if it had recently flown in and alighted itself in Viola's white, sugar-spun hair.

Viola Uptergrove, David knew, was always the one to pray.

She finished traversing the aisle and came near to him right as Nelson Hull took to the pulpit again and brandished the microphone. David glanced up and saw Nelson waiting, watching Viola's progress with his patient, loving smile.

When she spoke, her voice was so gravelly David had to bend close to hear her. She patted his hand a long time. "You have such a beautiful family," she said at last, her rheumy blue eyes shining up at him like stars. "Happy Father's Day."

He waited for more, but that was all she said before she began her journey to her seat again, trundling her walker back across the aisle.

As soon as Viola got back to her seat, the sermon began. Because Nelson Hull had long been his friend, David felt in harmless hands whenever Nelson preached. He settled into the pew, making himself comfortable. But for some strange reason, Nelson's eyes caught David's from the pulpit. And David didn't feel quite so safe anymore.

"Often, we are convicted in our lives that something needs to change," Nelson began as David sank lower into his seat. "But a man who hears and feels convicted of something, and equates that with having changed and *done* something about it, is like a man who sees himself in the mirror and then walks away and doesn't remember what he looks like."

On the back of David's bulletin, flat against a hymnal, Braden began to sketch timid outlines on paper. Desperate to break eye contact with his pastor, David focused on Braden's drawing instead. At first he thought Braden was drawing a picture of a pitcher on the mound. But as the shape began to take form, David recognized a man crouched in a warrior's stance with a huge belt, sword drawn for battle, shield upheld.

A little boy's picture.

"The more we know our heavenly Father, the more we love Him. The more we love Him, the more we trust Him, and the more we trust Him, the more we want His advice and counsel. The more we seek His advice and counsel, the more He'll give it to us."

David wondered what sort of a picture a little girl would draw in a church pew on a Sunday morning. Little girls liked to draw flowers, didn't they? They liked those little houses. Or those big green scribbles of trees.

He raised his eyes. Unbidden, they locked immediately onto Nelson's. "You get stuck," the pastor's voice rumbled in much the same tone and manner as the thunder on the mountains the other day, "because you think hearing something and being convicted of it are equivalent to the *doing*."

Samantha's face swam before David, the way it had appeared in Susan's wallet photograph: sunny and irrepressible, her dark eyes studying him as if she could see into the core of his soul.

Desperate, David squeezed his son against him in a stupid, transparent gesture of fatherhood and held him there against his will until Braden squirmed away.

It wasn't only the thought of losing his family that left David longing and afraid. It was the thought of losing his courage. Of losing himself.

*What happens to me, if I bury this? What happens to an innocent child if I cover my own transgression from the one it will hurt the most?*

For a moment, just one moment, David felt Abby's chin brush against his shoulder and smelled a waft of her familiar perfume, the scent Braden called the smell-of-Mom. She uncrossed her legs, settled back, and placed her hand possessively upon his knee.

The poignant mixture of Nelson's words, of Abby's touching him, of Braden sitting beside him on a pew, swinging his legs and doodling, pushed David to a chasmic edge.

*Trapped. I'm trapped. I jump here, and I die.*

The truth seemed to come from every part of him at once, crying out in silence from the back of David's throat. It came from his heart, and from someplace larger than his heart, something beyond him that knew him to the very depths of his soul.

*You're standing still, aren't you, and letting mistake heap upon mistake? You're standing still and letting rubble pile upon rubble.*

Here today in their pew where they sat every Sunday near the front in the center of the third row—today while Nelson's sermon words pounded out over the loudspeaker—David felt the church members were surveying the knobs protruding from his backbone. They were measuring the flush of color that crept past the collar of his Teton Pines golf shirt. They were comparing the way he had clutched Abby's hand last week, how she made a point to reach for him today, and how he didn't respond to her now.

*Guilty. Guilty.*

God was telling him to do something impossible.

And everyone would see his deceitful heart.

# Chapter Seven

$\mathcal{E}$very Sunday afternoon Abby called her mother, Carol Higgins, to have a weekly chat.

"Oh, Abigail," the woman said. "It's so good hearing your voice."

"Yours, too, Mom. How are you? Have you had a good week?"

"Russell Smith came over and painted the shutters this week. They look so pretty from the street. Much better than before."

"Oh, nice, Mom. I'm glad you're pleased."

"Frank planted petunias in the big pot by the front door yesterday. Pink ones. They add such a nice splotch of color."

"How *is* Frank?"

Frank Higgins was her mother's second husband. It had been such a blessing, having Carol find someone special like him in her retirement years. Someone who would finally take care of her the way Abby's father never had.

"Oh, Frank is fine. Just fine. He's out washing the

front windows right now. I'll go get him in a minute. I know he'll want to talk to you."

"I want to talk to him, too."

Carol lowered her voice a notch, as if she was worried someone might overhear her. "It means so much to Frank, Abigail. Having you treat him the way you treat him—"

"Well, I wouldn't treat him any other way."

"—almost as if he were your real father."

Abby let this conversation taper off into nothing.

But Carol found something else to say. "He didn't wait to open those gifts you sent. He ripped into them yesterday, right after the postman left them at the door."

"Shame on Frank."

"And you chose for him real well, honey. Those huckleberry chocolates were just the thing. He's already eaten half the box."

"Good."

"And to have Braden sign the card in his own handwriting. That was really something."

"I'm glad he was pleased."

"Honey, thanks for working to make everything right with him."

*Oh.* A sigh. Abby shifted the receiver to her other ear. "It's like Frank is my dad, Mom. It's easy."

At that, neither of them could come up with anything more to say on the subject.

"How's David, dear? Is he having a good day?"

"I think so," Abby said. "Yes, he is."

"Well." A long pause. "I should get Frank."

"Okay."

"Honey—"

"It's okay, Mom."

"I know Father's Day is always a hard day for you."

"Mother, it's really okay."

"I'm sorry for the part I played in that."

"It's gotten better. It has. I hardly think about that part anymore."

"Abigail—"

"I just focus on David, Mom. I think about what I have to look forward to instead of what's happened in the past. That makes everything a whole lot easier."

David pulled the lawn mower out of the garage. He yanked the pull cord as hard as he could and took morose satisfaction when it wouldn't start. It meant he got to yank it again.

He had been waiting all day for the "right time." Only there was no right time to do something like this to his wife.

Every time he went inside she and Braden would tell him, "Happy Father's Day." And when he wasn't suffering through that he was remembering Viola Uptergrove's shining eyes, that surreal, flapping butterfly, and her frail hand patting him.

*You have such a beautiful family.*

When the engine finally chuffed to life, he aimed the mower at the ragged grass with hawkish precision and went after the lawn. He made one violent slash past the window, then another, widening his course, the mulch shooting out like coleslaw around his ankles.

He ran over a pinecone and took perverse pleasure in chopping it to smithereens. He shredded aspen leaves that lay like playing cards in the grass. Back and forth, on and on across the yard. On his last pass, he made a fierce right-angle turn and began again, cutting across the grain, one resolute swathe after another, dividing his lawn into checkerboard squares.

His shoes were green when he stepped inside, and he stopped to pick up a grass clump that had stuck to the carpet. He wiped his hands on the kitchen towel and realized he'd left grass there, too. Oops. Abby would go after him for leaving grass on the tea towel. He tried to brush it off and made a bigger mess of it instead. It left a green stain and landed in the sink drainer on top of clean silverware.

"Abby?" He heard her tromping up the stairs from the basement. "I need to talk to you."

Up she came with her full wicker laundry basket in both hands, headed toward their bedroom to put clean clothes away. She balanced the basket on her hip for a minute and poked a strand of hair behind her ear. "What, David?"

"Let me have that." He tried to take the basket from her. "I'll help you."

"You're going to get green all over everything. These are clean."

"See, I knew you'd be worried about grass getting on things. I cleaned it up in the kitchen."

"I've got this."

"You sure?"

"What is it? You're helping with the laundry now? That's a surprise." She stood on her tiptoes and gave him an unsuspecting little peck.

He hated that she was teasing him, hated that she didn't have any cares or any awful intuitions about him as he followed her into the bedroom. "Abby." He waited until she dumped the basket on the bed and began to sort through the laundry. Then he shut the door.

That stopped her.

She stood beside the trappings of their everyday lives—one masculine gray sock with a hole in the heel, her own frayed nightshirt, a tea towel from the kitchen that read *"Kindness is a special art of giving with a loving heart"*—and said, "You've shut the door. This must be serious."

He couldn't do this. He couldn't blurt it out and destroy everything they'd ever had together. *Father, if this is what you want from me, then you've got to help me do it. You've got to help me know what to say.*

"What is it, David? Why are you staring at me like that?" Her smile shone unprotected, as happy and unwary as a child's.

Braden and his friends went dashing around the side of the house. David heard skateboards rasping over asphalt and the slam of wheels on the plywood incline that he had hammered together beside the garage. The thump of a hard landing, the tumble of a fall.

David picked up something to fold, some flimsy silk thing that he'd seen Abby wear underneath her sweaters. He tried to match seam to seam, corner to corner, but the thing slithered formless from his grasp like something alive.

If he didn't have anything to fold, he didn't have anything to do with his hands.

He considered sitting down on the bed before he told her. But, no. He felt more comfortable, more in control, standing up. "I don't know how to say this, Abigail. I don't know where to start."

"At the beginning." She rescued the shiny silk thing

from his knee and pressed it into a perfect, tiny square. "Just start at the beginning, David. It's as good a place as any."

"This is important, Abby."

"Well." He could see she was confused. Her expression became neutral. "Okay." She waited. "Go on."

*Lord. Is this the way it is with you? Giving up everything good I know in exchange for failure I deserve? Sacrificing something that I understand for everything that I don't?*

Outside, the boys had abandoned the skateboards and turned on the hose. In the grass out the window, the yellow sprinkler threw up May Pole ribbons of spray. Braden ran through, the water beating against his bare legs. He skipped and yelped, running back for more.

"They're getting their clothes wet out there," Abby complained. At first David thought she wanted him to tell them to stop. But he realized she was only talking, filling the space between them. "I'm not doing laundry again until next weekend. This is my only day."

David turned from the window, back to his wife, back to the awful matter at hand. "I need you to listen carefully and not to interrupt me with this." There wasn't anything he could say to cushion the blow for her. "Because I have difficult news."

She stopped folding and rested her nose in the vee between her thumb and her pointer finger. "Okay."

"I've gotten into . . . well, it can't be helped, Abby. There's going to be some trouble."

She lowered her brows. "Go on."

"It's something you have to know. In order for us to . . . go forward."

"Okay." She waited.

He took a deep breath and launched. "I've had an affair, Abby."

"What?" For a moment she seemed disoriented, as if she had lost her bearings. She gave one half-witted, awful-sounding hiccup. "That's the most ridiculous thing I've ever heard." She removed a pair of his socks from the basket and matched them, toe to toe, heel to heel, before she rolled the tops together, one inside the other. David had an absurd thought as he watched her: here was why he didn't help with the laundry. He could never fold things quite right for her.

"No. It isn't ridiculous. It's true."

She stopped folding.

"Abby, listen to me."

She waited, those eyes of hers dazed, bewildered, still. "You're crazy, you know. Saying things like this. It isn't in very good taste."

"No, Abby. Maybe then I was crazy. But not anymore."

"This isn't funny."

"I didn't intend it to be."

She cocked her head to one side, staring at him, her eyes turning hard. Her face showed slow recognition, slipping into a mask that didn't look like Abby anymore. "Suppose you tell me again, David. Suppose you tell me again and this time I won't be stupid enough to think you're kidding."

He could see a tendril of her hair that had escaped, curling against the nape of her neck. He wanted to reach for it and tuck it away from her face. Only, now, he didn't think he had the right. "Please. I don't want to tell you again."

"You're lying—"

"I wish to God that I were."

"You are."

David shook his head slowly. He branded her eyes with his own. "I'm not lying."

*Until now it's been a lie, Abby. Now, this time, it's finally the truth.*

Slowly, methodically, she began to take the few pieces of laundry she'd folded, wad them up, and pitch them back into the basket one piece at a time. Each word she spoke was punctuated with tossed clothing. First the silk lingerie she had smoothed into the little square. The socks, landing like a Scud missile on the floor. His khaki shorts pinwheeling through the air, like some bodiless person turning a somersault.

"Why are you telling me now?" In went a pair of his burgundy BVD's. "Why on a Sunday, when we've been to church?" A washrag and the green shirt to Braden's little league uniform. "Why, on Father's Day?"

When he answered, his voice was grave. "Because it couldn't wait any longer. Because I'm doing what I think the Lord wants me to do."

She stared at him in disbelief. "You're doing what the Lord wants you to do? The *Lord?*" He watched her draw in on herself, her body language tightening, her emotions pulling in. She gave one slight rock of her chin, one small robotic flick of her hand. "Well, then. Thanks be to the Lord," and her voice gave one broken little cry, to be saying such familiar words when her heart felt so little. "I don't know what we'd do without Him."

"Abby, I'm sorry."

Her face had gone pale. How he hated himself for the numb shock in her voice, the deadness in her eyes.

"I don't want to talk about this right now. I have to ab-sorb this."

"Please."

"You need to leave me alone."

"No, I can't." He took one step toward her. Just one step. No more. "There's too much at stake."

"I should say so."

"Things have gotten messed up."

"An affair. What does that mean exactly? Were you *attracted* to someone besides me?"

He had the grace to look at the toe on his left shoe.

"Did you . . . did you spend *time* with someone else?"

"Please, Ab," he said. "Don't make me have to spell this out."

She looked deeply into his eyes and he could tell she didn't trust his words anymore, only his expressions, and she was trying to read the truth in him. "You didn't. Tell me you didn't—"

Outside, Braden must have picked up the water sprinkler and aimed it. Spray pelted the side of the house and made them both jump. Water spattered like pancake batter against the windowpane.

As powerful as Abby's gaze had been to search him out, so was his need to break it and turn away. He re-fused to meet her eyes. "I did."

"When, David?"

"A long time ago."

"*When* a long time ago?"

"It doesn't matter now, does it? It's been over for years."

"It matters, David."

He struggled against himself, trying to wrangle a way to protect her from any more pain. He owed her so much more than deception. He owed her the truth. "It was nine years ago, Abby. I met her at the bank. She was a grad student spending her summer here and I . . . I got way too involved."

Her voice tightened. "Nine years ago?"

"Yes."

He watched her counting back. "I was pregnant with Braden nine years ago."

"Yes."

"We were just getting started, David. We were practically still on our honeymoon." She twisted one of his favorite Denver Bronco T-shirts into a wad, then pulled out a pair of his sweat shorts and yanked on each leg like she was unfurling a flag. "I was *pregnant*."

"I know that." Even in David's own ears he heard how feeble his story sounded. "If I had to do it again, Abby, I wouldn't."

"That's noble of you. Don't you think you should have thought about it then?"

*Don't say any more.* He wanted to shake her. *Don't take us farther than we can go.*

"I just cracked, Abby. You were eight months along and I got . . . freaked out."

*When does it stop? This hurting people?*

It doesn't, the answer came. Never.

Abby's face had changed. She looked transparent, as if mistrust and anger and fear were waiting there right beneath her skin. "Did you fall in love with her?"

"No. Not, that way, I guess. I just . . . well . . . Oh, Abby, she was *there*."

"You risked us for some woman who was just '*there*'? You risked us for somebody you didn't love?"

He hung his head like a wayward child.

"When . . . when the baby was born, when we brought him home, had it changed by then?"

Almost impossible, making himself say the words, "That was the middle of it," he said. "She called the hospital. To see if we had a boy or a girl. And I told her. A boy. We had a boy." He hesitated, remembering. "And she cried."

Abby's eyes were intent and numb and sad. "What would Braden think?" She asked it as if she knew it was the very question that would most torture David, as if she knew exactly how to make him pay. "What would he think if he knew his father had done something like this? If he knew his father had betrayed him? Even while he was being formed in the womb?"

His father. As if they were talking about someone who wasn't standing in the room. A third party. Someone Abby hadn't known before.

David heard his own voice, thin, like a thread of smoke. "Braden's going to be involved in this, Abby. There's nothing I can do to change that."

"Why?" she asked dully. "Why would Braden have to be involved?"

He saw it as a movie going slowly: him saying the words, "I have a little girl whom he needs to know." Abby letting out a cry and picking up her basket, still just as full as it had been when she'd come in. Walking past him like he wasn't in the room, leaving him standing there, gaping at the empty spot where she used to be.

# Chapter Eight

The last place David and Abigail Treasure would have chosen to go, the next evening after they'd discussed David's having an affair, was to The Spud Drive-In with the entire Elk's Club baseball team.

For time immemorial, for as long as anybody could remember—for as long as anybody's *parents* could remember—The Spud Drive-In had been the place to gather during summer twilights in the mountains. The screen stood like a great white slab above the farmland. Its red-and-blue sign was shaped like an Idaho license plate. White paint peeled from its ticket booth, where a hand-lettered price list read, "Carload $10. No foot traffic."

It was called The Spud because, for people from Wyoming, everything in Idaho begged to be called a spud. People who worked in Jackson Hole but lived eighteen miles across the pass in Idaho were called Spud Brothers. Anyone who drove to Idaho Falls to the mall said they were going to Spudville. And any baseball team that came back victorious from the Madison

Grand Slam tournament in Rexburg bragged for weeks about how they'd been Spud-bashing.

The Spud was frequented by hearty souls who didn't mind staying wrapped inside sleeping bags to stay warm while they watched a movie. It was filled every night with those who didn't mind seeing something at least five months old and those who didn't mind swarms of moths and bats drawn by the huge projector's stream of light.

On this night, of all nights, the Elk's Club Little League had defeated Jedediah's House of Sourdough at Mateosky Field in a game in which Braden Treasure homered twice and sparked a five-run outburst from his teammates.

But during the showdown, Abby Treasure had cheered from the third bleacher on the left portion of the stands, sitting conspicuously away from the bevy of other moms that she usually socialized with on the sidelines.

David Treasure had rooted for the team from behind the north fence-line, standing alone.

Nobody understood why Abby didn't jump to her feet at the first homer, lifting her fists in victory and proclaiming, "Yes, that's *my* kid. I taught him everything he knows."

Nobody understood why David didn't step forward and high-five the other fathers and speculate with the usual false modesty, "Yep, it was a nice pitch, all right. Brade really got ahold of that one, didn't he?"

Nobody understood why, with the game ended and Braden begging them to come to The Spud, David had said, "Maybe tonight isn't the best time, sport." And Abby had said, "Honey, I'm just not in the mood."

Braden wouldn't give up. "But, Mom. I hit two homers. *Two*."

"I know that."

"Everybody's going. The whole team. Even Wheezer."

Wheezer was Sam Jacoby, who suffered asthma attacks every time he inhaled dust while base running or had to slide in at the plate. He kept his inhaler in his sock, and nobody could understand how a boy could suck something into his lungs that smelled like his feet.

Cindy Hubner, the coach's wife, gave Abby a long look. "Are you okay? You were really quiet today."

Abby tried her best to answer, but no words came. Her lips felt as thick and useless to speak through as sponges. "I don't—"

"You have to come, Abby. It won't be as much fun without you."

And so they were coerced. Two people driving over Teton Pass to Idaho, sitting in the front seat of a shiny late-model Suburban, and there might as well have been a fissure in the earth between them. The man, who'd satisfied himself at the expense of their covenant. The woman, who saw her life changing forms and boundaries, melting away like a Salvador Dali painting. She was standing on empty air. Nothing around her was what it seemed to be.

As the road descended past outcroppings and moss gullies, Abby longed for the place she wasn't trapped, she and Braden wrapping gifts on the floor, honoring someone she trusted.

As the car crossed Moose Creek Bridge, Abby tried to touch the wound inside her, to examine it, but found it was too frightening to try.

As David signaled their turn into the drive-in, she

relived the click of the lock as she'd shut their bedroom against him, realizing that the place she wanted to run from was the only place she knew to be.

They passed the ancient flatbed Army Dodge with the huge papier-mâché potato nicknamed "Old Murphy" on the back.

They bounced along the gravel driveway to the booth, where David had to pay ten dollars for just the two of them because Braden had ridden with somebody else.

They rattled in over the metal teeth that would shred tires if anybody tried to go in the wrong direction without paying.

It wasn't until they'd backed into three different spaces, looking for a spot where they could see the screen beyond the sleeping-bag races and boys tussling on the weeds, it wasn't until they'd tried three different speakers for sound quality and the moon had ridden over the hood of the car, that she saw he'd noticed what she had done.

"Abby?"

She'd lifted her left arm to fasten the unwieldy metal box to the edge of the window glass. She fiddled with the volume knob, trying to get the speaker to play, and began to roll up the window.

"You've taken off your ring."

"Yes."

"Why?"

Her voice, quiet and cold and broken. "I think you ought to be able to answer that question for yourself."

He reached across the front seat to her, but she recoiled against the door.

"Don't even think about touching me, David."

"We have to handle this like mature adults, Abby. We can at least talk about it."

"No," she said. "We don't have to talk about it right now."

"If it makes you feel any better, Abby, nobody knows. Nobody. Nobody *has* to know about it." Then, "We were very discreet."

With a kind of terror, Abby felt her grief welling up, overtaking her, shoving her emotions into the forefront—all the anger and betrayal and shame. Devastation hit her with such force it drove her voice out of her in a sob. Her shoulders sagged against the door, her knees trembling against the seat. *Oh, yes*, she thought. *Nobody knows. Only* him. *And* her. *And* me.

"Where is it?" he asked. "Where did you put it?"

"What?"

"Your ring."

"It doesn't matter where I've put it," she said, her body shaking but her expression still wrought of stone. "I took it off at work. I gave myself permission."

Earlier today, through blurred vision, the delicate twine of white gold had glimmered like a joke on her left ring finger. This cold piece of jewelry, this one statement, had been so much a part of her for so many years that for at least seventeen hours after David's admission Abby hadn't once thought of removing it. There at the Community Safety Network, in a shelter room that had been made to look like a home but wasn't a home at all, Abby allowed herself a momentous thing: in a wonderful, therapeutic act of defiance, she had taken the ring off and had dropped it inside her skirt pocket, a loose and dangerous place for a precious stone.

Now she flexed her ring finger once, twice, marveling at the naked feel of it. She hugged herself against the Suburban door.

David's voice was harsh again, his mouth tight and thin. He said defensively, "I knew you would go off the deep end when I told you."

Abby kept rubbing her bare finger. "Surely you can't expect me to act as if everything's still the same, David. Not anymore."

"Look," he said ridiculously. "We have a lot of things to discuss. A lot of things we have to deal with. There's a woman that gave birth to my child."

"You betrayed me," she said, her voice careful and quiet. "You betrayed our marriage vows. *You* have a lot of things to deal with. I have things to think about."

"What is that supposed to mean?"

Abby stared through the bug-splattered glass at the massive screen. "I have some serious decisions to make, David. Until I make them, I don't know what I'm going to do. I don't know how I'm going to deal with this."

"You have to think about Braden."

"I am thinking about Braden. And you should have thought about him, too, a long time ago."

David glared through the yellow bug guts. "How is anybody supposed to watch a movie in a place like this?" He brandished an old napkin tucked into the door carryall, got out, and applied all his frustration to scrubbing the windshield. Each stroke squeaked against the glass.

"Turn off the light," somebody yelled at him. "We can't see."

He got back into the car. His attempt at cleaning had been fruitless. Smeared bugs were everywhere. "That day at the hospital—"

"David, please—"

"I wasn't there to find you and Braden. I didn't know the two of you would be there."

"I don't want to hear details now. I don't want to know everything." Abby just wanted to crawl away somewhere and die.

"I was there for a blood test. Trying to help my daughter. She's got leukemia, and Sus—. . . I . . . they thought I could help her. But I can't. I didn't match."

*Oh.* So that was it. Abby unfolded her arms, but she couldn't stop herself from the know-it-all lift of her jaw. "You need Braden for a match, don't you? Because they're brother and sister."

Blue light from the screen flickered on David's face, illuminating his frown. "That's about it."

"I have to get out of the car," she said, her voice soft but panicky. "I can't breathe."

"Abby, stay here. Don't be stupid."

In the same wavering light, Abby could see their boys, the entire Elk's Club baseball team, aligned along the ground.

"I can't breathe, David. I have to get away—"

The dome light flashed on again when she climbed out. She grabbed the blanket they kept for emergencies and slammed the door.

He opened his side. "Abby, get in the car."

"Don't follow me, David. Whatever you do, don't come after me. I don't want you to."

He climbed out and shut his door, too, to shut off the light. The SUV hood curved between them like a military bulwark. "Abby," he said. "Don't do this. Try to think of what we've *had* instead of what we *haven't*." He watched the screen for another moment, as if he had to search there for ideas.

"It's pointless talking about things like that, David. Don't."

The two of them stood there, caught over the hood of their family Suburban like two shell-shocked soldiers stunned to see the whites of an enemy's eyes. Then, rising unbidden out of her anger, came the very thing he'd told her to think about. What they'd had.

Three months after Braden arrived, she'd been weeping while nursing him, the bliss and pain of the baby's insistent tugging absorbing her. In those days she'd been so thirsty she carried a hospital mug of grape juice everywhere she went, filled with grapey ice chips that stained her mouth.

She turned on the television for noise to soften the stillness and found a movie playing, the sort that always came on at two in the morning—giant ants fighting one another with their monstrous pinchers. While huge black ants took over colonies of huge red ants and terror reigned in the streets of Manhattan, Abby's tears fell, dripping on her own hands where she held Braden, on his terrycloth sleeper, the downy fuzz of his hair, the working of his cheek.

*I don't know if I'm doing okay*, she thought. *I'm supposed to be a wife to him and a mother to this baby and I've forgotten what it's like to be* me.

David padded in, barefooted and barechested, his face colored by the flickering light of the television.

"Your lips are purple."

"Yeah."

"Won't he go to sleep? You've been up with him forever."

"Stay with me," she said. "There's a movie on that will make you laugh. Giant ants taking over the world."

"Oh, Ab, honey," he'd said, stifling a yawn. "Don't make me do it. I'm so tired."

"But I feel so alone," she'd told him.

"We'll do it some other night, okay, Ab? It's been a crazy week. I need to get some sleep."

Maybe that day—that day, too—David had been with the other woman.

She said now, very quietly, "Get back in the car, David. I've had no reason to trust you for a very long time."

For long moments after he did, she wandered around in the Spud parking lot by herself, her eyes prickling with tears as she skirted fenders and stumbled over runnels in the gravel that had been dug so vehicles could park tilted upward toward the screen. Pebbles sprayed and clicked beneath her footfalls. When at last she sensed she'd found softer ground, she kicked off her shoes and felt the lacy cool of weeds between her toes. She slumped into an empty spot of grass, away from the others, and sank down deep. She wished the earth would consume her.

*Oh, Lord. Oh, Lord. No. Not us. Not this.*

Her heart felt like an empty cavern, trackless and strange. *I can't. I can't.* There wasn't anything left inside her that was capable of prayer. Nothing to ask. Nothing to say.

Nothing to keep her safe.

David, liking the warmth of someone else's mouth on his. David liking the sound of another woman whispering, the smell of her.

Some parts of marriage were so sacrosanct, so inviolable and beyond price, no one was supposed to be able to touch them. Those parts weren't tangible. They weren't supposed to be stolen.

Despite the warm wool blanket, Abby couldn't stop shivering. The only thing she felt now was cold, deep cold, as her hair clung in tendrils to the nape of her neck.

David, having a daughter.

David, sacrificing their son.

"Mom? What are you doing laying here in the grass? Why aren't you in the car with Dad?"

*Braden. Oh.*

She shoved against the dirt, lifting herself an inch or so out of the blanket. Her teeth chattered. "What, honey? What are you doing over here?"

"Jake wants to know if he can come over and spend the night."

She didn't know. How to cope with another child in the house? How to cope with *Braden* in the house?

"Honey, I don't know. Why don't you go ask your father?"

"I can't find the car in the dark, and you're right here."

"Go ask your father, Braden. I don't *know*."

So many moments in their lives she'd believed in. So many memories she had counted as joy.

How many of those moments, those memories, had been lies?

"But, Jake—"

"I don't care what Jake does," she said. "Jake can do whatever he wants."

Abby heard her son leave, but didn't watch him go. She fell back heavily against the earth, trying to lose herself in the stars that buzzed overhead. Shifting formations of moths danced in the movie light and occasionally blundered into her face with a velvet wing. Beside her cheek, a beetle as shiny as an orange bead waddled up a stalk of grass on thread-thin legs.

And who knew that stars had so many colors? Abby had always thought them simple and plain, identical markings of the heavens. But tonight they ebbed and flowed before her, showing their iridescence in the pastel colors of Easter eggs and nurseries—baby blue, soft yellow, powder pink, a white as pure as lamb's wool.

*My whole life is gone.*

For only a moment, only one short inkling, in the colors and the sky and the glistening, Abby perceived the stars' distance and her own size.

The universe shone huge, unfathomable, overwhelming.

And she was a speck of nothing on the ground at The Spud Drive-In, insignificant, a tiny lost thing in a nightmare, swallowed whole.

# Chapter Nine

*H*ow quickly the numbness in Abby's heart changed to the acknowledgment of betrayal.

How easily she converted to mistrusting David, after the complete confidence she'd held in him for over a dozen years.

She counseled women at the shelter all morning, keeping her expression a mask of indifference while inside her heart justified grievances began to line up like militiamen.

*While we chatted across the table in the candlelight, you wished you could be somewhere else . . . While we practiced deep-breathing exercises on the floor in Dr. Sugden's office, you wanted it to end so you could go to her . . . While we were lying close at night, you wanted to be lying close to somebody different . . .*

These emotional disloyalties, and Abby hadn't yet even considered the consequences of David breaking a marriage vow. Bits and snatches of the solemn pledge they'd shared on their wedding day fluttered in and out of her head like paper streamers.

*For better, or for worse.*

*To have and to hold, from this day forward . . . to love and to cherish . . . according to God's holy ordinance; and thereto I pledge thee my faith.*

At lunchtime, Abby drove home and—in a fit of irrationality—searched like a madwoman for clues.

She searched because she didn't want to believe it. She searched because she didn't want to find a thing. If she couldn't find proof, maybe he'd say he really hadn't done it. Maybe he'd say he'd played a cruel joke to see what she would say. Yes. *That,* she would forgive him for.

Abby stood in their bedroom with the closet door open, facing the queues of David's shirts. She slid open his top drawer and stared at BVD underwear and socks. There, shoved back inside one corner, she found sacred treasures from boyhood he'd managed to save: a fishing lure, a marble, a ski pin from Winter Park in Colorado.

Nothing here had changed. There was nothing that might be a gift from someone she didn't know. Eight years gone by, and the trail had gotten cold.

*Nothing here that I should have seen and deciphered. Dear Lord, please. Nothing here.*

*I don't want to be like my mother, with a household I have to fight to keep together and a spirit that has been crushed within me.*

*I don't want my son to be hurt the way my father hurt me.*

Not until she'd sifted through the game closet, past the dilapidated boxes of Pictionary and Mouse Trap and even Braden's dreaded Hi-Ho Cherry-O with red plastic cherries that spilled everywhere. Not until she'd pawed through the Christmas supplies with swatches of wrapping paper and tangles of ribbon she would never throw away and would never use. Not until she followed with

one finger along the row of titles in the bookshelf—
*The Book of Goodnight Stories*, *The Food of France*, *The Grapes of Wrath*. Not until then did she find the evidence that she had prayed she would not find at all.

Braden's baby pictures. She pulled them out and thumbed through.

Here was the naked bathtub picture they'd teased him with, telling him they'd blackmail him with it in years to come. Here was Braden in the safe cage of his crib, staring up at the mobile of primary-colored bears. Here was the shot of him sleeping on a shoulder at four months, wearing an expression that belonged to a wise old man and not a baby.

Here was the proof, in Kodak color. Indisputable.

Abby wasn't in any of these pictures.

Oh, parts of her were there. The shoulder was hers. The hand holding Braden upright in the water. Even the knee, the ankle, and the Avia athletic shoe in the photo of Braden bouncing like he was riding a wild Wyoming pony.

The camera shots never focused on her face. Not one of them depicted her completely from head to toe, with a smile and her half-exhausted I'm-glad-to-be-a-mom eyes. He'd been hiding from her all that time. He must have been thinking, *If I never look fully at her, then maybe she won't look fully at me.* With the exception of one photo snapped on Braden's dedication day at church— that matched David's in his office and had been posed by someone outside of the family—Abby might as well have been the headless wonder.

Abby looked fixedly at the photos, seeing with bewilderment and horror what their lives had been.

*Oh, David.*

Another question rocked her as she sat staring at bits and pieces of herself. A question that felt almost comfortable because at least it would take some of the blame off David.

*Did I do something to make that happen? With the baby and all, wasn't I enough for him?*

No.

*No.*

For hours each week, Abby worked to draw the answer to this from hurt, broken women who sought her advice at the shelter. Once, long ago, Abby had heard her own mother ask the very same question. And how well she remembered an aunt's thoughtful, sad answer, because it had become the same answer she gave over and over herself at the shelter.

You can't be responsible for anybody else's actions.

You are only responsible for yourself.

He made his choice and now you have to make yours.

Harm and injury closed in around Abby like water closing in over her head.

When Sophie Henderson walked back into the door at the Community Safety Network, she toted a blue, plastic trashcan, transparent enough to reveal a canister of Super-Hold hairspray, a hairbrush, two pinecones, and a packet of panty hose.

"I grabbed what I could on the way out," she said, the tremor in her voice belying the defiant lift of her chin. "I told Mike I was taking out the trash." She fished deep inside the trashcan with one arm. "The truck keys are way down here, too." With a sleight of hand, she pulled them out, two Dodge keys dangling from the chain-link body of a cutthroat trout. She tossed them onto the desk with shaking fingers. "That's the only chance I had."

"Sophie!"

Abby took two steps forward and stopped, torn between throwing her arms around this woman to welcome her back or throwing her arms around her in heartbreak because she'd returned. She waited and did neither. Instead she spoke words she'd spoken at least a hundred times before—the same words she'd already said to Sophie the *first* time she'd walked in the door.

"Oh, Sophie. You did the right thing, you know. You've gotten yourself to a safe place again."

"I know."

Abby gave a calm half nod toward the blue, transparent trashcan. "We haven't moved anybody into your room yet. Bring your things and we'll get you right back in."

Sophie held the trashcan higher as if she was apologizing for it. "I know what you said, Abby. I know you said to plan ahead no matter what. A packed suitcase with necessities. Kept at a neutral site."

"A packed trashcan. It's almost the same thing, isn't it?"

"I kept thinking what I'd do if Mike looked inside and saw this stuff," Sophie jabbered on, hugging her belongings against her, disoriented and panicked as she followed Abby through the frosted door. "I kept thinking how he'd say, 'Sophie, what are you doing? You can't throw all those *pinecones* away.'"

"Oh, Soph—"

"I never packed a suitcase this time because I

thought I wouldn't need it. He was so sweet when he begged me to come back. He promised about the counseling. He promised that everything would be different."

Together they walked through the courtyard and Abby's own dull senses awakened slightly—to sensation, to pain. She heard outdoor sounds: bird cheeps and bee buzzes, the screech of an un-oiled swing-set, the distant chime of eleven o'clock from the city hall clock tower. The resident shelter cat, a brown-striped tabby with the look of wild Africa in her face, waited at the door to be let inside, her body ribboning curves against the wooden jamb. "Oh no, you don't, Phoebe." Abby picked up the cat and set her aside. "You know you can't go in there."

"Hey, cat. I missed you." Sophie bent down and scratched her ears.

Through a tiled hallway and up a narrow, hardwood flight of stairs, Abby led Sophie Henderson to the place she didn't need leading to at all. "That cat remembers me."

"There are clean towels in the bathroom down the hall."

"Thanks."

So many arrived at this shelter without hope. So many struggled to find it, and never could.

"Oh, Sophie." They hugged each other at last, tight and swaying. "I wanted it to work for you and Mike so badly."

Sophie flinched. "Don't squeeze too hard."

"You're hurt. He really hurt you this time."

"Guess I should unpack or something, huh?" Sophie gave a raw, bleating laugh and pulled away. She extracted the packet of panty hose, still shrink-wrapped in cellophane, and spun it like a Frisbee onto the bed. "Have you ever thought about this? What you would you take," she asked with downcast eyes, "if you had to leave your house without any time to plan? I couldn't even think. I live in Wyoming. I haven't worn panty hose for fifteen years."

Both of them stared at the package where it lay, with its dramatic photograph of two lacy, curvaceous legs, the toes *en pointe*—an impossible position that would have sent anyone but a prima ballerina to a chiropractic clinic. "You know I need to fill out paperwork again. Are you up to that yet?"

A deep breath. Another meeting of eyes. "I can be. Guess I'm as up to it as I'll ever be."

Abby retrieved her notepad and pen from inside her big skirt pocket. Vaguely aware of how miserable this was, she pulled out a copy of the official admittance papers and began writing fast.

*Sophie is depending on me. They all depend on me.* Today, for the first time in Abby's life, these burdens seemed more than she could handle.

"It started when he shot the TV."

Abby's pen paused.

"It wasn't that big of a deal, you know. I was watching *ER* and in the summer they're all reruns. Before I knew what had happened, Dr. Corday and Dr. Kovac were gone and there wasn't anything left but a gray hole and shards of glass. Glass everywhere. My legs got cut when I stood up, from the slivers in my pants."

Outside the window, far above the town, Abby could see the Tetons standing as high as heaven, with slopes spiked above the tufts of trees. The magnificent Gunsight Notch of Mount Owen dominated the view—a

U-shaped cleft with sun-touched gray cliffs, a straight-edged shadow streaming down.

"Even Elaine's starting to believe me now," Sophie said, as the hum started in Abby's head again.

*When do people ever stop hurting each other? When do marriages ever stop falling apart?*

Sophie reached for the buttonhooks on her blouse, and showed her the bruises and welts. They strung across the crest of her collarbone in various stages of healing, from pale yellow-green to the freshest one, shaped like a fiery purple sunburst.

"At least this time I knew I could come back here," Sophie said to Abby. "At least this time I knew I wouldn't have to be alone."

⌒

A week ago, Abby had taken such joy in puttering around her own house. A week ago, she'd pinched fresh rosemary and thyme and dill from the terra-cotta pots she kept on the windowsill in the kitchen. She'd changed the colors of the candles in the entry hall, restocked fresh d'Anjou pears in the wooden bowl, and rearranged the frayed, gold-imprinted spines of her favorite novels she kept on the shelf.

A week ago, the windows would have been thrown open to the light and the Dutch lace curtains would have been riding a touch of breeze. The teakettle would have been on the front burner for a last-minute dose of Cascade Mint Herbal. The birdfeeders would have been laden with thistle and grain.

Today, no one had bothered to throw open the curtains or the windows. One pine siskin chattered angrily at the empty feeder. The pears in the bowl had long since been thrown out because they had withered. And the little pot of rosemary and thyme in the window was sorely in need of water.

Abby couldn't bear to stay inside a house that felt empty and joyless, a house that didn't feel like a home anymore.

More often than not this past week, with Braden out playing at the neighbors and David gone into town, Abby had traipsed through the grass along Fish Creek where a path hadn't been beat down. She found herself a hidden, grassy spot on the riverbank and there she sat, her knees drawn beneath her jaw, her arms wrapped around her shins, her bony chin propped hard upon her knees. She sat still long enough for the life of the creek to resume around her—an occasional mallard floating past, a chorus of red-winged blackbirds in the branches of a willow, the *ker-thop* of a muskrat as it surfaced, saw her, and smacked itself back under.

Today she watched as a grasshopper fell in. The current picked it up and it struggled, flopping its legs in vain against the film on the creek's surface. *Struggling like me*, she thought. Just as she compared herself to the besieged thing, a cutthroat trout rose to take it; the insect was swallowed whole in one ribbony swirl of water.

*What do David and I do now?* Abby asked the river, because it was the only thing she felt close enough to to ask. *Where can any of this go from here?*

Nothing. Only silence, and one little thump as the trout rose farther upstream to feed.

Abby unfastened the buckles on her sandals. She tested the water with one toe. Cold. Icy. She slid first one foot, then the other, all the way in. She put her

weight on them and stood, biting her bottom lip because her feet had already begun to throb. Black mud
oozed between her toes, tiny specks of mica floating
over her skin. Her persimmon toenails sat magnified in
the water and sunlight, looking twice as big as they
really were, while the current rushed against her ankles
as if it wanted to push her along.

She was still standing in Fish Creek when she heard
David calling her across the lawn. A week ago, she
would have splashed out of the water and started toward
him, eager to welcome him back. Today she only stood
with her toes in the water, welcoming the fierce cold
that had made her limbs go numb—the way she wished
her heart could be numb.

What had David said? *I'm doing what I think the Lord
wants me to do.* Well, if the Lord wanted David to do
this, he could just as well do it without her.

"Come on, Abby. Why can't you walk where there's
already a path?"

"I didn't expect you home."

"I called you at the shelter. They told me you were
here."

If she had been alone, Abby would have climbed out
of the water. Instead, she stood staring at him, her jeans
hiked up in her hands, not moving.

"We live in the same house," he went on, "and we
can never talk because of Braden. I can't wait any longer
for this. We've got to decide something."

"David. This has been years in the making. I don't
know what it is you want from me *today.*"

"I want you to forgive me. I want us to go forward on
this together."

Her shoulders moved as if she'd felt a chill. "Well, I don't think it's going to happen that way."

"It has to," he said. Then softer, "It *has* to, Abby."

Abby began to clamber up out of the water. She sloshed up on shore and stood in the grass with wet, muddy toes. She stared at them a long time before she spoke. "You made your decisions about this nine years ago. And you made them alone. With no regard for what it would do to your family. There isn't anything that says I have to stand beside you now. The Bible even says I don't have to stand beside you. I looked it up this morning." And then, probably to his horror, she quoted. " 'I tell you this, a man who divorces his wife and marries another commits adultery—unless his wife has been unfaithful.' I say that would apply to the husband, too. Or, maybe not. What do you think?"

"You're using the Bible against me."

"I'm using the Bible as . . . the *Bible*."

"You're thinking about divorce?"

"I'm thinking I have some options. It's nice to have options."

David slapped his hands together once, twice, glancing toward their house. "If you won't go forward with me, then I'm going to have to go forward alone."

"How can you do that? How can you go forward on a marriage alone?"

"I'm not talking about marriage anymore, Abigail. I'm talking about Braden. I'm talking about having him tested."

She stared at her husband. "You can't do that. That means he's going to have to *know*."

"I wanted us to stand together on this. I wanted you to be beside me when I explained it to him."

"Oh, David. No."

"You know I've got to do it. To see if he could be of some help—" David stopped, as if he couldn't say the other child's name in front of his wife. "—for my daughter."

The words "for my daughter" struck a deep blow. Abby felt her stomach go weak. This mention of David's daughter brought them both to a singular, more fragile, territory—one in which she did not dare be self-righteous. Dissolving a relationship was one thing. Saving that child's life was another.

"David, I'm really trying—" She swallowed hard, her stomach heaving, clinging to reason as a rush of salty liquid filled her mouth. *Please don't tell Braden. Don't let him know all that his father has given away.*

"I've already phoned Susan in Oregon. She knows that you know, and that I'd like to proceed with tests on Braden." David's voice stayed cool and deliberate. "They've sent a second test kit to St. John's by special courier. It will be here this afternoon. I'm going to pick him up after ball practice and take him over to the lab."

*Oh Lord, please,* she wanted to cry out. *My son.*

"I'm going to talk to him," David said. "Maybe he won't have to know so much of it. Maybe I can tell him . . . just enough." He paused and sought her face. "Do you want to be there when I do?"

"I don't think—" Could she trust David to handle this well, to be gentle with Braden's heart? *If he expected me to trust him, he never should have betrayed me in the first place.*

"You weren't ever going to tell me you had an affair, were you, David? You were going to die with this. If something like this hadn't happened, I was never going to find out."

He thought about that, shook his head. "No. You wouldn't have."

"Braden is the only reason."

"Yes."

*Oh, Lord. Oh, Lord. What have I missed? What could I have had until now, if I hadn't had David? What did you want me to have?*

Abby pushed her painted toes into her sandals, bent to buckle them. She shook her head sideways, tossing her hair, afraid to look up, as if she were trying to deny something to someone who had shamed her. "When you talk to him, David, I want you to measure your words with your *life*."

"I'll tell him what he's got to know, Abby. I won't go any further than that."

Abby felt as though her life were rushing away from her, as if it were water tumbling and thrashing past her, and the only way to be a part of it was to leave the bridge—to jump in, to let it tumble her along, too.

"Will you say that I love him? That we—" She stopped, furious at her husband. "This is asking way too much of him."

"I have no reason to exclude you, Abby."

She met him head on. *Of course you have reason to exclude me. You've been excluding me ever since you touched that . . . that paramour.*

"Abigail—"

"You just don't let him be scared."

They waited with nowhere to run, both of them facing consequences, terrified suddenly at how they could discuss these details this way.

It didn't feel like a beginning anymore. It felt like an end.

David shifted his weight from his right knee to his left. "Do you want me to move out, Abigail?"

The memories came back to Abby, a flood of them spinning out of control: two silhouettes standing in the driveway, her mother crying in the dark.

*"I've already told Abigail good-bye, Carol. We had a day together yesterday. We drove all over the park. I bought her souvenirs."*

*"How could it be a good-bye, when you didn't tell her you were going to leave?"*

*"She'll figure it out after awhile. You know Abigail. She's a smart girl."*

Abby leveled her eyes on David's face and said, "What if that's what I wanted? What if I told you that I wanted you to go? Would you come back to see him? Or would you go off with *them* and start a new life?"

"Abby." He looked horrified. "Braden means *everything* to me."

He looked, for a moment, as she remembered him from a vacation in California, his bare toes curved over the edge of the diving board as he stood, taking two breaths, three, before screwing up the courage and concentration to jump. "Okay. I'll pack up some things tonight."

"Well, I *do* want you to go. There's no place I can go to have a clear head or to get a perspective on things when you are near like this, pushing me."

"Maybe I can stay with friends for a while."

She took one step forward, as if she might grasp his shirtsleeve. Only she didn't. "Is it as easy as all that, David? Both of us asking for what we want?"

David shoved his hands into his pockets and looked at her. "I don't think *easy* is the word."

"You can't move out right now. You can't leave at the same time you tell Braden about your other child."

*Abby's mother at the kitchen table with an untouched coffee cup before her. Tears streaming through her fingers, running down her wrists to wet the cuffs of a blouse the color of dishwater.*

"He'll read too much into that," Abby said. "He'll think you're leaving *him* instead of me."

# Chapter Ten

David and Braden Treasure sat together on shiny chrome stools at Jackson Drug, elbow to elbow on the black countertop. Their bottoms—one swathed in a pants suit with button-down pockets, one with a dirt smudge the shape of a pear from sliding into second base—kept a slow, synchronized pace, twisting right and left, right and left, in rhythm with the sucking they did on their straws.

"Hm-m-mm." David extracted his straw from his chocolate malt, licked it lengthwise, and laid it aside. "It's too thick for this. I'm killing myself. I say dig in with the spoon."

As little boys are prone to do, Braden copied his father exactly, wrapping his tongue around the curve of the straw with the same effort as a Hereford going after a salt lick. "Hm-mmm."

"You like the shakes better? Or the malt?"

"I like the shake. You just like malts better because you're an old person."

"Watch it, sport. This is your father you're talking to."

Braden sat as tall as he could manage, watching his own face in the mirror behind the malted-milk machine and the Coca-Cola clock and the little shelves of Tazo Tea. He made a face, pulling the skin below one eye down until veins appeared. "So what did you bring me here to talk about, Dad?"

"Oh, you know." David laid his long-handled spoon right in the center of the napkin, which he'd never unfolded or used. He wrapped both hands around his malt glass and leaned into the counter. "Seems like we never have time alone anymore. Time to talk boy things. *Man* things."

"Oh, no." Braden slumped on the stool. "Not *that* stuff. Charlie Kedron said you'd want to talk about that stuff. All dads do, and it's eeew, yuck, *nasty*."

David's glass clattered on the counter. He had to catch it or it would have gone all the way over.

"I don't even *like* girls, Dad. I like baseball."

"That's good," David said, popping the spoon in his mouth and talking around the ice cream. "At least a man can *understand* baseball."

Their feet sat together, baseball cleats and Hush Puppies, toes resting on the metal bar that ran along the floor. Shoulder to shoulder, father and son plunged in with spoons again. Together they reached bottom with a huge clattering noise that would have made Abby cringe.

"Braden," David said at last, pressing his forehead with his palm, half out of desperation and half because he'd finished his malt too fast. "I'm going to ask you to do something that most dads don't have to ask their sons. I'm going to ask you to do something courageous."

"What?" Braden sat up straight again.

"There's a lady at the hospital who's waiting for you to come over. She wants to test you for something."

That didn't go over well at all. The color left Braden's face. "Test me for something? Does that mean I've got to have a shot?"

"Yes."

Braden turned away and began the process of bending his straw, tucking one end inside the other so the straw became a triangle. "Why did you bring me here first?" he said. "Mom always makes me wait to have ice cream until after I've done that. Then I have something to look forward to."

"I did it different than your mom. I thought it would be best to have you prepared. I wanted to have time to explain it to you."

"Why didn't Mom come? She always goes with me when I do something like this."

"She thought it would be best if I went with you today instead."

"Why you, Dad?" His voice, small and worried. "Is it going to be scary? You always go with me when things are scary."

"No." David held the top of his nose with thumb and forefinger. His shoulders lifted and fell with a resolute sigh. "Not as scary as all that. Not really."

"But it will hurt," Braden said.

"Yes. It will hurt as much as shots hurt. And it takes a while."

That most important of all details out of the way, they scraped the aluminum soda-fountain glasses with their spoons again and took stock of each other in the fountain mirror. A lady stepped up to the cash register and paid for a refrigerator magnet with a bison head that read I GOT GORED IN THE TETONS. At the pharmacy on the other side, someone had opened a roadmap and was asking the pharmacist for directions to Jenny Lake.

"Why does that lady want to test something about me?"

David regretted afresh what he'd done, regretted how he now asked his son to pay for it. Here was betrayal, pure and simple. If he'd anguished over baring his soul to Abby, then telling the truth to his son felt like slicing out his very heart.

*Here goes nothing.*

"Because there's a little girl who's sick and we think you might be able to help her."

Braden's straw, lying on the counter beside his baseball glove, popped out of its geometrical shape. "Does she go to my school? Who is it?"

"You don't know her, Braden. She doesn't live here."

"But then, if I don't know her, why do they think I'm the one who can do it?"

David's heart clubbed hard, high in his chest. He started to say it and he couldn't. *Not yet. Not this way.*

"They think you might have the right kind of something in your bones, that's all."

Braden's eyes, as big around as skipping stones, locked on his father's in the mirror. David opened his mouth again to try and explain the rest of it, the logistics of Susan Roche and Samantha, his wrong decisions, the sins he'd committed long ago. But when he saw his son's expression, he snapped his mouth shut.

"Lots of people check to see what kind of blood they have. I did it, too. Only mine wasn't quite right. They need you."

"Why?"

"Well." He stumbled. And gratefully used the lame explanation that parents have been using since the beginning of time: "God just worked it out that way."

"Where does this girl live?"

"In Oregon."

"How come you know about her?"

"Because I know her mom."

Braden gave his father a dark look. "How do you know her mom?"

"She used to be a friend. A long time ago."

"But that doesn't . . ."

David watched his son ponder while his own heart stopped, his breathing ceased. His very existence depended on this one little boy and his reaction.

"I don't . . ." Braden scrunched on the stool and reached across the counter. He popped three more straws from the dispenser and studied them, perplexed, as if they were the question. "That isn't very good."

"Don't take more straws than you need. You know Mom never lets you play with straws at restaurants."

"Does Mom know that you have that lady that's your friend?"

"Sport. Braden." Uncharted territory, all of it. He'd never done anything like this before; he had no idea how to tread this new ground. "Yes. Mom knows. There isn't any big secret or anything. Not anymore."

"You know what I dreamed last night?" Braden asked out of the blue as he tucked his baseball glove beneath his armpit. "I dreamed I could walk on water. When I stepped off the shore and into the water, the soles on my tennis shoes floated. I walked way out and I was just standing there."

"Okay, Mr. Walk-On-Water." David laid several bills

and a pile of quarters on the counter, took one more gulp from the silver ice-cream glass to make sure he'd gotten everything from the bottom, and wrapped one arm around the width of Braden's shoulders. "We'd better get going. We've got people waiting for us over there."

"I'm scared," Braden said, "but I'll do it."

"Thanks."

Father and son wiped their mouths with napkins that before this moment hadn't been made use of. They slid off their stools together. As the plastic seats refilled with air, they made a sound like two whoopee cushions.

The deed was done. Enough of the story confided to his son. *Secrets revealed, but not too many.*

Braden looked up at his dad and grinned about the noisy seats.

David rumpled his son's hair with a host of gratitude.

~

The delivery truck with the magnetic sign that read BLOOMS 'N GREENS drove up fast and parked in the For-Staff-Members-Only space. In the office at the shelter, the staff scurried around closing things up for the day. Kate Carparelli glanced out Abby's front window. "Oh, my word. Look what's coming up the sidewalk!"

The van had opened and here came an enormous spray of roses—an entire baker's dozen of them splayed out in one perfect, symmetrical constellation. The arrangement was so big and extravagant that all they could see of the woman who carried them was her legs.

Somebody opened the door. The overpoweringly sweet smell arrived before the flowers did. "Delivery!"

came the disembodied voice from behind stems and leaves.

Kate dug into her purse and gave a two-dollar tip. Then, with the solemnity and purpose of a bucket brigade, everyone in the office passed the roses along from one to another, smelling them and oohing and aaahing over their fragrance and beauty. It didn't take long, though, before someone placed them smack dab in the middle of Abby's desk.

There the roses sat in front of her. Petals as soft as a baby's cheek curled within blossoms as crimson and rich and perishable as blood.

The betrayal, sudden and living again, seared through her like heat. Abby lashed her arms around her middle. *David, how could you think roses would make up for what your unfaithfulness has done to our family? How could you think they would make up for what you're asking all of us to face?*

She lifted her chin at her colleagues at the shelter, daring them to say what they were thinking. They had to know by now what was happening. Jackson Hole was a small town, after all.

*He blew our cover. That's what he did.*

Braden, their innocent son. Braden, who, when he thought his father wasn't looking, speared four pieces of macaroni—one on each prong of the fork—just the way his father did it. Braden, who had begged to be the first nine-year-old boy ever to drive a Suburban, perched atop his father's square lap while David worked the pedals and Braden made shaky turns with small hands. Braden, who, when his baseball friends had complained that the color of their uniforms wasn't manly and powerful enough, had piped up in words that carried across the field like the chirp of a little bird, "My dad says green is the good-luck color. Green means 'go.' Dad says that way, when we look at each other, we should think 'We can go all the way and win!'"

Abby had never wanted to live her life in a web of suspicions. She'd never wanted to be like the rest of the women who sat in the rumpus room at the shelter, leaning forward in the donated chairs and whispering: "That's the one thing I'd never forgive him for. Sure, he hits me sometimes when he gets mad. But the minute he fools around with another woman, I'm out the door."

She'd never wanted to be the one at Bible study or prayer group whom people scooted their chairs close to, touched a shoulder in sympathy, and said, "Please. Let us. We want to pray for you."

Five o'clock came and Abby's colleagues began to gather their jackets and keys and thermal lunch bags, leaving without words in acknowledgement of the sudden uncomfortable distance. Abby's pluck-and-mettle filtered out of the room along with them. Finally, the last person whispered good-bye to her.

Abby realized she was alone. She leaned forward in her chair and searched for David's card among the greenery. She found the miniature envelope impaled among the roses on a pronged plastic fork. She read the two words scribbled there.

"To Sophie," they said.

Abby rocked forward in her chair and placed her feet firmly on the floor. Her body went limp with relief even while her throat went dry with disappointment.

The roses hadn't been meant for her.

David hadn't sent them.

*Well.*

The staff here followed protocol when residents received deliveries. The message on the card was checked; the recipient was notified. Abby needed to notify Sophie. She would be given the sender's name and the option of viewing the arrangement, no questions asked. After that, she would be given the choice of whether or not to receive them.

Abby slipped a finger beneath the seal, opened the flap, and tried to stay detached while she read the words:

I'm sorry for what I did, Sophie. I just wish you would come home. It'll never happen again, I can promise you that much.

*I love you,*
Mike

Phoebe the cat was nowhere to be seen when Abby made her trek through the courtyard. Her light tread on the stairs did not disturb anyone. She knocked lightly at Sophie's door. She could hear the cat purring even before the woman opened it.

"Sophie. Phoebe isn't supposed to be inside."

"Who?"

"The cat."

The door opened wider and Phoebe's smoky topaz eyes peered out from between Sophie's braided arms.

"Something's been delivered to you today. I need to take care of it before I go home."

The door opened even wider. "This cat remembers me, I can tell. She knows I was here before. I'm sorry I snuck her in here, Abby. I just . . . didn't want to be alone."

Abby thought of Brewster-dear, uncomplicated Brewster, who only cared about long-legged splashes into the creek and sniffing out starlings and demolishing a bowl of beef-flavored Purina One, the same flavor he'd joyously demolished last week, last month, last year.

She thought of David snoring, his lanky limbs draped over the arm of the couch, the thin blanket she'd given him never quite the right angle or the right size to cover his bony ankles. She thought about the loud click when she locked their bedroom door. She thought about spreading out as wide as she could in the bed, with her head on the pillow in Washington State and her feet stretched clear across to Florida.

"Some flowers came for you."

Sophie let the cat slither to the ground. "Flowers?"

"Roses."

Sophie thought about that. "I don't have room for anything else in here. Especially if they're from the person I think they're from."

"If that's what you want."

"They're from Mike, aren't they?"

Abby nodded.

"Are they pretty?"

She didn't answer directly. "People send things. You don't have to accept them."

"Did he write me something?"

"Yes."

"What? What does he say?"

Abby pulled the tiny envelope from her skirt pocket and handed it over.

Sophie's hands were shaking. "You know what it says?"

"Yes."

"What?"

"That he's sorry, that he loves you, that he'll never do it again."

"And?"

"And he wants you to come home."

There are moments between strangers and friends when words do not suffice. Long seconds passed while the two women stood in a silent shelter room, toe to toe, exchanging their heartbreak through their eyes.

"You know what I was just thinking?" Sophie said. "I was thinking how each day is like a capsule of our whole lives. Each day always starts with a morning, and a morning is a beginning. A morning always feels so clean."

"It does."

"Then there's the afternoon that gets filled with everything. And there's the evening, when everybody's tired and they're thinking how they'd like to get some rest. They're thinking how they've got some things they'd do over and some things they'd like to forget."

"It's a thought."

"If I could give you a present, Abby, I'd give a morning. I'd give Mike a morning, too." She laughed. "I might not *live* with him through it, but I'd give it to him."

"Mike's lucky, having you feel that way."

"You know how the TV shows always make you feel like it's these huge things in your life that matter? Those moment-in-time errors or victories that change everything?"

"Yeah."

"Well, I don't think that's right. I think it's the morning-times that change our lives, Abby. The times we'll give ourselves permission to start fresh."

"Maybe. Maybe so."

"You mind if I have a look at those flowers now? At least I can do that much."

"They're down in my office."

"I'll just come down there with you. No sense you carrying them all the way up here."

They took the cat out with them and went down to the office. There they stood with arms crossed, surveying the monstrous bouquet from every angle, shifting their weight from one knee to the other the same way they'd survey some imposter artifact in a museum.

"Well, I know what let's do," Sophie said finally. "Come with me." She gathered up the vase in her arms, spilling water and bits of greenery on the pine floor. "Here." She started out the front.

"Soph? What are you doing?"

"Come with me. You'll see."

"I don't know if you should go outside in plain view or not. Mike knows you're here."

"What is it? The cat can't come in? I can't go out?"

A rust-riddled pickup jostled up the street toward them, one window halfway open and the other broken out and covered with tape and Saran Wrap. The music system inside, which had cost probably three times more than the truck did, belted the Dixie Chicks.

"I've seen them do this in Cheyenne."

Sophie stepped right in front of the truck. Brakes screeched.

Abby flew off the curb toward her. "Sophie!"

"Hey," Sophie called out to the driver. "You want to take a few of these roses home?"

The disconcerted man, who'd managed to stop with only inches to spare, turned down the music, stuck his head out the window, and spit tobacco juice in the street. "How much you want for a rose?"

"Nothing. They're not for sale."

"Then why are you standing out in the middle of the road, lady? You're going to get yourself killed."

"I'm giving these away."

"*Giving* them away? Why?"

"Because of what day it is."

"What day is it?"

"Today."

"Oh." He laughed. "I was thinking this was something on the calendar I had missed. Some new Hallmark card or something. They're always doing that so they can sell more cards. New things to make you feel guilty for if you forget."

"How many do you want?" Sophie licked her fingers and tugged one thorny stem from the oasis inside the pot. "I've got plenty."

He thought for a minute. "How about three? Could I take three?"

"Sure." Triumphant, she found two more pretty ones and handed the stems through the open window. "Just be careful not to stab yourself. Those thorns can get you."

"This is great." He waved out the window as the

truck started rolling and the Dixie Chicks began rocking again. "Thanks a lot."

All in all, after Abby had charged out into Hall Street and begun to hand out flowers alongside Sophie, they gave every last rose away. They gave some to a man who jogged past with two kids in a long-distance baby stroller. They gave one to a husband walking along with his wife and holding her hand. Sophie presented several to a businessman in a Lexus who was in a hurry to post flyers for a Western-art gallery walk over the July Fourth holiday. And last of all, they detained Floyd Uptergrove, Viola's husband from church, who sauntered past them commanding a team of three anxious Chihuahuas.

"You think I need to give Viola roses?" he asked as the Chihuahuas strained to overpower him. Several small, unused poop-bags protruded from the brim of his fishing hat. "I've been taking care of that woman for fifty-nine years now, and look where it's gotten me. It's made me bald as a bedpost and she calls my family outlaws, not in-laws. Oh, and my feet aren't allowed on the couch, but the dogs are."

"Viola's a beautiful woman," Abby said.

"You bet she is. Especially when she dresses up for church with that butterfly in her hair. I wouldn't trade her for anything."

He accepted a final rose and walked on, so slowly that it took him five minutes to get past the next house after he left them.

*I wouldn't trade her for anything. Fifty-nine years.*

Sophie and Abby watched him for a long time as he ambled out of view.

*David and I will never have anything like they have. I always thought we would, but not anymore.*

Sophie led the way back to the shelter and pitched the pretty urn into the dumpster beside the garage. They both heard it shatter.

"One afternoon, well lived." Sophie laughed and dusted her hands together with spirit. "Guess that takes care of that."

# Chapter Eleven

As Abby poured Brewster's kibbles into a bowl, she heard the patio door open, sensed the oppression, and knew David had come in from his run.

For several dense, smothering moments, he didn't speak. Neither did she. Then, finally, "Abby—" He spoke in undertones so Braden wouldn't hear them.

"No," she whispered. "Don't say anything."

So, for a while, he didn't try. The two of them went about their morning as they'd done for the six mornings since David had started sleeping on the sofa. They were insufferably aware of the other's whereabouts, their backs thrown up as protective barricades, repelling one another like opposite sides of magnets.

She stayed carefully in the kitchen while he hurried to get his clothes from the bureau drawer.

He stayed in the bathroom while she straightened the bed.

She ducked away when he came in to pour coffee.

He rummaged through the junk drawer to find a pen, refusing to meet her eyes.

Saturday morning, a summer morning, and they had all the time in the world.

He waited until she was sectioning a grapefruit, slicing the fleshy part of the fruit with a knife that had been a wedding gift, before he said in a hushed tone, "Braden took it all right, Abby. He didn't ask too much. You would have been surprised."

Her knife paused. Then, pointedly, she cut one more triangle before she acknowledged what he'd said. "I don't want to discuss this right now, David."

"We have to discuss it sometime. We can't hide from it anymore."

"I'm not the one who's been hiding."

"Come on, Abby. It's Saturday. It's the first time all week we've had time to begin this conversation when we could finish it."

"I'm not the one who ignored my marriage vows."

There. Let him have *that* to think about.

Silence settled in again like fog, close and sultry and difficult to navigate. "Look." He spoke in a low baritone. "We're both adults. You've got to help a little bit here." For the first time in days, he came around the table, moved close against her rigid spine. "Ab."

"No." The knife clattered to the floor. Abby jerked her hand to her mouth and sucked the tender skin between her thumb and pointer before running cold water over the wound where she'd cut herself, her whole body throbbing with the sting of it.

"Don't push me like this. Don't do it."

"Abby—"

"You don't know how Braden took it. You know how you *think* he took it. You just know what *you* think he knows."

"This isn't my fault anymore. It's yours."

"His whole world is falling apart and he doesn't know it yet."

And David said, very quietly, "It doesn't have to, Ab, if you don't want it to."

Of all the things he'd done—telling Braden before she'd even had the chance to assimilate this, demanding a confrontation with her by the stream—this subtle shift of blame to her lap hurt worse than anything.

"Oh, no you don't," she hissed through bared teeth as she turned off the faucet. "I've spent years counseling women who try to blame themselves when a man wrecks their marriage. I'm not going to let you do that to me."

"Okay," he said, backing down quickly. "Okay."

Sorrow engulfed them, capturing them there, holding them together and apart. There could be no escaping this that had come upon them while they'd been so settled and smug and serene.

Abby found the tin of Band-Aids on a shelf above her head. As she thumbed through them to find the right size, morbid curiosity finally got the best of her. She asked the question that had been needling her for days.

Paying full attention to the tiny adhesive strip as she peeled off the wrapper, she asked, "You've talked to her, haven't you?"

"What?"

"You've talked to her. That's how you found out about the little girl."

He lifted his head, tossing it high like a stallion. From that one defensive movement, Abby already knew his answer. "Come on, Abby."

"Have you seen her, too? How many of her phone

calls have you taken? I know you've taken one because I answered it. That night when we grilled outside. And then you lied. You said it was somebody from the bank."

He took a breath that seemed to go all the way to his Nike running shoes. "Yes. I've taken her calls," he said with great command. "I have seen her. And I will continue to do so until we get this worked out."

"When?" she insisted. "I want to know all the times."

"Don't do this to yourself. Don't do this to us."

"No, David. I'm not doing this to us. You are. I'm only asking you to be truthful."

She'd spent years counseling, and he hated being analyzed. She made him feel so cornered and wrong. He practically growled at her, "Look, Abigail. There's a little girl's life at stake here. You seem to have forgotten that."

He couldn't help himself; just the mention of the other child softened his voice. David heard the change himself. Deep within him, a natural human instinct had taken hold: paternity, as irrevocable as what he felt for his own legitimate son, and impossible to control or evade.

He had a daughter.

He'd never met her; he'd only seen her face in a photo, but their lives were inextricably bound by generations of family heritage and ancestors.

She had a right to know he cared about her.

No matter what mistakes he'd made, he had a right to love this new person who had been born of his own flesh and blood.

"You can answer the question or not," Abby said. "I don't care."

"She called me on our anniversary. While we were

gone that night and Crystal was babysitting. That's when I heard from her first."

"Our *anniversary?*"

"Yes."

Another memory gone. One more thing taken away that she'd thought she could hold dear.

"That's when she told you everything?"

"No. She called so we could meet later."

"She called so you could meet? She came to *Jackson?*"

"Yes."

With meticulous attention, Abby stuck one end of the Band-Aid to the outside of her hand and one end to the inside. So she'd been right. He *had* spoken to that woman, several times. When a phone call would have sufficed, she had traveled hundreds of miles to see him instead.

For the first time today, she met her husband's eyes. "It happened because you had second thoughts about marrying me, didn't you? The baby scared you and you weren't sure how to manage so much responsibility. So you did the most irresponsible thing you could think of." *Please say that isn't it, David. This is your chance. Tell me I'm wrong.*

David plunked on the couch, presenting his spine to her at exactly the same stiff, contemptuous angle she'd presented hers to him. He brandished the remote control like a weapon and turned up the TV as loud as it would go.

———

At least once a week after practice, the entire Elk's Club baseball team rode their mountain bikes from Mateosky Field to Snow King Ski Hill, for a ride on the Alpine Slide.

They would dart in dangerous, unpredictable angles across the streets, their matching black-and-green caps pulled low over their noses as they shouted to each other. They would fish in their pockets for money to buy tickets and be off up the lift to the top of the hill. Once there, they would disembark, choose a plastic sled with metal wheels, and plunge headlong down the winding cement half-pipe. When the mood struck, they would race each other, leaning left on a left turn, leaning right on a right turn, and bursting with a yell from under the bridge. They yanked hard on the brakes before they smashed into the rows of tires for safety at the bottom, then started all over again.

It was a nine-year-old boy's heaven.

Today, halfway up the lift, two abreast and strung out fifty yards from each other, the Elk's Club baseball team carried on a conversation.

"Hey, Wheezer!"

"What?"

"Chicken's butt."

"Shut up, Jake. Go back to your hole."

"I'll race you!"

"I'm in my hole. Jackson Hole."

"You're gonna go down!"

"No, I'll take *you* down."

In the chair beside Jake Fisher, Braden sat without saying a word. He stared past their dirty, dangling cleats at the ground, getting a topside view of hikers heading up Snow King. He rode with his lower lip folded between his teeth and his baseball cap slung low over his eyes.

"Hey, Treasure!" Jake lifted up his shirt to show off his latest bike-wreck laceration with pride. "Look at this. It's nasty, isn't it? Look at the pus."

Braden didn't look. "Sweet."

"I got it on that turn going by Cache Creek. Tire went right out from under me."

Again Braden didn't comment.

"I hit the handlebars."

"Sweet."

Braden wasn't admiring the lesion nearly as much as Jake might have hoped he would. Jake touched it gingerly once more, trying again for sympathy. "My mom thought I might have smashed my spleen, but I didn't." He gave up and pulled his shirt down. "What you thinking about?"

"Nothing much." Which was a lie.

Braden was thinking about all sorts of things. He was thinking what good stories he could tell about the vials and the tubes and the needles he'd seen in that hospital lab room. How they'd given him a cotton ball to hold against his arm and how a nurse drew a bear face on it. How they'd made his dad lean down and put his head between his legs right in the middle of everything while the nurse said, "Mr. Treasure, take deep breaths. You are about to faint!"

Braden was thinking he could say, *That needle was as long as Lick Creek going into my arm. And then they sucked out so much blood that they filled up five containers, and those containers were all rolling around on a tray. It was eeew, yuck, and I was brave to let them take it out and they took so much that I think they might use it to save somebody.*

It would make for a good story, all right.

But for some reason, Braden kept thinking maybe he

ought not to tell it. He kept thinking maybe he ought to keep it quiet, with how stirred up he felt in his heart about his dad and mom fighting with each other. He didn't want *anybody* to know about that.

Almost every morning of Braden's life, Brewster had nosed open Braden's door, creaking the hinges and barging his way in. Almost every morning, Braden threw back the covers for him and Brewster jumped in, nestling down low in the bed so no one could find him. Two mornings ago Braden had taken the dog's big, scruffy neck in his arms and hung on for dear life, ignoring the dog-food breath and trying to ignore the anger in his parents' voices and the words he didn't understand.

"Hey, Brade. We're at the top of the lift."

Jake gave him a shove because he'd almost missed getting off. When he jumped down, he carried his questions with him, low in his middle, along with a slight tinge of fear. His friends were already warring over the best sleds—the orange or the blue, or the one with the skid marks that Chase had commandoed and won races with last week.

At first, Braden hadn't understood what his mom and dad had been talking about. He hadn't understood the hurt in his mom's voice, nor the defense in his dad's.

As he listened, though, he'd begun to realize what they were whispering about. They were whispering about that little girl he was supposed to be able to help.

It made him want to shudder, hearing how unhappy they were. He had heard them fight before, but he had never heard them talk to each other like that. Fear had chilled him; even the panting dog under the blankets hadn't kept him warm.

"Hey, Treasure. What's wrong?" Jake lifted a sled and dropped it on the track. "Are you mad about something?"

"No."

"Then what are you holding the line up for? It's your turn."

Braden took the first available orange sled and settled himself feet first. He leaned forward into the course and hung on to the sides of the cart as it started moving, its metal wheels bumping over the seams in the concrete with a rhythmic *thunk thunk thunk.*

Once, when they'd been in the third grade, Charlie Hessler had said, "The worst thing that could ever happen to me would be if my mom and dad broke up." Three months later, Charlie's dad got an apartment on Pearl Street and Charlie went to visit him on Sundays to watch football.

As he went down the slide, Braden passed a patch of harebells, and thought of his grandma who loved harebells. He began to go faster, bursting through the quick sun-and-shadow of the pines. The brim of his baseball cap caught air and he almost lost it. He yanked it off and stuck it between his legs where it would be safe.

Even though he'd been sad for his friend Charlie, even sadder because Charlie had talked to him about it beforehand, Braden couldn't help feeling just a little bit proud.

*My dad kisses my mom when they think I'm not looking. My mom wraps her arms around his neck like she never*

*wants to let go. Sometimes they pinch each other and pop
each other with rubber bands and laugh.*

Although that part was yucky and mushy and he
tried to ignore it, it made him just a little happy, too.

*My parents would never break up, not in a million years.*

Braden picked up more speed. He rode the turns hard
all the way. The mottled shade felt cool on his face, and
aspens zoomed by in flashes of white.

A chiseler paused on the side of the half-pipe, and
Braden couldn't resist aiming the sled for it. The rodent
raised its front paws and chattered at him, its tiny body
a question mark. It scurried away just in time.

*Maybe it's my fault they're so upset. I must have done
something wrong.*

Braden leaned further forward. He was flying—too
fast, breaking the rules of the slide. It didn't matter.
Today he didn't feel like obeying rules anymore. Water
streamed from his eyes along the sides of his face. He
squeezed them shut and tried to remember the prayer
everybody wanted him to memorize from Sunday
school.

*Our Father, who art in heaven . . .*

Hm-mm. He couldn't remember any more. He took
a running start at it and tried again.

*Our Father, who art in heaven . . .*

That's as far as he could get. Certainly not far enough
to do any good. Nothing like calling God's name and
then leaving Him hanging.

The bottom of the Alpine Slide loomed ahead of
him. On the bridge beside the miniature golf course,
mothers held their children tightly and pointed at him.
He narrowed his eyes at them, pleased with himself, and
leaned into the downhill, thinking again that maybe he

was to blame. He wasn't thinking about the slide any-more. No one could catch him, or match this speed.

He passed beneath the shadow of the bridge and someone shouted at him.

That's when Braden finally looked up.

Just ahead of him on the track, Wheezer, his own teammate, had stopped at the end of the track. He was slowly climbing out of his cart.

"Wheezer! Jacoby. Out of the way!"

Braden wrenched the brakes. Metal wheels screeched against concrete. Wheezer bellowed and rolled out. Braden hit Wheezer's sled with a crash that sent it top-pling violently into the grass. Wheezer stayed on all fours, his head drooping toward the ground as Braden's cart bashed into the tires at the end and, with an awful jounce, flew end over end in the air. Braden's Elk's-Club cap went soaring. He tumbled safely into the grass.

"Too fast!" hollered the man running out of the ticket booth toward him. "Too fast!" He caught Braden by the arm and yanked him around. "What's your name?" the man demanded. "You tell me, what's your name? You were riding dangerously. You could have hurt somebody. You aren't riding here anymore."

Charlie said, "Did you see all those chiselers on the track? I almost hit one."

"Hey," Jake bellowed from behind them. "Wheezer can't breathe."

Wheezer crawled on the ground in no apparent di-rection, his nose low to the grass, his fingers desper-ately spearing the blades. His gasps for breath came labored and hollow—the same eerie, rattling whistle as a flute.

"He's lost his inhaler," Charlie shouted. "Come on!"

Braden tried to help Wheezer but the ticket man held on and wouldn't let him go. He stood watching, helpless and terrified, as eight of his team members worked through the grass like starlings, getting in one another's way.

"What does it look like?"

"It's orange."

"It's a little bottle that you push."

"There's a prescription thing on it with his name."

Wheezer gave up and rocked back on his heels, sucking and rattling for air.

"I've got it!" Chase leapt from the lawn, clenching the medication in his fist. "Here, Wheezer. Here. I found it. Take this!"

Jake held Wheezer's shoulders while he and Chase fumbled for what seemed like an eternity with the small plastic spout. Then came the *hiss*, and another *hiss*, and Wheezer gasped and gulped in a great lungful of air.

"Yeah, Wheezer!" they all shouted, applauding their friend, paying tribute to their own relief.

"Way to go."

"Good job."

Wheezer took three more deep, satisfying breaths before he could speak.

"Thanks for my inhaler, dude. I must have lost it."

"Wheezer—" Braden tried to wrench free.

"Oh, no you don't." The ticket man gripped Braden's biceps. "You're not going anywhere." He pulled a radio out of his pocket and keyed it. "Call for Snow King Security. Call for Snow King Security. Security needed immediately at the Alpine Slide."

"Oh, c-come on." Braden tried to choke the words out, and they weren't very respectful. It didn't matter, though; his protest wasn't loud. He couldn't breathe, either. His own windpipe was choked with tears.

# Chapter Twelve

Nelson Hull and David Treasure jaywalked across Cache Street, dodging the two Clydesdale horses and red tourist stagecoach making the same slow, circuitous route it made at least three dozen times each day. Nelson mouthed a Dum Dum lollipop he'd picked out of a teller's jar in the bank lobby. "David, you're my climbing partner. This is hard. I don't know how to start this."

"You're good at starting things. They pay you to start things. You're a preacher."

"You want a Dum Dum?" He pulled several out of his pocket.

"How many of those did you take?" David asked. "The bank can't afford you much longer."

"Here." Nelson tossed him a green one, David's favorite. Only a good friend would have known what flavor he'd want.

"Thanks." David caught it in midair and jabbed it into his pocket.

"Well," Nelson started again.

They passed through the famous elk-antler arches

that curved over each entrance to the town square. Just as they did, a gentleman in Bermuda shorts handed David a camera.

"Here we go. Sir, would you mind taking our picture for us? I've got five rolls of vacation, and there isn't a one with me in it."

"Sure. No problem. I'll take it."

David and Nelson both watched as the man took charge and arranged everyone. He had a certain place he wanted them, on the rock pedestal beneath the landmark tangle of horn. For a moment, David was distracted again, listening as the fellow gave him instructions on how to focus and which button to push. He lifted the camera to his eye and saw a family very much like his own inside the viewfinder. The father hurried around to take his place, spreading his arms wide to encompass his wife and children.

"Okay, are you ready?"

"Yes!" they all chimed.

"Okay. Say . . ." By this time, just looking at them, David had to clear his throat and start over again. "Say 'cheese.' On the count of three."

"Cheeeese," the children said, before he'd even gotten ready.

"Okay. One. Two. *Three.*"

"Cheeeese!" they all shouted, their arms wrapped around each other, their grins as broad as the MacKenzie drift boats used by fishing guides on the Snake River.

David snapped the picture and handed over the camera. "Here you go." He thought of all the family Christmas card portraits he, Abby, Braden, and Brewster had posed for. Under the antler arch. On the balcony of the Old Faithful Inn. In a raft, riding the white-water called Lunchcounter.

"Thanks so much."

David watched them a few moments more, then he and Nelson walked on. They came to the veterans memorial statue in the center of the square—a bronze cowboy busting a bronco over a listing of Jackson Hole heroes from each war. Some of these family surnames went back ninety years. Warren Watsabaugh. Bert Schofield. Pete Karnes, Harvey Hagen, and Clinton Budge. Nelson sat down beside those names and said, "When you hear what we're going to talk about, you'll wish we'd gone mountain climbing instead. It would have been easier."

"Well, then. Go ahead."

The affection and regard in his eyes spoke of something larger than himself. "I think we need to talk about what's happening between you and Abby."

A beat. David offset his jaw then righted it again. "Well, I don't know why we'd need to talk about that."

"Maybe we need to discuss it because I'm your pastor. Maybe we need to discuss it because I'm your friend."

David picked up a stick lying beside his feet in the grass. "Seems to me that's Abby's business and my business, Nelson." He hurled the stick, watched it soar aloft. "It isn't yours."

When David turned back to Nelson, the gentle, careful expression he loved was gone and in its place sat frustration. "Don't close me out, buddy. You need a friend right now. And I'm here. I'm your climbing partner."

"Stop saying that. Stop saying you're my climbing partner."

"I thought you might need some guidance."

David picked a piece of grass and examined it. "Abby and I . . . well, I don't know what we're working toward, Nelson. She's got every reason to feel the way she feels. I've committed adultery and the verdict is in."

Nelson stared in stunned surprise. "That's what's happened between you? You cheated on Abby?"

"Yes."

The expression on Nelson's face had slipped. He wasn't the caring pastor anymore; he was the concerned and incredulous friend. "C'mon, man. What were you thinking?"

Both men settled in on their bench as if they were settling into themselves. David slouched a little, shifting his weight from one buttock to the other. Nelson leaned his chin into his left hand with elbow propped on his knee—the thinker's pose.

David puffed out his cheeks and blew. "Well, I guess I had my reasons."

"Which were?"

David rocked back and leaned his weight on the heels of his hands. "I was thinking I'd gotten married too fast, is what I was thinking. All of my buddies were playing in the Montana Hot Box baseball tournament and camping by the Platte River over the weekends and making all-night road trips to Denver for the Bronco games, and here I was with a kid on the way. And Abby wouldn't . . . I don't know." He stared at the sky, searching for words. "Sometimes she lived *around* me instead of *with* me. I had a wife but it often seemed like she wasn't there."

He waited for some response from his comrade and got none. At the corner, a START bus loaded passengers and pulled away from the curb with a sheer billow of diesel. Behind the bus, the town stagecoach made another slow circle of the square, the horses' hooves clattering on the pavement.

David added quickly, "But none of that is any excuse, is it?"

Nelson didn't answer that question. "Sometimes it's the hardest thing I have to do, being both a pastor and a friend."

That admission made them both look at the sky again. Then David let out an uncertain chuckle. "If I had to pick between one or the other, you know which one I'd choose." He threw another stick. "I could find a different pastor."

Two men sat on the rock ledge, leaning on the balls of their feet while the birds began to sing again. David clapped his hands once, twice, three times. Nelson slapped his knees and stood up. "I only wish I didn't have so many other people to worry about."

"Other people?"

"Yes."

"What do you mean by that?"

Nelson didn't want to answer. David could tell by the way he fisted his hand at his side. "Well, I'm the pastor of a church. And others know there has been strife between you and Abby."

"What?"

"You're in the church leadership. People have been calling."

"They have?"

"Yes."

"About our marriage?"

"Yes."

David said, coloring faintly, "You know I was going to talk to you about it, Nelson. I was just waiting for the right time."

"You waited too long."

"Who's calling you?" David pressed. "Who's talking?"

Nelson scrubbed his forehead. "If I were to tell you, it would only make it worse, and you know it. But I have the health of the church to think about. There are chasms beginning to form."

"Who?" David asked again, even though he knew Nelson couldn't answer. So David began running over the hit list in his head, trying to answer for himself. Grant Fisher, Jake's dad from baseball. Hal Carparelli, Kate's husband from Abby's work. Larry Watt, his administrative assistant's brother. In his mind, they all became suspect.

"How can people in the church know? Braden doesn't even know. Abby and I don't want this to be all over town." David hated the way everyone, including himself, thought of them as a pair.

Abby and me. Me and Abby.

"The presbytery committee is coming to meet with you, David. I asked them if I could speak to you first because we're such good friends."

"Meet with me?"

"You need to be prepared. They're going to come to you and ask you to step down. From the finance committee, too."

His anger erupted. "What?" He leapt up, his breath

coming in another heavy chuff. Nelson's expression didn't waver. "Fine."

But it wasn't fine.

*Sure. I'll quit. I don't have to be an elder.*

He broke off a branch from the cottonwood beside them and began to snap it apart in inch-long increments.

*All this time I've served and this is the thanks I get?*

He kicked a pinecone with the toe of his Hush Puppies and watched it skitter away.

*I don't have to teach the sixth-graders either. Let them try to find somebody else who can handle Scott McComas.*

That made David smile, if a little viciously. The boy was a handful, and everybody knew it. Three weeks ago, after David had prepared and prayed over a middle-school lesson the entire week, he'd asked the class to share ideas how they could reach other kids for Christ. He'd called on Scott immediately, impressed by the arm high in the air and the waggling fingers. "Go ahead, Scott. What do you want to say?"

"You know how to hypnotize a chicken?"

Eight pairs of eyeballs had locked on Scott McComas. Eight heads had scrambled to figure out if this had anything to do with leading friends to Christ.

"My uncle was here from Iowa and he taught us to hypnotize a chicken. Hold its face close to your face and look it straight in the eye."

Sure, let somebody else listen to those barnyard stories. "Nelson, if they had problems with what was happening, why didn't they come to me? Have they had phone calls? Meetings? Have people been discussing it as a group?"

David had been in a leadership role at the church

for over nine years. He'd even sat on the committee that had hired Nelson Hull. *How could they ask me to step down as elder? How could Nelson let it happen?*

"It's wrong, how people go about it, David. They talk because they want to make sure they're right. They win others to their side without realizing what they're doing."

David felt like he'd been booted in the gut.

"It's in 1 Timothy, the part about a church leader managing his children and his household."

"Stop it," David said. "Stop it. You and Abby both quoting Scripture at me. I know what the Bible says."

"David—"

"This is the only thing I'm doing right for God anymore. And they want to take that away from me, too?"

The Dum Dum was long gone, but Nelson still wheedled the stick around in his mouth. For a long moment he didn't say anything. He looked at his friend with all the care of heaven in his eyes. "Are you really doing this for God, David?"

David stared him down. "That's a ridiculous question. Of course I'm doing it for God. Who else would I be doing it for?"

"Yourself."

"Right," he said with no small hint of sarcasm. "I sit through meetings two nights a week during the school year and stay past nine o'clock at night. I miss Braden's Junior Jazz basketball games at the rec center. I miss Abby's Chorale concert and the night Braden gave his speech for student council at Colter. Sure, I miss all those things. And I do it for myself."

"Or maybe you do it for your wife."

"Right."

"Maybe you've been doing all this, trying to be worthy of something from Abby."

"That's ridiculous."

"Maybe you've been trying to earn her love and trust because you know you don't deserve them anymore."

"You're nuts." David rose and jammed his fingers through his hair in frustration. "I know *exactly* what I'm doing. And I know exactly why I'm doing it. For nine years I've been serving the *Lord*."

"Maybe you're trying to be acceptable to Abby," Nelson stayed right with him, "and maybe you're trying to be acceptable to God."

Silence formed a wall between friends.

"If that's what you want, here's my resignation. Officially. I step down. Tell them they don't have to come—that I've already done it. Take me off the elders' board and the finance committee. Take me off all the other lists, too. Especially sixth-grade children's church. I really don't want to do that anymore."

Nelson spread two hands in the air, helpless. "You have to resign to the presbytery committee, not to me."

David began to walk away, his shoulders sagging.

"What you're doing this minute might be the only thing you're doing right for God. Being honest with yourself. Admitting to the world where you stand."

"God forgave me a long time ago for what I've done." Why wasn't Nelson telling him the things a pastor was *supposed* to say? "Don't you think that?"

"Frantic servers. That's what I call them. Trying to make up for something they won't ever be able to make up for."

"I'm not frantic," David insisted, following him. "I've just been busy."

As if David wasn't already smarting enough from his conversation with Nelson Hull, when he walked into the lobby of The Jackson State Bank, there beneath the mammoth taxidermy head of a bison that had been the bank's logo and mascot for the past seventy-five years sat two security guards flanking his son. One of them hefted himself from the chair, his leather belt squeaking as he hoisted it. "Mr. Treasure? Is this your boy?"

Heaviness, rock-solid, bore down on him. What next? The other guard stood, too. Still sitting between them, Braden pursed his bottom lip, brought his elbows close to his ribs in shame, and stared at the floor.

"Is this your son, Mr. Treasure?"

"Yes, it is." A pause. "Braden?" Then, back to the intimidating men, "Is there some problem here?"

Two dozen pairs of magnetic eyeballs locked on them. From the personnel at the customer-service cubicles and the tellers lined up behind the long, narrow desk to Francisco, head of maintenance, who was busy rearranging velvet ropes, everybody was watching.

"Yes, we have a problem." Security Guard One locked his forearms across his chest. "Even though the police were not called, Snow King management did not want this boy released to anyone except his father."

"Released from what?"

"He's a minor, so it hasn't been determined which charges will be filed. But it might be reckless endangerment, Mr. Treasure. Your boy injured someone on the Alpine Slide."

As often happens to a parent when his child stands accused, David's thoughts pendulumed between defense and blame. First he thought, *Oh, good grief, sport. Why did you do that?* Second he thought, *My child would never behave that way! Who do you think you're kidding?*

But the misery on Braden's face warned David that he'd best get the whole story before he passed judgment. "Would you both like a Dum Dum? Here. Have one." He lifted a jar from a customer-service desk and offered it to the guards. "Try the green. They're the best. Yellow is good, though, too. You might think it's lemon, but it's pineapple."

They declined, one of them soundly and one of them looking like he would rather have said yes.

"Why don't we go to my office? We can hash this out."

They started toward the stairs with Braden in tow. As David panned the room, all gazes withdrew to their proper duties. Except for Francisco, who accidentally knocked over a brass post in his haste to occupy himself.

Once they'd closed the door and all the pomp-and-spectacle of the guards had ended for everyone, David sat in his thick swivel chair and motioned for Braden to join him. When his son came, he gave him a place to perch on his knee and hugged him. There he sat, hanging on to his son for dear life, as if they were both dangling over a dangerous cliff.

"Now, who's going tell me what happened?"

The two guards stumbled over each other to recount the details—how they'd been called from their offices by two-way radio and how they'd found everybody so upset and how they'd seen the injured kid still breathing hard beside the picnic table.

"Braden? Is this the truth?"

Braden bit his bottom lip and nodded.

"That boy—" Guard Number Two adjusted his belt around his paunch. "—is not allowed to come back to the Alpine Slide for the remainder of the summer."

"Braden? Is this what happened?"

When Braden finally spoke, his voice was thin with shame. "I did it to W-wheezer, Dad. I did it. It was my fault."

"But I—" David stopped. What had he been about to say? *I expected you to say it was an accident. I expected you to say it wasn't your fault.* "Are you sure?"

*I expected you to stand up for yourself!*

Of course it was what he expected. That's exactly what he would have said for himself.

"You did it to Wheezer on the baseball team?"

Braden nodded, tears pooling in his eyes. "He couldn't find his inhaler and h-his lips turned blue. I d-didn't know what to do."

It just came out of David's mouth, that phrase men use with each other when they're surprised, the same one Nelson himself had relied on when he'd found out what was wrong. "Braden, sport. What were you thinking?" A lowered head, a prodding gesture of the chin. "What?"

"Nothing important."

"Well, there must have been something."

So there they sat, father and son, one chin propped on top of the other one's head, while Braden began to try to answer.

"I was thinking . . . I was thinking . . ." His entire face crumpled and his words came out in sobs. "I heard you and M-mom when you thought I was asleep . . .

and I was thinking w-what I did . . . to make you and Mom be mad—"

When David realized, the truth felt like a boulder, crushing him. *No.*

"—be m-mad at each other and fight all the time—"

"Braden. No."

"—because Brewster opened the door and came in and I h-heard you and I know it was s-something—"

"Sport."

"—I did."

"Listen to me, Braden. Stop. Listen to me."

"What is it, Dad?" Braden's voice wavered with hurt and concern and responsibility. "Why are you and Mom mad all the time? What did I do?"

The security guards had discreetly left the room at the start of Braden's sobs. David clamped his son against him so hard that he knocked the air out of his own chest. "I'm sorry, sport," he said, his insides twisting with love for this boy. "I'm sorry, I'm sorry, I'm sorry." How could he say it? How could David reassure his own son when he had no reassurances himself? "It isn't anything you've done. It's just that your mom and me—"

He didn't know how to go on. *This is Abby's doing, not mine. I've been honest with her and she's the one erecting walls of defense. Abby's to blame for this.*

"Daddy," Braden whispered against his shirt. "I'm scared."

David's heart lurched. The only thing he could feel, after the other parts of today, was the complete possession and life of this boy. He grabbed onto that one reality as if it were a climbing rope, saving him from the abyss. "Brade. Oh, sport." He dislodged his son and was down off the chair in an instant, balanced on the balls of his feet on Braden's level. "You haven't done anything."

"Why, then? What's wrong, Dad?"

"Sometimes parents fight, and there isn't anything to worry about. They just do."

"This isn't the same as that. I know the difference. Mom's mad and you're mad and I don't know what I've done."

"Braden, it isn't you."

Braden's little face crumpled and his grimy fingers curled around his dad's wrists. "Are you and mom breaking up? Mom's talking about it on the phone to her friends. I've heard her."

"You've—?"

"Are you and mom falling apart or something? Charlie Hessler said his parents argued all the time before his dad moved out and they got a divorce."

"No," David lied. "We aren't falling apart."

It was Abby who was doing this, and no one else. Abby on the phone with her friends. Abby who had refused to discuss the situation with civility and who flung his broken marriage vows into his face like stinging cold water. Abby who accused him of making the world fall apart for Braden, when she was the one who heaped kindling on the pain.

Sure, he had had an affair with another woman once. Sure, he had fathered another child. But Abby was the one who held his offense against him like a fur trapper with live bait, goading a coyote forward. Abby was the one who brandished full-time bitterness against him like a punishing sword.

Lord, I don't want any part of this. We're so broken

that maybe it would be best if we just ended it and went our own separate ways. Maybe it would be best if we hurt our son once now so he could start healing and he wouldn't have to be hurt anymore.

Maybe.

*Do You hear me, God? I don't want this. I don't want this.*

"Dad?"

David gripped Braden's shoulders in helpless abandon. "Let's go home, son. What do you say?"

⌒

June 23
Dear Susan,

I am waiting anxiously to hear the results of the blood test that should have been sent to you via the lab at St. John's Hospital on June 19. I didn't tell Braden much about the situation. Children are so perceptive, especially smart children. He has sensed the tension between Abby and me, and it has begun to become a problem with him. It is time we made some decisions in our family. I have made one decision on my own. This is what I'm writing you about today.

I would like the opportunity to meet my daughter.

I know you have kept her secure and well taken care of. For that, Susan, I offer you my respect and my thanks. If we are measuring good things from our relationship, we will measure the life of Samantha as one of those things. I regret that I didn't get the chance to know her when she was young. But one can never know how things would have turned out. Even if she's said she's never wanted a father, do you think she might want one now? I want to offer her good things, nothing bad. But she needs to be the one to choose. Maybe Braden can give her life. Maybe I can give her some fun.

Please respond promptly. We both know that time may be of the essence.

Yours in massive respect,
David Treasure

~

June 23
Dear Mother,

I am writing to let you know that it might not be best for you and Dad to drive to Newcastle for the Little League Wyoming Shoot-Out Baseball Tournament this year. I don't think it'll be a problem to cancel your reservations at the Trail's End Motel. If you need the number I've got it. Remember, that's the place we stayed last year where the air conditioners in all the rooms had to be turned off in the morning so the maids wouldn't blow the fuses when they did the laundry. I'm sorry to have to make you miss that experience this year!

I need to be frank with you and Dad. Abby and I are having some problems. It wouldn't be a good time for any of us to be together. I know what you're saying as you read this, Mother: "God can work miracles in a marriage if you'll only let him." But there is a lot involved here, so many different sides and, above all things, we feel like we have to protect Braden. At least, I feel that way. Sometimes two people get so hurt that nothing can help them see their way out of it. We bring out the worst in each other. Maybe we can't go back to where we were before. If we could, I don't think I would want to.

So you see, that baseball tourney isn't going to be very much fun this year.

I know you'll call when you get this letter. Please call me at the office. This is something that I cannot discuss with you and Dad over the home telephone.

Your son,
David

June 23
Dear Members of the Presbytery Committee,

Upon receipt of this letter, please accept my official resignation as elder from the Jackson Hole Christian Center. Please also accept my resignation from the finance committee at this time. I am stepping down per a conversation with Pastor Nelson Hull on June 22. Per 1 Timothy 3:12, I have a situation in my household that demands attention and I do not feel I should be serving the church in this capacity at this time.

I look forward to continuing in service at a later date. It has been a privilege to preside with you in servanthood to the Body of Christ.

Sincerely,
David Treasure

P.S. Please also remove my name at this time from teaching sixth-grade Sunday school. Thank you.

# Chapter Thirteen

*A*s Abby commuted along Hall Street toward the shelter the next morning, she happened past Floyd and Viola Uptergrove's house.

There stood Viola on the front porch as Abby went by, teetering up on the second rung of her walker, trying to hang a bird feeder beneath the eaves.

*Goodness, that thing could go right out from under her!*

Abby screeched on the brakes and hopped out. As she ran up the sidewalk, Viola stood with her legs straddled, one on each side of the walker, holding the feeder at arm's length. Abby ran to her, grabbed the walker beneath her, and held it steady. In another moment, she supported the woman's elbow. "Why don't you let somebody else help you with that?"

Viola, who had stretched to the full extension of her slight body in an attempt to attach the feeder, grasped Abby on the shoulder with one feeble, impassioned hand. "What a dear you are, thinking you need to rescue me." She wore a Mexican dress with puffy sleeves and silver rickrack, as bright blue-green as turquoise stones. "Isn't this the most lovely feeder? Floyd built it for me this weekend. You know how the songbirds always come out this time of year."

"I'll get it up for you, Viola. I'll fill it, too, before I go. It would be awful for you to take a fall."

Viola tried herself once, twice again, before she acquiesced and handed the feeder to Abby. "Honest to John." She climbed down and brushed her hands together with purpose. "I don't know why everybody around treats me like I'm ninety years old. I'm only eighty-five." She thumped her walker, which had wheels on the front legs and neon-yellow tennis balls on the rear ones, into the house. "The thistle seed is in a paper sack in the refrigerator. I've got it labeled. Be careful not to get that critter crunch. That stuff brings the magpies."

"I'll find the thistle for you." Abby followed her into the kitchen and rummaged around the refrigerator shelves.

"Since you're taking so much trouble, you've got to stay for a cup of tea. Why weren't you at church this week, by the way?" The woman turned, a moose hot pad like a puppet on one hand and a pinecone teapot in the other. Her blue eyes glowed with light. "You and your husband have such a beautiful family. I love watching the three of you come into the sanctuary."

If Viola Uptergrove noticed how quiet Abby became at that comment, she didn't say a word. Viola scuttled around her kitchen like a little nesting bird herself, bringing out sugar and slicing up a lemon, digging in the breadbox for muffins.

Abby found the thistle. "I'll just—" She gestured outside. "I'll be right back."

"Good. You hurry. And don't fall."

Abby completed the task, without falling, in minutes. When she returned to butter, crème, and even lemon curd set out on the table, Viola took her arm and steered her to a chair.

"I know you haven't had breakfast. Kids your age never eat breakfast before they're out the door."

"If you lecture me about breakfast, then I'm going to lecture you about your walker." Abby laid her own fingers over Viola's on her arm. "It's dangerous to climb."

"Floyd will be back any minute with the dogs. He'll be so glad to see that the feeder's up. I certainly didn't want him to try to do it."

As Abby reached for a spoonful of lemon curd, she noticed an ancient flaking-leather photo album on the floor beside her chair. "What's this?" She bent to pick it up.

"Oh, the funniest pictures. You wouldn't believe."

"Can I look?"

"Of course you can."

Abby flipped open the album and came face to face with the Uptergrove's wedding pictures from 1943.

There stood a handsome young man, his boyish face as scrubbed and shiny as a farm-fresh tomato, his shoulders square in his formal Navy whites.

"Is this Floyd?"

"Yes," Viola answered. "Isn't he handsome?"

At his side, wielding a cake knife with lily-of-the-valley waving from the handle, stood a minuscule girl with dark hair, glowing eyes, and lips emboldened by deep lipstick, who looked like she might take on the whole of the German army if it kept her from getting her man.

"Oh, Viola." Abby sighed. "You were so beautiful that day."

One never knew exactly the right thing to say when examining pictures a half-century old. When someone looked so lovely, it seemed a shame to voice surprise.

"Of course I was beautiful that day," Viola said. "It was my wedding day. A day when a woman makes a covenant to her love and to her Lord, meant to last a lifetime."

"Oh." As if she'd touched something forbidden, Abby drew her hand away.

"All those bride magazines, selling fancy lace and satin dresses. All to capture what can't be captured: the reflection of a woman's face looking into the face of her God."

Abby began to gather her things. "I'd better go."

"Nothing can be more beautiful than that."

"I'm already late for work."

"The kids have already given us a golden anniversary party, and now they want a sixtieth, too. I hope you and your precious family can come."

"I-I hope so, too."

"My family is coming from Kansas and they can get wild, so beware. At our fiftieth, Miley put gunpowder in an eggshell. The cat went too close to the fireball and got its whiskers burned off. Did you know that a cat without whiskers runs into walls?"

They made their way outside again. Pine siskins and chickadees had already begun to feast at Floyd's hand-made feeder. Abby stopped to watch, reticent at the old-fashioned innocence of it, not wanting to head out into the reality of her own life.

Viola stepped up beside Abby, her brow furrowed

deeply. "Is there something—" She paused, as if she hadn't any right to ask. Then, as gently as a hand might be offered to a frightened mongrel dog, Viola offered her hand again to Abby. "Oh, my. I can see it in your face. There is something, isn't there? Something new to pray about."

"Covenants are sometimes hard to keep," Abby said.

"Covenants are always hard to keep," Viola said. A clasping together of fingers, older woman to younger one. "Has he done something to hurt you?"

As the chickadees and the siskins and the sparrows bobbed and swayed on the feeder, tears pooled in Abby's eyes. She nodded and for a moment the words wouldn't come. Then, "I don't think I'll be able to talk to you about this, Viola." Old grievances mixed with new ones. "You and Floyd have had such a wonderful life together."

*A woman called him on the phone on our anniversary, and he phoned her back. She stayed in a motel. She made a trip here, and David agreed to see her.*

"Abby?"

*Right when I needed my husband the most, he didn't think he loved me.*

*He's thought about that for nine years—nine years— before he said anything.*

The birds twittered in the tree for a long time while they watched. At last Abby said aloud, "When I asked him if he had second thoughts about marrying me, he wouldn't deny it. He wouldn't say that I was wrong."

Viola leaned forward on the walker, which tottered with her slight weight. "Oh, honey."

"You know what happened yesterday, Viola? Braden forgot his baseball cleats for practice so I had to drive home to get them. Down where the road makes that jog by Puzzleface Ranch, this . . . this moose came out in front of me. The whole time it was happening, I kept remembering David saying to me, 'Apply the brakes and hit the animal square, Abby. Worse thing you can do is to try to swerve. When you swerve, you catch the right front fender on it and then you flip.' The whole time it was happening, I was saying, 'Okay. Okay, David. I won't swerve, I promise. I'll plow right in.'"

"When you asked him about it, about him having second thoughts, he didn't say he was *sorry* he had married you, did he?"

"This policeman saw me slam on the brakes and he stopped me to make sure I was okay. The moose was fine. But, I couldn't . . . I started crying . . . and I said, 'My husband's had an affair and isn't this ridiculous? I've been so strong in front of everybody, and with a total stranger, I break down?'"

"Because there's a big difference in that, don't you know? Between David having second thoughts then, and not being sorry now?"

"He had his affair after we got married, Viola. And he's a Christian man."

"Well, goodness. You think just because he's a Christian man, he's got to be perfect?" Viola left her walker on the sidewalk and began to make her way without it. "You think because he did it after he got saved instead of before, you think that makes him any less forgiven?"

"No," Abby said, "but it ought to make him changed."

Viola had settled herself on the pine stoop. She slapped the planks beside her. "You just set here a minute and listen. You just set here. Those ladies over at the shelter can keep."

Abby sat as she'd been told.

"The worse trouble you can get into, you know, is feeling something strong and lecturing yourself that you're not supposed to be feeling it. Christians have a bad way of doing that—thinking they're supposed to live above something and not letting it touch them."

"I'm not even trying to be good, Viola."

"Disappointment? I can't feel that, I'm a Christian. Hate? I can't feel that! I have to be good."

"I feel betrayed. And angry. And rejected. And hurt. I thought we had been happy. I thought we had done so well."

"You feel what you've got to feel and you admit you're feeling normal human things and then you tell God you're willing to let Him stir around with those human things and do something supernatural with that. You certainly don't try to stir around with them yourself."

Abby bent forward on the steps and gripped her ankles. She turned her face toward the sun. Viola continued.

"Because if you don't, if you nurture that betrayal and anger and hurt, that's when you get separated from where you're supposed to be. That's when you get separated from the Father."

*Nothing I'm standing on is solid, Lord. Nothing around me is the way it seemed to be.* Abby began to rock, hanging on to her ankles. "I don't know how to have it and not nurture it, Viola. I don't know how to stop it from playing over and over again in my mind."

"Humph," Viola snorted. "I can tell you a story about that."

"What?"

"You know Hoyt and Alvie Strong down the street?"

"Sure I do."

"Well, Alvie got excited about planting herbs not long ago. Brought this long terra-cotta pot home from Spudville. Filled it full of dirt and set it out on the porch. Then her sister came to visit and she never got time to put anything in."

Abby still rocked.

"Something started growing up out of the dirt. They were asking all the neighbors 'What's this?' and nobody knew. Not until Deputy Clarkson stopped by and said, 'Go get rid of that thing, Hoyt. You're growing marijuana on your front porch like it's an herb garden.'

"'How can that be marijuana?' Hoyt said. 'Alvie's been feeding it Miracle-Gro.'"

That story brought a little smile. Abby wagged her head, laid her chin on her knees.

"That's the way it is, then," Viola said. "Let God do the rest. He already knows what you're thinking. He already knows what's growing in your dirt."

"Oh, Viola."

"You just don't look for anything extra to feed a weed with. You don't give it anything that'll make its roots go deeper."

# Chapter Fourteen

The telephone call came early Wednesday, only minutes after David had left for the bank and Abby had stepped in the shower. When she first thought she heard a ring, she had soap in her hand and was working up a wet, loose lather over her shoulders, dousing off the suds. *Lord, what does it matter if I'm nurturing what I'm feeling? I'm angry and I'm hurt and I'm . . . I'm justified.*

She drizzled water over her knees and focused on soaping her feet. *Lord, how could I ever lay that down?* She ran a washrag along the sleek curves of her arms, and passed it twice, three times, around the nape of her neck.

The phone rang again. And again. Abby turned off the water and listened.

Whoever it was wasn't giving up. She climbed out of the shower dripping wet. She toweled off as best she could and wrapped the towel around her middle, then opened the door to the bedroom and picked up the phone. She balanced the receiver between her ear and her shoulder blade. "Hello?"

A beat went by, then two, and no one said a word.

"Hello. Hello?" The whir on the other end, which meant long distance. "Who is this?"

"I'm sorry," the voice finally came, as breathy as a whisper. "I'm calling to . . ." The woman hesitated. "Mrs. Treasure?" Another long pause. "Abigail Treasure? Is this you?"

Of course it is, Abby almost said with sarcasm. Who else would it be answering my phone? "Yes, this is Abigail."

She hadn't dried off nearly enough. Droplets were sliding down her legs. She shivered and futilely tried to swipe them with a corner of the towel.

"This is . . ." A pause. A woman's voice, one that Abby vaguely recognized. "I don't know if you know me. But I think you do."

Abby froze, her towel clutched in her fist. Reality hit her and her legs turned to mush. *Of course. Of course.* "Yes, I know who you are."

"This is Susan. Susan Roche. I didn't know if you knew my name."

Abby made a long, slow descent to the floor. "No. I didn't." She flattened her back against the bed and sat there. "Now I do."

A rush of words. "I know David has explained it all by now. He said he did."

"Yes." How strange, hearing another woman speak her husband's name in such an intimate way. "He has."

"Is it . . . ? Do you go by Abigail?"

"Sometimes I do. Yes." Abby waited. She listened, interpreting the other woman's silence. "I'm sorry," she said after there was nothing left to do but to speak again. "I really don't want to talk to you."

"I can understand that. I feel the same way."

"Perhaps you'd better tell me why you've called, then."

A moment, and then all pretension of pride was gone. "Well, I need—" All false respect gone, any false posturing Susan Roche might have intended. "I need you to tell David something. I need you to tell him that Samantha is missing."

"Who?" And then Abby realized. "Oh, I—I see."

"I thought he'd want to know."

A chill shot up Abby's spine. "Yes, I'm sure he will."

"Will you tell him?"

It seemed so surreal, discussing this subject in such a formal way. As if they were struggling through cloudy, chilling water together. "Of course I'll tell him. Of course I will." She hesitated. "Do you feel free to give me any details?"

"She was at camp. A good camp. Camp Plentycoos, where sick children go to spend a week and remember what it's like to be normal again."

"She disappeared from camp?" In spite of Abby's contention with this woman, she couldn't escape a mother's pity as well. *This is awful. What would I feel like if this were Braden?*

"Sam was so excited because they were sewing beads on moccasins this session. And she had a paint horse named Oliver with the sweetest brown heart on his forehead. I thought it was going to be so good."

"Do you have any idea—" Abby couldn't go on. *What did you ask at a time like this? Do you know if she left? Do you know if somebody took her?*

"She stuffed pillows in her sleeping bag last night so they'd think she was sleeping. No one realized it until she missed breakfast this morning."

"Did she leave a note or anything? Do you think she ran away?"

"No note. No nothing. If she'd gotten a ride from somebody and tried to come home, she would have been here by now."

"You know I'll tell David. I'll go tell him right now."

"That's what I was hoping. I would have just phoned him at the office, but I didn't want him to be alone when he hears—"

Abby glanced at the clock. Gooseflesh raised on her arms. Yes, that's exactly where David would be this moment. Susan Roche knew David's schedule just as well as his own wife did. Abby stared at the fist tangled around the phone cord as if the gnarled, curled knuckles twisted into a ball weren't her own.

"There's more for you, too," Susan stammered. "There's something else you need to hear."

"What?"

"I don't know if he's told you or not. David wrote me a letter last week."

Abby's voice, threadlike. "A letter?"

"In it, he said he wanted to meet Samantha, that he wanted a chance to be a father to her."

"I see."

*No, David wouldn't have told me about that. He wouldn't have told me. It's just another thing.*

Inside, Abby became dry bones, burned ashes; if someone tried to touch her raw edges, she would cave in on herself. More choices they hadn't made together. More deception and prevarication, while he struggled to cover what he'd done.

"I just—"

"It's okay. It's really okay." Although it wasn't. "You don't have to say anything else."

"I didn't show his letter to her. I didn't want to speak to her about her father at all. I was still thinking what I wanted her to know."

"You've been hiding her father from her?"

"What good does it do, to unsettle her life like that? When we don't know how long—"

Susan went mute again. It rattled them both, hearing each other's breathing on the line. Abby kept thinking, *Here she is. The one who has carnal knowledge of my husband. The one—besides me—who's given birth to his child.*

One minute of silence passed, then another and another. Their words hung between them, tangible, unspoken.

*My family is falling apart because of you.*

*My daughter has a right to get well, if someone can help her.*

*He was with you when I thought he cared about me.*

*He wanted your marriage to work so I never told him the truth.*

Two women who had knowledge of the same man, one for a season and one for a lifetime, trying to make sense out of where such uncommon ground brought them.

*It's so huge in me, Lord. It's everything I am right now.* Abby began to work on the knot in the phone cord. *I can't look at his hands without thinking how he touched this woman's body when he was also touching mine. I can't look at his face without seeing all those pictures of our child without me in them.*

Abby was still on the floor, sprawled out with her legs in two directions, leaning against the bed. "I don't know what I'd do if it was me," she said with sacrificial honesty. "David wants to meet her for David's sake, I think."

"I was looking for something else the other day. Digging through the cubicles in my secretary to find an address book with a phone number. When I went back to check for that letter, it wasn't where I'd left it. I think she may have found it and taken it. Maybe it hasn't been there since she left for camp."

"Oh, Susan." Abby's heart practically stopped beating in her chest. "You don't think Samantha might be trying to get to him? To come here?"

A horrifying thought, one that left them both in silent dismay.

Susan's voice, even over the miles, rang with terror. "An eight-year-old girl traveling alone? How dangerous is that?"

When the hush fell between them again, Abby's mind raced to a scary, unbidden place.

Pray for her.

*Well, how would that be? I can't do that. Here, let me pray for Samantha to be safe. And then, worst of all, what if she isn't? Here, yes, let me pray for your daughter while you know my marriage is crumbling around me.*

*When you know my marriage is collapsing because of you.*

Abby couldn't turn away from it, this thing bigger and stronger than herself, this thing that compelled her, that made her lungs ache. All the talk that might have come, and this arrived like an apparition, from someplace outside of herself, the hardest to grasp of all.

My love never fails.

The single word came with the riffling of the breeze

through the blinds and the rustle of the blue-spruce branches against the window.

*I don't have your love in my heart, Father. Not for Susan Roche and her daughter. Not for my husband, David. They've hurt me. They've taken down all I believed in about my marriage and myself.*

"Abigail?" came the voice from the other end of the line. "Abigail, will you tell him?"

"Susan?" Abby asked, her voice trembling, feeling terrified. "I'd like to pray for Samantha. Will you let me do that? While you're on the phone?"

The silence was deafening. The distance clicked and hissed and roared between them.

Then, in a miraculous, gentle voice—a broken voice—Susan answered, "You'd do that for Sam?"

"And for you, too. Please."

"After all we've—" Susan Roche broke off.

"It isn't me doing this," Abby answered very quietly. "I couldn't."

"Oh, please." The voice became a child's voice, eager, desperate. "Please. Yes. There are so many things—"

"Okay," Abby said. "Okay."

Over the miles, two women clasped their hearts together before God. One who'd believed in her marriage once and who'd had her trust torn away, the other who'd thought for nine years she might not ever be worthy to be prayed for. And God gave Abby the words to speak, because they were not in her own heart.

David walked into his office and found Abby waiting for him. She stood beside his desk with the photograph of their family in her hand.

She set it down fast. The gold frame toppled and fell flat with a metallic smack on the desktop.

"Hello, Abby," he said as he stood the picture up again, with an odd twist in his gut because he'd caught her looking. "Amazing how times change, isn't it?" And he looked at it, too.

"Or how times stay the same," she reminded him, her voice low. "That picture is the only one from the whole year that had my face in it. Do you realize that, David? I think you went a whole year without looking at me."

David didn't doubt it. He didn't want to look at her now. He'd gotten so tired of defending himself while she accused him, while she carried her betrayed heart aloft like it was a float in a parade.

"You didn't even take that one, remember? Floyd Uptergrove did, so we could be in it together."

"Abby, let's don't do this to each other anymore." He lifted his eyes to hers and she glanced away, as if she hadn't meant for them to go to this place now. But there could be no other place for them to go. Every time they ended up in a room together, it reared up between them. "It's hurting Braden more, us trying to hide it. He thinks it's something that's his fault. He's heard us. He's heard you."

"Please. David. There's something that's more important than this."

"What could be more important than this?" he asked with acid irony. "What, Abby? Because your pride has cost us everything that there is. Your pride is costing your son's heart."

Oh, she wanted to say it. She wanted to bite right back at him and ask, "Who's pride? Who's pride is doing all this? It takes more than just one!" It served him right, building up to it this way. He'd been defensive since he'd walked in.

Abby tried for a false lilt in her voice but couldn't quite pull it off, not with the somber news she bore.

"Susan called."

That got him. He sat hard in his swivel office chair and his defenses went down. "She did? Susan called? What did she call about?"

Their gazes splintered on each other.

Of course, he thought he knew. "Braden didn't work? The tests didn't match?"

She shook her head. "That isn't it. They don't know about the test yet. The tests take at least five days. And this one had to be couriered. There's—"

He came up out of his chair. "Abby, is she . . . ?"

"She's okay. I—I mean, she's not . . . Oh, David. This is so hard." She began to talk and he could see she was hurrying through the story for his sake. She began with the camp and ended with pillows shoved deep inside a sleeping bag. And even as she shared something this important to him, he felt as if the whole world hung between them, an odd, clear wall like the visitation windows at a jail.

"Ab." It just slipped out, the endearment he always used with her when something was wrong. He called her his pet name with no hint of appraisal or judgment; he said it only with a sense of deep need.

"I don't know what to say, David. I'm sorry."

"Do they have any idea where she could be?"

"No. Nothing really. Her mother's posted all the information on an Internet site. And she's making up posters, getting them out the minute she can."

He raked his fingers through his hair, stared at the ceiling as if it would give him an answer. "I want to go out there."

"David," Abby said. "You could have told me you had written Susan a letter."

Like an elk caught in headlights, he froze. "What?"

"That letter. You could have told me about it. You've finally told me about everything else."

"She said I'd written a letter? She told you about that?" He was reacting all wrong to her finding out, and he knew it. He was playing a game—offense, defense, then offense again, trying to keep his footing.

"I'm tired, David. I'm tired of fishing, asking questions, trying to figure out what you haven't told me."

"Well, you know the truth?" he asked. "I'm tired of it, too."

"Samantha may be trying to get to you." David realized how odd it must feel to her, being the one who knew of Susan, being the one to talk to him about his child, his mistress. "The letter's gone, and Susan thinks she might have taken it. Susan hadn't told Sam about you."

"Oh, man." He stared at the wood grain of his desk. "Oh, man."

"David, I'm sorry."

"Sorry for what? Sorry to tell me? Or sorry that she's missing?"

"How dare you? How dare you ask such an unfair question at a time like this?"

Yeah. Abby was right. "She's out there alone somewhere. That or worse. I could get in the Suburban. I could drive west, see if I could find her."

"The state patrol told Susan to stay home where Samantha can reach her. I'd imagine they would tell you the same thing."

He stopped wrangling over it for a moment and looked at Abby hard. "Thank you for being willing to get involved. Thank you for coming to tell me this."

"Maybe I'm not willing," Abby said. "Maybe I don't have any other choice."

# Chapter Fifteen

There were probably over a dozen places one small girl could conceal herself inside the lockable nooks, crannies, cubicles, and bins of a twenty-seven-foot Jayco camping trailer, especially when that trailer was packed for a camping vacation with blankets and pillows and at least fifty pounds of tuna cans, Rice-A-Roni, Ritz Crackers, and marshmallows for S'Mores.

Especially when a friend was helping her.

"Okay," one small girl whispered to another. "This will work. You can hide here."

"Are you sure? Are you sure they aren't going to find me?"

"It'll be fine. Dad'll be home right after five and then we're driving all night long. He never stops except to get gas. And Mom will be sleeping."

"Will we be there in a day?"

"No. Sixteen hours, that's what Dad says. It's perfect. You hide here all day, we leave tonight and get there tomorrow about eleven in the morning."

"What if I make noise or something? What if I sneeze?"

"Last time we went on a trip, we hid Jess Cavender's Welsh Corgi in here for two days. They never knew a thing until we got to California and it was too late to send him back. I think he probably barked. Of course, he peed on the floor. You won't pee on the floor, will you?"

An insulted shrug. "It'll be hard, but I'll try to do my best."

"If you have to go, push this button before you do." She gestured toward a little plastic panel on the wall behind the tiny sink. "And after you've gone, you have to punch it again to turn the pump off. Dad always gets mad when we forget to turn the pump off. It wastes water if you don't."

"I'll turn the pump off, I promise."

"Okay." A deep sigh of conviction. "I guess that's it, then."

"I guess."

"We'll leave in about an hour, I think. Right when he gets home."

"I'm right here. I'm not going anywhere." But then they stood staring at each other, knowing how wrong those words were because, yes, Samantha was going somewhere. She was going to Wyoming as a stowaway.

When the door shut, Samantha Roche waited alone, a deserter from camp, locked inside her best friend's trailer. She looked around for a place to get comfortable and decided on the corner of the bunk bed, propped in a corner with a pile of corduroy pillows. She unzipped the front pocket of her Camp Plentycoos backpack and pulled out the letter, tattered and pressed flat, with a Rock Springs, Wyoming postmark. She pulled the blue stationery out, unfolded it once more, and read the words her mother might never have showed her.

"Even if she's never wanted a father, do you think she might want one now? . . . I can give her good things."

Samantha held the letter to her chest with both hands and squeezed her eyes shut. She held all of her uncertainty and all of her fear and all of her hope in one small, bursting bosom.

"What do you think?" she whispered aloud to no one. "What do you think about this?"

And from somewhere, into her, the sureness came.

⌒

As the setting sun silhouetted the Tetons and scalloped the underbellies of the clouds with gold, Abby poured lemon oil on a rag and began to polish the coffee table. Tonight, horror of horrors, it was the Treasures' turn to host prayer meeting. Tonight an onslaught of committed couples, including Nelson and Sarah Hull themselves, would arrive on their front doorstep shortly after six-thirty P.M. After a fifteen-minute round of visiting, they would get down to business, petitioning the heavenly Father for everything from new shelves in the church pantry to protection for the church missionaries in Benin and Somalia and Uzbekistan. After that, they would lean in to the circle and get very personal, laying hands on the ones who requested it—some of them weeping with joy or grief, some of them giving praise reports on what the Lord had done this week in their lives.

And here we are, Abby thought. So many layers of

damage and danger and deception in our lives, and people are starting to know about it.

She made careful circles over the table with the cloth, smelling the sharp incense of the oil, watching the deepening richness as it soaked into the pine, and thought of how even dead wood could be polished and refurbished with a loving hand, but hearts sometimes got weather-beaten beyond repair.

She refolded the towels in the guest bathroom, put out a fresh box of tissue, and thought, Why had it been easy to discuss David with some friends and be silent to the ones in church?

She lit a candle in a holder shaped like a moose and thought, How easy to light a flame in wick and wax, when the light has gone completely from our lives. In came the prayer group at seven and there they sat, and the whole time they were holding hands and singing— a part that Abby always loved—the questions wouldn't stop sounding in her head.

*What are we going to do if Samantha comes, Lord?*

*What are we going to do if she doesn't?*

*Oh Lord Oh Lord Oh Lord.*

As their church family circled hands in their living room, she noticed that David sat as stoic and motionless on the sofa as she did. When someone began reading Scripture, he didn't follow along in his Bible; he stared at the gold wedding band on his knuckle instead.

Several times she noticed Nelson watching David. Once during the evening, Betty Sailors said, "It's such a shame David resigned from the finance committee. That was such a nice letter he sent. We're really going to miss his expertise."

"He's resigned?"

Betty nodded. "From the presbytery committee, too. From all of it. You didn't know?"

Abby shook her head.

"Well, that's a surprise," Betty said. "You're his wife."

*Well, he didn't tell me.*

That night, they laid hands on Nelson and Sarah and prayed for the power of Nelson's Sunday messages. They prayed for Sarah's sister who had been diagnosed with diabetes. They prayed for Joe Anderson who had gotten laid off from his job at Sunrise Lumber. They prayed for Victor Martinez who was looking for a new place to live. They prayed for Hannah Saunders who was in angst, listening for God's instructions, trying to decide whether or not to move her mother into an assisted-living center.

From the reflection in the window, Abby could tell that the candle in the little holder in the bathroom was burning low. "Is there anyone else who has needs?" Nelson asked, his Bible held clenched between two able hands. Abby saw her pastor glance pointedly at her husband.

*Nelson knows. David's been talking just like I have.*

Something caught in her throat.

*But, has he been talking to be transparent with his sin? Or has he been talking to win others to his side?*

They had both lost so much. She didn't even know what David was thinking anymore.

There is nothing emptier than an empty profession of the mouth when the words spoken aren't what is inside your heart. So Abby sat in painful endurance, her ears roaring as she kept a stiff upper lip and said nothing.

Samantha Roche had checked her Fossil watch three times before she finally heard the family loading up and the slamming of doors and the revving of the engine. The camping trailer jerked as they started off down the sloping driveway, and something crashed onto the floor. Samantha pressed herself into the corner of the bunk, thinking she could burrow beneath pillows if anyone came searching.

But no one did and eventually she must have fallen asleep because when she opened her eyes next everything had gotten dark. Through the window, reflected off the walls and the windows of the camper, she could see arches of amber light as they passed beside ramp exits and the beginnings of towns. In the clacking of the tires on the highway, something seemed to be whispering, "Your father . . . your father . . . your father." Wind buffeted them. It washed all the way over them each time another vehicle passed.

They must have turned off the highway at some point because she felt them slow and turn and stop. Sam lifted her head just high enough to see the glaring hooded halogen tubes of a service station. She could hear the gas pump clicking. They'd parked right beside a sign that read TUMBLEWEED'S THRIFTI SAVE AND GAS! WELCOME TO HOPE, IDAHO! RESTROOMS FOR PAYING CUSTOMERS ONLY!

The power of suggestion. *Oh, my.* If she did this, she would have to turn on that button. She'd promised. She waited until the car door shut and they pulled away again and, when she punched the little button on the wall, she felt like she had performed a magical feat. She did what she'd wanted to do. She was terrified to flush but she held her breath and did it anyway. She kept thinking of Jess Cavender's dog. She burrowed into the corner of the bunk again and had just touched her father's letter, hidden beneath the folds of her sweatshirt where she'd put it for safekeeping, when the horrible banging started, vibrating beneath her.

*Blee lee lee lee lee.*

For long minutes she held her breath, waiting for the trailer to pull to the side of the road, waiting for something to be wrong and for them to be stranded, waiting to be discovered and punished, waiting to be told she'd never get where she wanted to go.

*Oh what do I do what do I do what do I do?*

Then she remembered. The button on the wall behind the sink! She'd never punched it, never turned it off.

Samantha scrambled down and hit the panel. The awful vibration stopped. Silence roared in her head. Someone had to have heard that; she was sure of it.

But the twenty-seven-foot Jayco trailer didn't stop. The miles kept rolling beneath them. For all the fear, this plan was working! And Samantha Roche felt for the envelope still hidden inside her sweatshirt, warm and wrinkled and safe against her breastbone.

⌒

When the telephone rang at nine P.M., David was staring at the Weather Channel on cable television. The meteorologist pointed to a high-pressure system moving down from Canada that would hold rain at bay for at least another four days.

"David?" Susan's voice. He recognized it now without having to grasp for it.

"Yes?"

"I'm sorry to phone so late."

"It doesn't matter. No one is sleeping here anyway." He'd heard Abby turn off the shower only moments before.

"I just . . . needed to talk."

For an inkling, David felt that flash of guilt again, that awful touch of a cheater's unwarranted fear. But that disappeared inside the vast worry that played inside him now, this thing that had consumed him since Abby had come to his office and told him his daughter was missing.

*Lord, You gave this child life through me and now You've got her where she might lose her life again. I don't understand. I don't understand You!*

He remembered a woman in the Bible who had grabbed the prophet Elisha's feet and cried out to him because her son had died.

*I didn't even ask for this child, Lord, but my hopes are crushed. Why would you do something like this? Why?*

Elisha had laid upon the boy, mouth to mouth, eyes to eyes, hands to hands, but nothing happened. Elisha had turned away in disappointment and had paced back and forth in the room. Then he'd climbed on the deathbed a second time and stretched out upon the boy and the child's body had grown warm with life.

"Have you heard anything, David?"

"No. Have you heard anything there?"

"No."

"If I find out something here, I'll call you. I promise."

"David, what if something awful has happened to her?"

"Don't think that, Susan. Don't think the worst. Neither of us can afford it."

"I can't help it, David. With everything else that's happened, I can't think anything else."

"Susan."

"There's a whole website, did you know that? It tells you what to do next if you're looking for a missing kid."

"I don't—"

"I made posters with her picture on them. The police will circulate some, but that site said they don't get them out as fast as they ought to. Every minute counts, that's what the site says."

"This camp ought to be helping you look," he said.

"They're afraid I'm going to sue them."

"They ought to be. Losing a camper. Just like that."

"There's no courier service tomorrow because of the July 4 holiday. If I fly some to you tonight, would you put them up?"

"Of course. Tomorrow's the day all the tourists are in town. Maybe someone has seen her."

"Delta has a freight service. A hundred and sixty-nine dollars and they'll have it to you at seven in the morning."

"Did they tell you that on the site, too?"

"No," she said. "I called Delta myself." Then, with a softening of voice, "David, is Abigail nearby?"

That tinge of guilt again, as he listened for the whereabouts of his wife. "No. She's in our—" *She's in our room, where I used to sleep, too, until she found out about you.*

"She prayed for me, David. She prayed for me and Sam both. Did you know that?"

"Who?"

"Abigail. Your wife."

"Abby? Abby prayed for you?"

"Yes. And I can't help thinking maybe it helped. I just . . . maybe Sam's going to be okay because of it."

*How can she be living in her faith like that, after everything I've done to us? How can Abby be living in her faith like that, after everything she's said to me?*

Long after Susan had hung up the telephone, David sat in his chair, helpless, thinking about how uncalled for it was. Abby wouldn't forgive him, but she was praying for Susan?

This thing he'd found out about Abby. It rocked him. One more thing to think about as he laid awake nights feeling every lump and loose spring in the cushions, his soul like an empty mine cavern, ready to cave in.

⁓

For the past twenty-four hours, law enforcement agencies all the way from Lincoln County, Oregon, to Teton County, Wyoming, had done everything they knew to do. Calls went out as far north as Canada, as far south as McAllen, Texas, as far west as Washington State, and as far east as Quoddy Head, Maine.

Everybody was looking for the little girl with the long brown hair flying over her shoulders and the little-girl grin as broad and open as the Powder River Pass.

On July Fourth morning, Samantha Roche's mother sat by the telephone in her home near Siletz Bay, gazing out over a gray mirror of backwater, billows of marsh grasses, and tiny birds leaving fanlike feather etchings where they'd taken off from the sand.

On July Fourth morning, Samantha Roche's father, who had just returned from a trip to pick up posters at the airport, gazed out at a mountain he'd set his feet upon as it stripped mightily toward the sky. As the sun rose higher, it mantled the Grand Teton in pink light, draping lower and broader over the pinnacles and snow-fields as it spread toward the trees. David sipped hot chocolate with Brewster flopped beside his feet. The giant lab's ears flopped over his paws. He wasn't asleep; his eyes stayed halfway open to keep watch. He didn't quite relax as his master scratched his neck, because dogs know when their households are unsettled.

In front of them Braden Treasure, armed with the packet of billposters, laid them out meticulously in rows on the floor. "The earlier we can get these out, the bet-ter, don't you think? Jake can take this many," he said to his dad. "Wheezer said he'd put one up at the START Bus stops on the square. Chase said he'd ride his bike to the stores in town. And Charlie's putting these up over by the skateboard park."

"Tell everybody I said thanks," came David's mut-tered reply. "It means a lot, you getting your friends in-volved. Maybe these will help."

"Missing," the posters said a hundred times, spread out the way they were on the floor. "Samantha Linda Roche, Age: 8, Eye-color: Brown, Height: 4'4", Weight: 68 pounds. Disappeared from camp July First or Second. May be heading to Jackson Hole, Wyoming." Across the bottom of the notice, in blaring forty-eight-point Times-New-Roman type, the words read: NEEDS MEDICAL ATTENTION. NOTIFY PHYSICIAN IMMEDIATELY.

Who can say if Braden would have noticed if not for a hundred identical placards laying in order on the floor? Who can say if Braden would have seen it if not for a hundred reproductions of her very precious, very familiar, grin?

He stood over the stacks of posters, his baseball cap screwed in the direction of his left ear, small blond brows furrowed, small fists knotted at his sides.

"Dad?" he asked after long minutes of studying. "Is this the girl you wanted me to help?"

"Yes," David said.

"She has a dimple on her cheek, the same place as yours."

David said nothing.

"Do you see it, Dad? It's really funny. Look."

David bent forward in the chair as if he hadn't really looked at the picture before, his adrenaline surging and stinging, making him dizzy. A meeting of gazes. A scant rush of breath.

"Dad? How come she looks like you?"

Brewster raised his head from his gigantic paws and looked at them both with liquid amber eyes.

David's attention dropped to his left thumbnail. He surveyed the quick of it, the small lavender half-moon, without turning toward his son.

Braden waited for his answer. The air held an almost theatrical silence until David broke it by moving to his chair and patting his knee. "Braden. Come over here."

David set his mug on a tile trivet with the word "DAD" printed in green marker. Braden had made it when he'd been in kindergarten. Beside it stood a pottery alligator Braden had formed long ago with his own tiny hands, each of the six pointed teeth almost as big as the tail. For a breath, one refined moment after Braden climbed on his knee, David refrained from hugging him. Then, as completely and wholly as armor would encircle a warrior, as if to protect him from something he couldn't be protected from, David curled his shoulders over Braden's. No more lies, Lord. I can't do it. No more.

David spoke the words quietly, as simply as he dared. "She looks like me, Brade, because I'm her father. She's your sister."

"She is?"

"Yes." An encouragement, a nod.

Braden only waited. After a long time he said, "Wow."

There would be more questions later. Later, Braden would ask, "So she's your kid, too?"

And David would answer, "Yes."

"Does Mom know about her?"

"Yes."

"If she's my sister, why doesn't she live in our house?"

"Because she has another mom."

"How can she have another mom? Did you get divorced from somebody or something?"

"No, sport. I've never been married to anybody except your mother."

Later they would discuss those uncomfortable things. And even in the eyes of his son, David might have to suffer an excruciating fall from honor. But for now they sat together in solemn quiet, with Braden absorbing this mysterious, unusual thought.

A sister. He had a sister.

Reactions came rushing out almost too fast for him to sort. His whole body went quivery, and the ceiling got misty in the middle from the tears in his eyes. He didn't understand exactly why he was crying.

"Is she like me?"

"I think so, sport."

"Do you think we'll find her, Dad?"

"I hope so, son. I really do."

There weren't many other questions Braden could ask that couldn't be answered by the papers on the floor. There lay the pictures of her grinning up at them, with a listing of vital statistics everyone needed to know. Samantha Linda Roche's face. Height. Weight. Eight-years-old. Brown eyes. NEEDS MEDICAL ATTENTION.

Braden slid out of his father's chair and gathered the posters into his backpack. "So, you're really a dad to two people, not just me?"

"How do you feel about that, sport? What are you thinking?"

Braden stooped and gave Brewster a deep scratch between the ears. "That's why I'm the one who can help her, isn't it? That's why I'm the one who can do that bone thing you were talking about."

"Yes, that's what we were thinking."

"Who was thinking it? You and mom?"

"Well, no. Me. I was thinking it. And Samantha's mother. Somebody you don't know. But she knows all about you."

Braden asked, "If they need one of my bones to help her, which one are they going to take?"

"Oh, son. It isn't—"

"If they take one of my bones for her, Dad, can I still play baseball?"

*Oh, Father. Father. He puts me to shame. After all of my fighting, and look what he'd be willing to give.*

"It isn't a whole bone, Brade. It's some stuff inside your bones. Like blood. Only thicker."

"Hmmm."

"You'll still be able to play baseball."

"Okay."

"You might need to think about this some, huh?"

"Yeah. I need to think about it a lot."

Even though it was early morning, Braden left his father alone and went in search of his skateboard. He took a running start and slammed it with a clatter on the ramp his dad had built him, never intending to ride it all the way up. He backed off and flipped it again and again and again, the metal wheels grating and pounding the hollow plywood.

What would it be like to have his dad be a dad to another person?

What if his dad didn't love him as much, now that he had somebody else to love, too?

What would it feel like, having his dad divided?

Braden didn't know if he wanted to share.

# Chapter Sixteen

By the time the sun had risen high, Samantha Roche didn't feel good.

Along the way, she had tried not to touch anything that didn't belong to her. But after all those hours, her stomach felt like it might turn in on itself. She gave in to her empty belly and grabbed the first food she could find in the latched cabinet—a jumbo bag of Oreos. She'd planned to put most of them back. She was only going to eat a few. Only they tasted so good. She couldn't help pushing whole cookies into her mouth and, before she knew it, the entire package of them had disappeared.

They had to be in the mountains now, driving on meandering roads. Every time the trailer took a corner, the green-sprigged curtains flailed sideways toward the opposite side. The stainless-steel measuring cups that hung over the sink on intricate hooks swung out and clapped back against the wall like little hollow bells. The camper pitched first one direction around a curve, then the opposite direction around another.

Sam wasn't supposed to be eating sugar stuff. And,

after all this, she just felt so *tired*. She couldn't be sure whether the roiling in her stomach was from the winding roads or the entire package of cream-filled Oreos or from the choking fear that had lodged itself in her throat.

Now that she'd gotten this close to Wyoming, she couldn't help thinking about things she hadn't considered before.

What if her father had changed his mind? What if he didn't want to see her? What if he didn't care anymore about what happened to her? Or what if he met her and he was disappointed?

Inside the rolling trailer, Sam closed her eyes. She had no idea how many more hours it would take them to get to where they were going. Her belly hurt, just thinking about it.

She burrowed down in the pillows on the bunk again, anticipation keeping her awake. The letter, which she'd kept safely in the folds of her sweatshirt next to her heart, had now been tucked away inside her Camp Plentycoos backpack for safekeeping.

She kept herself satisfied with this thought: even if her father didn't like what he saw in her, she could have his words written on that page.

That much, at least, would belong to her.

⌒

"David?"

"Hello, Susan."

"Did you get the posters?"

"I did. I've already been to the Delta counter to pick them up."

"Did you sleep last night?"

"No, I didn't. Did you?"

"No."

David just kept talking about nothing because it was the only thing he knew to do. "I haven't heard anything. Not one word." A stutter-step of seconds, while he waited for her to echo his statement, which she didn't do. "Why so quiet, Susan? Have you?"

A long unbroken hesitation, which sent his hopes plummeting to his knees. Then, "Yes, David. I've heard something. But it's nothing good."

He came out of his chair, gripping the telephone receiver against his ear as if he was trying to insert it into his head. "What? Susan? Oh, Susan, is she all right?"

"I don't know about that part, David. We still haven't heard anything about that."

"But you said—"

"It's this, David." Susan's voice over the line trembled with irony and fear. "The tests. The doctor called a minute ago. Isn't that something? It's a national holiday, but he knew I'd want to know."

"The tests? Tests?" For one helpless moment, he struggled to remember what the tests might be, just as he'd struggled once to place Susan's name. *The tests. Braden's test, for Samantha.*

"They came back late yesterday afternoon. He didn't realize he had them until today. It's over, I think. Braden doesn't match. He's farther off than *you*."

Words failed him. There was nothing that could be said, only the deep sense of loss that crashed over David like a breaking wave. *"Oh, Susan."*

"So that's it," she said. "Just like that, David. There isn't anything you can do to help her."

Every year, the July Fourth celebration in Jackson Hole kicked off with a pancake breakfast in the square. Members of the Jackson Hole Jaycees donned red chef's aprons donated by the Silver Dollar Grille and stood in line behind a sizzling outdoor griddle that must have been a good fifteen yards long. They artfully flipped flapjacks, hash browns, bacon and sausage, and massive slabs of scrambled eggs that looked like they'd been run over by a John Deere tractor. By nine in the morning, striped awnings had been erected on the grass, the Bar J Wranglers were tuning up their fiddles on the flatbed trailer parked in front of The Gap, and the Teton Twirlers Square Dance Club was making their first official grand-right-and-left of the day.

It was a day for commemorating and honoring freedom in the United States of America, with what seemed like an entire nation of tourists who had come together to see one of its greatest treasures. It was a day for hanging red-white-and-blue bunting from the balcony of the Rancher Billiard Hall and Sirk Shirts, and waving flags from the doorways of the little shops lining Broadway and Millward Street. It was a day for children to roam in herds, devouring homemade scones while honey butter dripped from their chins, and snicker at the square dancers' goofy clothes while secretly wishing they could join in.

Because of his upstanding community rank as an officer of the bank, David Treasure had been invited to sit in the reviewing stand that day and judge the floats during the annual July Fourth parade. He fiddled with the knot of his patriotic tie just as he heard Abby passing in the hallway behind him, as lightly and as carefully as a shadow.

"I can't do this, Abby," he said, his voice sounding gruff and hard, resounding with a huge echo in a house that more often now remained futile with silence.

David felt, rather than heard, her pause behind him.

"Can't what?" she asked. "Can't tie your tie? Or can't go judge a parade with everything going on in your head?"

"Can't—" As he said it, the knot of his tie tightened pitiably somewhere below his shirt's third button. David gave up and stared at the dilapidated thing in the mirror. "Either of them, Abby. I can't do any of these things anymore. It's all so *hopeless*."

He saw Abby's face appear behind his left shoulder in the mirror. She stared at his tie without raising her eyes. This woman, whom I've married and who trusted me. Even the things I've tried to do right, I've done wrong.

"Turn around," she said. "Turn around and let me work on you."

He balked at first, his mind on his daughter and all he'd been unable to do.

All You asked of me, Lord, and it came to nothing.

He turned his pectorals toward his wife so she could fix his tie.

Abby didn't raise her face the entire time she struggled with his neckwear. He could only see the top of her head the way a bird would see it, the crooked part she'd combed into her hair, the double cowlick she'd gotten from her grandfather and was always trying to style away.

His skin went prickly with the nearness of her. He

ought not to swallow. Thinking about not doing it made him need to do it so badly, he had to give in.

His Adam's apple bobbed. He could tell by the way her hands hesitated against the hollow of his throat, even through the starched cotton of his shirt, that she knew why.

"Abby—" he began.

"Don't, David," she said. "Don't do this to me. Not now. Not with all these people who are needing us."

"Abby."

"You have *hurt* me. That isn't going to go away."

"Look at me."

"I've made a choice for now, David. I've made the choice to grit my teeth and get by. And that's *all* I'm going to do. I can't do it any other way."

"I need you right now, can't you see that? My life is in turmoil and I don't have a wife beside me. I can't take it day in and day out, you coming close to me and reminding me what I did. You even prayed for Susan, then you looked at me and accused."

While he held himself as unyielding as a timber post, she manhandled his necktie as if she were tying an outfitters' knot on the rump of a horse. She lashed it through itself with fierce intention and tightened it with little nervous jerks of her hand. In one gliding motion, she slid the knot, a perfectly formed triangle, into the notch of his collar at the base of his throat. She took three steps back from him. David inspected the results in the mirror. His tie looked so right the way she'd done it, they could have used it on the cover of *Gentleman's Quarterly* magazine.

"Lay blame where blame is due, David."

"Just stop," he said. "Don't say it."

"You should have thought about needing a wife beside you on the day you started your affair."

⌒

For the past three days, the women residents and workers at the Community Safety Network had been baking together in the kitchen to make goodies to sell to the parade crowds in the Jackson Hole town square. Sophie Henderson had made her famous zucchini buttermilk bread along with several batches of ginger snaps and chocolate-chip brownies. Kate Carparelli had baked her long-standing family-favorite rhubarb pie, as well as sticky buns and four-dozen lemon chess tarts. Thanks to several of the other shelter residents, individually wrapped gingerbread men, apple muffins, and slabs of peanut brittle stood in enticing rows on the table.

Sophie waved as she saw Abby weaving her way through the crowd. "Over here! We need you. We've made almost two hundred dollars so far."

"Great." Abby waved back. Here she came, with three plastic boxes from the bakery at Albertson's—chocolate cupcakes with industrial icing, pastel sprinkles adorning the machine-made, swirled tops. She set them down with an elaborate sigh. "And look at these. After everybody cooking all week, I didn't have time to bake."

Sophie wrapped an arm around her. "I'll bet those go faster than anything else on the table. Kids will always pay more money for things with sprinkles."

Abby hugged her back. "Go ahead, Soph. Make me feel better."

Kate had been watching them, her eyes somber, from across the booth. "Has anybody heard anything about David's girl, Abby? Have they found her?"

"No. Nothing new."

Hungry customers inundated them before they could finish the conversation. Quarters and nickels began to pile high in the cash box. Although Sophie had been a little off with her prediction about the Albertson's cupcakes with sprinkles, several children did select them. Kate's rhubarb pie brought a record seventeen dollars.

Just as a lull came, a man with dark hair slicked back, runnels still left from the comb, strode toward the table. He smelled of hair crème. A burgundy Cattle Kate scarf was knotted like an ascot beneath his clean-shaven jaw, setting off blue eyes that were the same color as a mountain summer sky. The man clamped Sophie's zucchini buttermilk bread in one huge paw. He fished a huge wad of bills and a snuffbox from his back pocket. "Here you go." He handed the bills to Kate.

Kate unfolded them and began to count. "Five . . . ten . . . fifteen . . ." She tried to return the rest. "You've given me thirty-five. This bread's only fifteen."

"I see the price." He poked his snuffbox back where it belonged. "But I say it's worth thirty-five."

At the sound of that voice, Sophie lifted her gaze from the tin box where she'd been counting out pennies for a little boy. Her body went rigid, her face drawn and looking almost ill. Abby saw the box-lid slam on her fingers. Sophie didn't even jump.

He said, "Hey, Snooks."

At the sight of him, Sophie shrank a little. She lashed her arms across her chest and took a step backwards. "Mike? What are you doing here?"

He touched the Saran-wrapped loaf to his belt buckle and Sophie physically flinched. Abby thought, *I wonder if he hits her with that.* "Oh, Sophie Darlin'. You know how it is," he said sweetly while Sophie kept staring at his huge hands as if she could see them knocking her around. "It's time to put this behind you and come home."

"This isn't going to work."

"Let's talk." He reached toward her and touched an arm that had been black and blue when Sophie had first arrived. "One more time. That's all. Just one more time."

Abby had seen this scene so many times, she almost knew what the next words were going to be. It always played out sugar sweet; then, when the men didn't get what they wanted, they turned angry. *Tell him, Sophie. Tell him. Tell him. You aren't coming home again.*

"Didn't you like my roses?"

*No,* Abby wanted to say. *She gave those away.*

"That's not going to work. Flowers don't make up for what you do. Mike—" Sophie floundered. The table and all those cupcakes stood in between them and, for the moment, Abby couldn't tell whether Sophie wanted to run toward this man, or away. A heart and a spirit in her, at war with each other, playing out on her face. "Abby?"

Abby nodded. "I'm here."

Sophie turned to her husband again. "This isn't fair, you cornering me like this."

"Why not? You're out here for all the rest of the world to see. Why can't I see you?"

"You could have made that bread yourself from your mother's note-card in the recipe box. You didn't need me to do it."

He was standing in everybody's way. Children elbowed in past him, and he stepped around several of them, pushing them out of his path. It was clear Sophie's fear hadn't gone away. Kate and Abby exchanged quarters for peanut brittle, making an obvious barrier between the man with the bread and this small, terrified woman in the booth.

Mike opened the wrap on his wife's bread, tore off a hunk, and shoved it into his mouth. "Humph," he said around the crust. "Good. Real good."

Abby said, "I'm afraid I'm going to have to ask you to leave."

"This is a public park."

"Yes, but your wife doesn't want to see you."

"Wait." He grinned suddenly. "Wait, Sophie. I got something." He set the bread on the table. "I got something you'll like." Without any further ado, he trotted away.

The air of fun and gaiety had left the booth the moment Mike Henderson arrived. Now Sophie, Abby, and Kate sold treats with quiet care, keeping watch over a hundred heads in the crowd.

"I wish he wouldn't come back," Kate said, "but I know he will. I've seen this happen about a hundred times before."

"Of course he'll come back," Sophie said in a pinched voice. "That's all he ever thinks about these days. Come back. Come back. Come back. And I just wish . . . I just wish . . ."

Abby touched her arm. "If you want the police, I've got my cell phone in my purse."

"No, don't do that to him. I don't want anything to happen to him. Please."

Here he came, lugging a heavy wooden crate with wheatgrass sticking out of the corners, his hands jammed through two holes for handles. Every few yards or so across the grass, someone would stop him and peer at the box with a stupefied expression, a glance of inquiry, and a careful hand reached inside. He approached the Community Safety Network booth with long, easy strides, and plopped the box on the ground with obvious pride. Sophie stood on tiptoe to look over.

"Uh-uh-uh." He stooped and reached inside where she couldn't see. "You let me be the one to present you with this little fellow. Hold out your arms."

"No. I'm not taking any live thing. You just want me to come home and take care of it."

"Well, I figure since the roses didn't do any good—" When he stood up, he'd lashed his arms around a big ring-necked pheasant. It craned its neck and flapped its wings in Mike Henderson's big hands, the most beautiful wild bird Abby had ever seen. Its tawny plumage glinted chestnut and purple and green, a corona of colors, in the daylight. Its eyes were round with surprise and wet with shine.

"How about this for a present? We were out with Ramey's Retriever, just giving it a run. Dog flushed this thing and we couldn't believe what we were seeing."

"Mike, that's a pheasant. A wild bird. Something people hunt."

Mike Henderson moved on impulse and not on logic. "Not until the fall, people don't hunt it. Serves all those hunters right who go out mid-week, when I can't afford to hunt until Saturday. Now I've got my own private stock."

"Mike, you're not thinking. You don't get it. I need a pheasant like I need a hole in the head."

The pheasant let out one double-noted crow, *kur-rik*.

"Looks like this one got his tail bobbed off. Looks like a coyote taught him a lesson. Bet he won't get in the way of a coyote again."

Abby moved in closer behind Sophie and pulled her cell phone out of her purse like a weapon. "Sophie has come to us for protection from you. If you don't leave her alone, I'm going to make a domestic disturbance call to the police."

"Mike," Sophie said. "I don't want that bird."

"I'm trying to make you listen, Sophie. I'm trying to make you see how much I love you."

"There's love that wins battles and there's love that loses them. I'm trying to figure out which one we've got."

"I said I wouldn't do it again, if you'd come home. I said I'd go see somebody."

"You keep getting it gnarled up like that. You can't make me do something that hinges on you. You can only figure out what two people's love is together when you know what two people's love is, separate."

"Sophie, you just need to get back home."

The crowd began to push in. "I want to pet that thing, mister. That's the weirdest bird I've ever seen." "Can I see it?" "Let me!"

The pheasant, which wasn't built much for flying anyway, flapped again, hard. With an airy whoosh against Mike's chest, it burst out of his arms and landed, wings threshing, on the bake-sale table. Dollar bills flew. Chocolate cupcakes with pastel sprinkles scattered in the grass. The bird's feet made tiny chocolate w's, evenly spaced, where it dashed for escape across the tablecloth. It took off tottering across the grass, its bare behind tucked under and waddling, its scarlet wattle seesawing back and forth with every step.

Every child in the town square sprinted in hot pursuit. In the corner of the square, the Teton Twirlers had broken into a fast rendition of "Oh Johnny, Oh!" One fellow, in the midst of a swing with his partner, had to wrench his cowboy boot sideways to keep from stepping on the pheasant and three kids. The pheasant took another flight and Mike jumped in to catch it. It fluttered up and forward like a hovercraft, escaping straight into the peril of a woman's square-dance costume, snagging itself in her bandana-and-tulle gathered skirt. There it floundered and no one dared disentangle it while it struggled to find the solid ground or sky, either one.

"Get it out! Get it out!" The woman stamped her Mary Jane shoes, desperately fearful, while an alien living thing rousted among her petticoats. As she tried to flatten it out of her skirt with her hands, the Bar J Wranglers on the flat-bed trailer broke into a rousing fiddle rendition of "Birds of a Feather."

"Hey, Henderson," somebody bellowed from the crowd. "Is that your new dancing partner?"

The pheasant scurried down the street, rounded a corner into an alleyway, and was gone.

In frustration, Mike slapped his big hand against his hipbone. When he wheeled back to face everybody, a vein protruded like a scar from his forehead. "Nobody makes a fool out of me."

"Mike—"

"You made a fool out of me, Sophie. Right when I was trying to do something good."

Abby wrapped her arm around Sophie's shoulders and tried to draw her away. "You don't have to do it," she said. "Sophie, you don't have to let him pull you like this."

"This is not what I wanted, Mike," Sophie said, her arms fastened against her chest again while Abby stood beside her. "No matter what parts of that bird are missing, it still needs to be set free."

"But that bird is a *gift*," he insisted.

"You can't give something as a gift if people don't want it," she said. "I want you to leave me alone, Mike. I want you to just go away."

# Chapter Seventeen

Braden Treasure's favorite part of July Fourth was the dunking tank that stood on the southeast corner of the square. All sorts of town dignitaries volunteered to take turns taunting customers and getting wet, all the way from the owner of the Mangy Moose restaurant to Mrs. Roehrkasse, a fifth-grade teacher who always traveled with her students to the dinosaur dig near Thermopolis.

Whenever Braden made his way to the front of the line, the hapless victim in the chair would moan. Being one of the Little League players, even though not its most accurate pitcher, had its distinct advantages. He'd been training all summer long to throw hard and fast and with newfound precision. If only he could hit the target this time, the unfortunate person perched atop the tank would plunge into the icy water below.

Today Braden would take aim at Ken Hubner, his own baseball coach. "You'd better not hit that, young man!" Ken bellowed, swinging his legs and waving while everyone jeered at him from below. "You just try to douse me! You just *try*."

Braden paid his dollar and was handed three base-
balls. He wound up to throw while Wheezer and Jake
and Chase cheered him on. But things didn't feel right.
He lowered the ball, lowered his chin, and readjusted
the bill of his Elk's Club cap.

*That girl might come here. That girl who's my sister.*

Braden reared his elbow back and let fly the first ball.
He stepped off to the left on his follow-through, just the
way Coach Hubner had taught him not to do. He
missed the bull's-eye target by at least six inches.

"Ha!" Ken shouted. "You missed me, you missed me,
now you gotta kiss me—"

"Hey, coach," Braden hollered up at him, teasing.
"You're going down!"He started a wind-up on the second ball.

*That's why Dad wanted me to put all those posters up. So
he could find her.*

The second ball missed, too. It smashed against the
backboard and bounced out of sight.

"Come on, Braden!" Hubner bellowed again.
"Throw that last ball like you mean it. I dare you!" The
coach grinned and raised his fists high into the air. "Hey,
I'm your coach. I know what you can do."

Braden adjusted his hat again. He hitched up his
elbow, cocked his knee.

*What if Dad finds my sister and he forgets about me?*

The baseball smashed into the bull's-eye target full
bore as spectators cheered. With a clatter, the wooden
platform burst open. *Splash*. Ken Hubner came up blub-
bering, with his clothes and what was left of his hair
plastered to his skin. He spit water. "That's the way to
pitch it in there, Treasure. Right down the pike!"

But Braden didn't stay for his coach's accolades. He was too busy thinking about Samantha Roche.

~

Calvin Baxter kept glancing into his rearview mirror, which extended like an arthropod feeler from the side of his truck cab.

"What is it with all these tourists?" he said. "You'd think somebody would let me into the lane I need."

"Honey," his wife pleaded with him. "Watch the road in front of you. If we can't get into the turn lane, you'll go straight ahead and double back. Your pride isn't worth risking our lives."

"I've been signaling for two miles."

Ahead of them, in the only lane where they could continue, three sawhorses loomed.

Calvin smacked the steering wheel with an open palm. "Oh, great. Look's like they're having a parade or something. No wonder everybody and their brothers are here."

"Well, sweetie. It *is* the Fourth of July."

"I've got to get over in that other lane."

From the minuscule backseat where she'd ridden for five hundred miles, one little girl propped her chin on her father's shoulder and said, "Daddy?" with the lilt in her voice she always used when she wanted to get her own way. "Aren't we going to stop someplace in town?"

"With all these people? You've got to be crazy. Our plan was to visit the wilderness, not the corner of Hollywood and Vine."

Before Tess Baxter could persuade further, Calvin threw on the brakes to keep from hitting sawhorses.

Streams of bumper-to-bumper traffic on either side didn't allow him to turn either way. Because he couldn't think of any other avenue to communicate his frustration, he pounded on his horn. A police officer on horseback gestured wildly at them with his hands.

Calvin said, "That's it, kids. Enjoy this trip. When we get home to Oregon, we're going to sell this Jayco. I'm never going to drive like this again."

"Well thank heavens for small favors, Calvin. That's a relief to every one of us."

"Daddy, let us get out somewhere. Please!"

With the officer's rather reluctant assistance, Calvin Baxter managed to maneuver the huge camper into the left lane. He lumbered them along Cache Street for two blocks or so, following the green road signs to Yellowstone, while everyone with him begged to be let out. At last he gave up and turned into a gas station, jostling the huge rig over a dip in the driveway.

"Fifteen minutes, that's all. That's it; everybody out. I can't stand it anymore."

Out of the fifteen minutes allotted, Tess needed approximately three. She begged the key from her father, saying she'd forgotten her copy of *Amber Brown Is Not A Crayon* in her bunk.

"*Hey,*" she whispered once she got inside. "Sam. Are you ready?"

"As ready as I'll ever be."

"You'd better do it quick."

"Okay."

Sam slithered out from her hiding place inside the bunk. Their faces met for the first time in five hundred miles. They gripped each other's arms, still children, with a child's plan, but with full-grown hope in their hearts. "I don't want you to leave," Tess said. "I want you to stay with us."

"If I stay with you, I'll never find *you know who.*"

"I want you to be careful, Sam. Really."

For one frightening moment, footsteps crunched on the asphalt beside the door. Tess slammed her friend out of sight behind the thin trailer door. They waited one long excruciating minute, while Sam counted the *kerthumps* inside her chest.

"It's okay." A hushed whisper. "Nobody's coming in here." They gripped each other's arms again. Tess whispered, "Be careful." Up front, the truck door slammed. Tess could see her own father checking the road map. "Go," Tess said. "Get out of here. If you don't do it now, they'll see you."

⁓

David Treasure sat on the back row of the reviewing stand, which was really nothing more than a set of choir risers from Jackson Hole High School lined with a dozen of the Elk's Club folding chairs. Even if he didn't still feel such nearness and such reproach from Abby, even if he didn't feel more helpless now than he'd felt when Susan Roche first met with him, he would be sitting in this exact same stance, with his chin raised and his shoulders set as square and firm as a rampart. He used his own body as a fortress against the world, against what seemed like absurd mirth on this day.

*You know I wanted to save her, Lord. I made the sacrifice, and it's come to nothing.*

Abby would never have even needed to know.

He'd always liked July Fourth and the way folks celebrated it here, in his hometown. After the breakfast and the parade would come the music-festival orchestra concert on the middle school lawn, its appreciative, sunburned audience laden with blankets and sunhats and watermelon and picnic coolers. Then tonight, as soon as the sky above Snow King darkened to its perfect, infinite depths of navy blue, without announcement, a torchlight would come alive in the center of the ski run. Thousands on every corner in town would wait with their hopes in their throats. A ghost of a hiss, a small smoke projection into the air and, with a heavy, single sound that echoed from Rendezvous Mountain to Blacktail Butte, the first rocket would explode, red, green, gold, or blue, a chrysanthemum burst of sparkles that tinted the mountains and the groves of aspen and the faces of everybody watching. The torch on the mountain would glow more and more often. Another boom. Another echo. Occasionally a flurry on the hill while someone put out a small spot of fire.

And all over town, on every corner, people would applaud or laugh or sigh and wait for more.

The annual Jackson Fire-In-The-Hole would have begun.

But for now David was trapped in the celebration, his chest yearning and his nerves tingling with sorrow, head swimming while he baked in his best clothes.

"Here are your ballots." A parade official handed him a thick sheathe of papers.

"Ballots?"

"For voting on the floats."

*I should be out looking. I should be out doing something to find Samantha. Not this.*

He glanced west toward the Wort Hotel, where three

sheriff's Jeeps proceeded slowly, their lights flashing, leading off the march.

*How can I be still? How can I just sit here?*

He sat and watched a parade go by, the way he'd sat and watched his life go by. Sat and watched, while God pried everything he held dear out of his fingers.

He'd fought so hard for so long, to atone for what he'd done. He'd fought so hard for so long, to deserve everything he'd been given.

He'd fought, and lost. He'd lost more than he'd ever known he had.

Down the street came the groomed mule team from Grand Targhee National Forest, brown beasts of burden with velvet, off-white muzzles, tied tail to nose with panniers and twisted yellow ropes. Identical forest-service mulepacks jolted with each step. In front of the reviewing stand, the muleteer shouted *Yah* and snapped a quirt over the lead mule's hindquarters. The team moved in synchronized formation, their hooves clattering on the pavement, their ears loose and listening for the next command.

Miss Rodeo Wyoming passed on her black Arabian barrel-racing horse, wearing a rhinestone tiara and a sash with glitter edges. Old Murphy, the red truck with its massive Spud Drive-In papier-mâché potato, rumbled by. A canvas-covered wagon with spoke wooden wheels carried guests from the Heart-Six Dude Ranch while they perched proudly on bales of hay.

*Is this how you are, God? Leaving me helpless? Setting this up to fail?*

A 1932 Ford Tudor Sedan, with pearl ghost flames on its side and wide rodder wheels, revved its engine as it approached the reviewing stand. Behind it came a shiny black 1966 El Camino and a gleaming 1949 Mercury, chopped and shaved, with a Desoto grill. But David didn't notice any of the polished front ends or the engineered chassis or the Flowmaster exhausts.

The parade marched past him in a jumble of hazy color, and all he could see was his pain.

~

Samantha Roche lowered her backpack to the ground with an exhausted sigh. She dropped it on the grass and stared at it. It wasn't all that heavy, but carrying it exhausted her. She got tired all the time now, for the smallest of things, and she knew it was because of the leukemia. It made her mad. One minute she'd be fine, and the next she'd feel like she couldn't stand up.

All she wanted to do this moment was sleep.

A man walked by with a bouquet of tiny American flags in his hand, and extracted one for her. "Here, little lady. You look like you could use something to wave."

"Oh." She took it from him. "Okay. Thanks."

Its fabric was thin as parchment; she could see light through from the other side. She held it in front of her face, a limp, gauzy curl that she ought to have been pleased to have.

Only, she wasn't pleased.

She was too tired and too uncertain and too alone to be pleased.

Sam thought of her mother, sixteen hours away and not knowing where she was. She wondered if anybody besides her mom might be looking for her. She thought of Camp Plentycoos where her counselor, Katherine

Tibay, had said every morning, "Make it a great day or not. The choice is yours."

She leaned her head against the tree trunk, closed her eyes, and felt with her fingers for the precious letter she carried there, from David Treasure.

She loved even the sound of his name.

Beside her on the grass, a father rocked backward with his baby in both hands, holding it aloft while he laid flat on the grass. He tickled the baby's belly with the top of his fuzzy hat, the baby's arms and legs flailing in mid-air with joy.

Over by the fence, a boy had just dropped chili dog down the front of his Jackson Hole T-shirt, and his dad was spit-shining his chin with a hanky.

Across the way, a dad and daughter opened the packaging on a plastic quiver of arrows and aligned one on a little plastic bow. Samantha watched as the dad showed the daughter how to cock her elbow and draw back the bow, shutting one eye and squinting down her nose to sight it.

Her whole life, as long as she'd been old enough to understand, Sam had never thought anything like that could happen to her. Having a dad to tickle her or to sight an arrow with her or to help fix things when she made a mistake.

All she wanted to do was to find him.

All she wanted was to say, "I'm glad you wanted to see me because I wanted to see you, too."

Samantha felt a little better now, after stopping to rest. She decided she'd better get up and walk more, because walking helped her think.

She didn't know what to do, being eight years old,

when you needed to sleep over for the night and you didn't have a place to stay.

She wandered. And looked at faces, to see if anybody looked like somebody she knew. But nobody did, and everybody was busy with their own families, as they skittered around or stepped in front of her and made her jog sideways to get out of the way.

Just when she thought she needed to sit down again, she came to a huge crowd lining a road. Just as she stood on tiptoe to see what was happening, a stranger approached, two huge hands extended toward her. She looked behind her, because she didn't think he'd be talking to her.

There wasn't anybody behind her.

"Just who I'm looking for," the man said.

"I . . . what? Me?"

"Yeah. A pretty little girl with a flag."

Her hopes skyrocketed. "Are you Mr. Treasure?" she asked, because her mom had taught her never to call grownups by their first names.

"No. That isn't me."

"Oh. I was just hoping—" She decided she ought not say any more.

"Are your parents here watching the parade?"

"Yes." Well, it wasn't *exactly* a lie because her dad *could* be around. "They're here." She pointed into the crowd at nobody. "Right over there."

"I'm out scouting for extra kids. We've got a big float coming up and we'll score better from the judges if we have a whole passel of people hanging from the sides, waving at everybody."

"Really?"

"How'd you like to take a ride in a parade?"

"I don't—"

He eyed the hoard of people where she'd gestured, maybe trying to figure out to which parents she belonged. "C'mon. We need you. If they'll give you permission, there's barbecue at the end of the run. Good food, too. Catered by Bubba's."

"I don't know what they'd say."

"Well, ask them. Tell them I'm Lester Howard, director of the community band, and they can pick you up at the rodeo grounds in an hour. That's when we'll be done."

Five other kids came jumping up and raising their hands to volunteer. Because he wasn't watching, she had her chance. She waited the right amount of time, disappeared into the milling people for three seconds, and came back to touch his wristwatch.

"They said it's okay," she lied to him, her voice gone soft and careful. "They said they'd pick me up later, where you said."

"Good. That's settled. What's your name?"

"Sam."

With no further ado, his huge hands wrapped around her. He lofted Samantha so high over the side of the wagon, she felt like she was flying. Next thing she knew, she was sitting on a bale of hay with a man playing a tuba right beside her head.

"Thanks for helping us out!" Lester Howard waved them off. "Oh, wait." Out of his pockets he pulled fistfuls of hard candy and piled it into her hands. "Throw lots of candy when you see other kids! That's the way to be the most popular float in the parade."

"You aren't marking your score sheet." Edna Clements, who was sitting next to David on the grandstand, elbowed him and directed his attention to the papers in his lap. "How can you pick a winner if you aren't giving them any points?" The muscles of Edna's mouth were stiff with reproach.

"I don't need to mark them," David said, feeling ashamed. "I can remember it in my head."

"Oh, really?"

"Yes."

"Don't you think that float from the Jackson Hole Playhouse was best? Don't you think it should be given the award?"

"Which one?"

"The one with the player piano on it."

"Oh. I don't remember that one."

Edna settled back in her seat, her face gone slack now that she'd proven her point. "That's exactly what I thought." She crossed her arms with pride in her lap.

David struggled to focus on the task at hand. Directly in front of them this moment paraded Deanna Banana the clown, with her big painted grin, her beautiful dark eyes and her rainbow striped hair. She walked along in long, slappy shoes, tying balloon animals without even having to watch her own hands. Whenever she finished one, she handed it out. Behind her a dog-sled team, made up of eight yipping huskies with red felt stockings on their paws, mushed against their harnesses and yanked a Volkswagen along.

"I like that one," David said smugly to Edna. "I think it should win."

"You think so? That one?"

"Yes."

"All it is, is a bunch of dogs pulling a car. That's their job. Those dogs run in Alaska in the Iditarod. No effort put forth to decorate the car or make anything festive."

"I like them, Edna. They're impressive."

But even as he argued halfheartedly with Edna Clements, the sight in the street sent David reeling deeper into his uncertainty. Perhaps it was the sight of those huskies barking and straining against their fitments. All their combined effort as they followed a master's command, and all it got them was another few inches up the road.

Over and over the dogs gathered their strength and struggled forward. Over and over they surged and rested, surged again.

David saw himself in them, the way he'd made such effort to pull himself ahead of what he'd done, to drag himself away from the wrongfulness that had for years held him back and weighted his soul. The same way that Volkswagen held back those huskies.

*Lord.*

Ridiculous. A grown man talking in his head to thin air. Who had he been following all these years? A figment of everybody's imagination. Something that Nelson and the men on the presbytery committee and his own parents had said would change his life.

Well, it hadn't.

*How is it that everything everybody else seems to do with you works, Lord, and every time I try to listen to you, something else falls apart?*

This moment, as he sat in a chair with his tie bound like a hangman's noose around his neck, watching a parade going by, his faith made him feel like an outsider looking in, wiping the fog from the window, seeing everyone else inside without him.

His final shred of hope and purpose, that Braden might have been able to save Samantha, gone. Gone. With Susan's latest phone call, even that remaining shred had been ripped away.

He felt so entirely isolated from God this moment that all his years of belief might have been a game.

*I don't want something in my life that's empty. I don't want this, if I've only been wasting my time. I don't know if anybody really hears you, Lord, even when they say they do.*

Up Broadway rolled one of the old standbys of the parade, gleaming green trucks from the Teton County Volunteer Fire Department, lights pulsing red and blue. The firemen aimed their giant water hoses skyward, and streams of water arced and rained down on the hapless people below. Behind that, still in the distance, David heard the beginning strains of the sparse but zealous Jackson Hole Community Band.

The band float was in sight by now and, behind it, the town street sweepers. The massive round brushes revolved on the pavement, with a light hiss of water, cleaning up the dropped remnants of horses and mules.

"That's the one I'm pushing for." He elbowed Edna. "The street sweepers get my vote every year."

The Jackson Hole Community Band passed before them, its brassy music making people extend their arms, jump sideways, and cheer along the curb. On the rear fender, two children held spinning disco balls high, the reflection of the July sun flickering over the bystanders with light.

*I am light, Beloved. In Me, there is no darkness at all.*

*But, Lord. There is darkness all around me.*

The lone tuba *oom-pahed* while children from the wagon threw fistfuls of candy onto the street.

"Oh, the community band isn't getting my vote this year," Edna commented beside him. "I hate this song so much, if they played it at my funeral I would stand up and walk out."

David turned away from the float and shot his neighbor a wide grin. "Edna, I doubt seriously that anyone would ever play 'The Macarena' at a funeral."

"With all the new people who keep moving into this town, you never know."

David's attention fell to his knees. He tamped his float ballots there, fingered his pen, and made several notations. It was high time he made some decision about the parade. "I want those huskies. They're really good."

*I am good, Beloved. My love endures forever. I am faithful through all generations.*

*Oh, Lord. Are you? Are you?*

*If you can bring good from this, Father, what could you have done with me if only I had remained faithful?*

David wrote two words before he laid down his pen and looked up. Directly in front of him, an eight-year-old girl with long brown hair flying over her shoulders shyly tossed a Tootsie Roll to a tiny girl holding her father's hand on the sidelines. Because the child on the sidelines was too little and the parade too big and the girl on the float hadn't thrown the candy quite far enough, the father dashed out, retrieved it, and handed it over.

The girl on the float grinned with pleasure, revealing

a dimple beside the left corner of her mouth and a teasing jut of her chin.

*My, but she looked like . . .*

David's heart leapt as high as the knot in his necktie. He felt as if his breath would never come again.

The child on the float—the exact image on a poster that Braden and his friends had tacked on every telephone pole and every fence in town.

She was the exact likeness of the small school picture that had tormented him ever since Susan had opened her wallet and let him see it.

David stumbled up from his chair; his parade ballots scattered into Edna's lap and he didn't even notice. He tried to get around the man in the folding chair one step down from him, but it couldn't be done. He moved sideways, crashing into John Teasley, who threw an arm sideways to keep himself from being pushed off the side of the reviewing stand.

David didn't notice. "Sam." Frantically, he tried the name on for size as she passed directly below him. *"Sam."* The band crescendoed below him. When the child didn't respond, he yelled louder. Louder, still. *"Samantha!"*

She turned toward the sound of her name. He saw her eyes searching, full on. And, he knew.

Every doubt in David Treasure's mind fled at that moment.

"I'm sorry," he apologized to the man in front of him who was right in his way. He fumbled and kicked and pushed, trying to get around. "I've got to get down from here," he said to John Teasley as he shoved the man's metal chair aside.

"You're knocking me off, David. Can't you wait until the end of the parade?"

"No, I can't." He almost shouted it in his frustration. "I've got to get down to the band."

Sideways he went, and a chair clattered to the ground. Three steps forward, between two people where there wasn't any room. As a final resort, he climbed over the top of somebody's head.

"I'm sorry, sir." A policeman on horseback cut him off. "The street sweepers are coming. No one is allowed in the road during the parade."

"But that's my . . . that's my . . ." David couldn't get it out; he was breathless from fighting his way through people and chairs. "That little girl is *lost*," he gasped. "She's my daughter."

The officer followed David's desperate gesture. He brought his horse around, and stared, peering from below his hat brim. "She's that one, isn't she?" he asked. "The one that's all over town in all the pictures."

"Yes."

The officer reined in his mount. "Don't let me hold you up. I'll help if you'd like. Me and this horse, we can stop that float. You'd better not let that young lady out of your sight."

David ran, catching up, falling back, catching up again, until he reached with his hand and seized the lip of the wagon. By that time, the officer had drawn to the front and the horses were slowing. David passed the pounding bass drum. He passed the trio of uplifted trumpets and the lady who tooted her piccolo.

"Sam?" he cried, gasping out her name before he'd quite gotten to her. His sweat-stained shirt had come untucked. The shoulders of his sport coat had worked their way down to his forearms as he ran. His necktie flew to one side like a sail.

She looked at him.

"Samantha?"

She'd been doling out candies to the littlest kids along the route, who looked like they weren't big enough to get much, and wanted it most. The candy scattered to the ground when she heard him calling her name. Tootsie Rolls and Jolly Ranchers and Atomic Fireballs bounced on the pavement like pearls, crunching to pieces beneath the wagon wheels.

"Is it you?" she whispered. "David Treasure?" He could read her lips even though the music played too loud for either of them to hear.

"Are you Samantha Roche?"

She nodded.

With no hesitation, he lifted his arms up for her. "With all due respect," he said with a good amount of reverence in his voice, "I think you're somebody I know."

# Chapter Eighteen

Oh, what it felt like for David to embrace his new-found daughter. He'd wanted to hold her like this, he knew it now, from the very first minute he'd known she was alive. It was a moment of wonder for him, more poignant to David because it was something he might never have known.

He felt himself when he held her.

He felt his own mother in her, and his grandmother, and the women his grandmother had known when she had been a girl, gone before. She smelled like chocolate and Atomic Fireballs and dust when she leaned close to his ear. "I was afraid," she told him. "Do you think I should be?"

He held her out a bit, his heart aching, thinking of all she had to be afraid of in her future. "Afraid about what?" he asked.

"Afraid of having you know me. Because you might not think I'm the way you wanted me to be." He examined her face. *They just don't make them much cuter than this*, he thought. She *did* look like Braden.

One beat passed, two, three, before David could answer her question. He'd lost everything that was solid and stable in his life, for this. Miraculously, being with his daughter now, it seemed worth that much. "So far, you're exactly the way I thought you'd be."

"Yeah?"

She cocked her head sideways at him like a puppy, and he spoke with an amazing feeling of possessiveness in his chest. "When someone is your father," he said, "he doesn't love you because he's gotten to know you. He loves you because he's your father—because you belong to him, no matter who you are."

For a long time she didn't move. She only looked at him with quiet reverence. "You really think so?"

He nodded. "I know so. Because of you." Then, "You're heavy, you know that? Bigger than I had imagined."

"I used to be even bigger. I've lost five pounds, because of leukemia." If she felt his arms tighten around her at that, she pretended it made no difference.

"Let's take care of you now," he said. "Get you something to eat."

That's how they found themselves at the end of the parade route. As if, for the time being, this might be nothing more than a normal day. Samantha wanted a hot dog. David sidled down the barbecue line with her, carrying her backpack and helping her load her plate. She wanted ketchup, a wiener without any black on it, and two spoonfuls of chili.

He watched while she consumed the entire thing in less than four minutes.

When she dribbled chili down her chin, he found a napkin for her and wiped it off. When she guzzled red Kool-aid from the paper cup it made a mustache that wouldn't wipe off no matter how hard either one of them scrubbed.

"Marked for life," he teased her.

"Nah." She laughed. "In one day, it always goes away."

"Well," he said, slapping his hands on his knees.

"Well," she said, slapping her hands on her knees, too.

And that seemed to be the end of the conversation for a while.

Around them, horses were being unhitched and the jangle of bridles and buckles rang out like bells. The entire roster of huskies had been fastened to a truck with individual ropes. Each dog chowed down from its individual bowl, its name inscribed like royalty on the side: Smoke-Fur Luke, Maggie, Tucker, Annie, Buckie, Heidi, Red Lady, and Tom. Above them the sky shone blue and clear, a color so deep it made David's head throb.

"I like Tom for a dog," he said, slapping his knees again, fighting for something else to talk about. "That's a good name."

Silence hung between them for longer than it had before. Samantha suddenly seemed shy to him. "So, what do we do now?"

She stared at a butterfly that had landed on the grass beside his knee. He steepled his fingers in front of his lips and looked at her. "Let's see. We ought to think about that. We really should."

And, as he laid the list out for her, David laid it out for himself as well.

"First, we need to get to the house and phone your mother to let her know you're here. She's been worried sick about you. After that, we'll call the police and tell them we've found you and they can stop looking, too."

"The police were looking for me? Where?"

"People were looking for you everywhere." He'd said enough. He knew by the way she glanced at the ground beside the cuff of her khaki shorts. He switched the subject. "You're going to meet—" He tried to figure how best to say it. "—my wife. And your brother. Did know you have a brother?"

Her head shot up, her expression full of disbelief.

And grandparents and aunts and uncles and cousins, too. But that would only come if some miracle gave Samantha more time.

"Most of all," David said, "you and I are going to spend some days together. Now, how does that sound?"

⌒

Abby stood at the bottom of the empty grandstand, her hair in disarray, chocolate footprints of pheasant running like tire tracks down the front of her jeans.

"Where is David?" she asked the empty chairs. Out of deference to the crowd on the square, they'd only brought one vehicle. He had told her crisply that he'd wait for her here.

"Good heavens," Edna Clements commented behind her. "You look like you've been run over by a stampede."

"Oh, Edna," she said. "Have you seen David?"

"Good heavens. Seen David? Oh, yes. I've seen David. Everyone's seen David. He practically *marched* in the parade."

"What?"

Edna shrugged as if she was shaking off a mosquito.

"When you find your husband, I want you to tell him that I'm a woman of great integrity. I want you to tell him that, even though he ran off, I cast his vote for him anyway."

"Edna, what happened?"

"You tell him the vote was a tie between the player-piano float and the husky dogs. I told the parade committee he would have voted the huskies if he hadn't run away. The huskies took grand prize."

"Do you know where he is now? I need to pick him up."

"God only knows," John Teasley said as he passed by with a bouquet of balloons. "He went running off after somebody named Sam. He kept shouting and he pushed my chair off the side, trying to get off the stands. It was like playing king of the hill, sitting beside him."

"He went chasing after someone in the parade?"

"A little girl. Named Sam."

*Sam?* A tinder-spark of joy burned inside Abby, and then flickered out. She'd gotten here safe. *Thank you. Oh, thank you.*

Inside Abby there came an aching and pleasurable dissonance.

She's here and she's safe. But if I welcome her into my heart, then I'm welcoming what David did.

How can I do something like that?

"Thanks, Edna," she said lightly, as if the information they'd just given her didn't make any difference. She strolled to the Suburban that they'd left in the bank parking lot. As she headed toward the rodeo grounds where the parade had ended, she drove slowly, thinking that's how it always was with people who drove toward something they knew was going to change their lives.

Either you drove fast to find out what was wrong, or you drove slowly because you didn't know if you wanted to get there.

She arrived at the dusty lot and parked on the farthest row away. At a smoldering charcoal grill by the swing set, a family gathered and passed a bag of marsh-mallows around. A little boy, much younger than Braden, stood on the pitcher's mound. Abby watched as he wound up an invisible baseball, pretending to sail it over the plate in the red dirt of Mateosky Field.

Across the way, an anxious mongrel dog leapt on all fours to catch a spinning Frisbee in mid-air. And, there they were, her husband and his daughter, the child of his indiscretion some nine years before, sitting together cross-legged in the grass.

$\backsim$

"Oh—" And, from his end of the line, David could hear Susan's astonished silence, then a little sob, then laughing and crying all at the same time. "She's *there?*"

"Yep. Weak, but fine. Every hair on her head accounted for."

She must have sat down hard on something because he heard the breath go out of her. "Oh, David. Thank you. Thank you for everything."

"No. Not everything. If I could have done everything, I might have saved her life."

"You've done so much, David. More than I ever thought you would."

"I haven't done anything."

Susan's voice came as little more than hiccups, as if

joy and grief took turns jolting her. "You've done every-thing you could do. That's enough, isn't it?"

"It isn't enough," David said of his whole life. "It's never enough." For a half minute or so, they were like two sad teenagers on the telephone, listening to each other breathe.

"While she's there," Susan said at last, "pretend she's normal, okay? Pretend she isn't different at all. And watch it when she starts getting tired. It happens quickly."

"I'll do that."

Then, "Thank you, David. Thank you for letting me come."

He thought about that as he stood in silence. "When are you getting here?"

"I won't have any luck flying," she said. "The planes are full to Jackson in July."

"What are you going to do?"

"I'll drive and then get a room at the Elk Country Inn again when I arrive. That will give you a little time with her, David. That's everything either of us could ask."

⌐‿⌐

Braden stood on one side of the driveway with his fingers jammed in his rear pockets.

Samantha stood on the other side of the driveway with her hands clasped in a knot in front of her, each wrist resting in the saddle of a hipbone.

Neither one of them knew exactly what they should be thinking.

Neither one of them knew exactly what they should do.

Braden pulled his hands out of his pockets and began to walk in slow circles.

Samantha swayed back on her heels and surveyed the sky.

"I don't know if I'm going to like this or not," Braden said.

"Yeah," she said back. "I guess I surprised you. I guess I surprised everybody."

That thought kept them both quiet for a long time.

"I like your skateboard ramp." Sam scrubbed the toe of her sneaker on the asphalt. "It rocks."

"My dad made it," Braden said proudly. Then, too late, he realized what he'd said. "Well, I mean . . . I guess . . . he's *your* dad, too."

"Yeah."

"Weird."

"I know."

Silence again. Braden asked with caution, "Is the place you live different from this, or is it the same?"

A scrubbing of the toe again. "Different."

"What do you like to do there?"

"My favorite thing to do is to chase seagulls. I go to the ocean every day."

That was an interesting thing. Braden softened. "You do?"

"My best friend's name is Tess and we walk to the beach from her house. She's the one who brought me here. They came on vacation and she snuck me into their camper."

"What's so good about chasing seagulls?" He couldn't help it; he still wanted her to prove her worthiness.

Then, with a hint of pensiveness, "I've never been to the ocean."

"We make sandcastles on the beach, too. Since you're my brother, I'll show you when I get the chance."

"Will you?"

"Yeah."

"What's it like?"

"What?"

"When they all take off like that. All those birds."

"Oh." Her faraway expression interested him. "When all those birds go at once, it seems like anything could happen, like there's more wings there than just the birds' wings, something I can't see. I feel so small and so big all at the same time, making so many things fly. Fifty of them at least."

"Really?"

"Or maybe even a *hundred*. So close I can feel bursts of air from their wings."

"I just play baseball."

"I'd like to learn how to play baseball."

"Would you?"

"Yeah."

"Okay. I'll pitch a few to you, then." He thought about it hard before he said it. "It'd be good to have a sister who could hit."

"Okay."

"Yeah."

They started sauntering toward the house, toward this new odd thing between them. "The ocean's so amazing," she told him as they scuffled along shoulder to shoulder. "You stand right beside it and it crashes all over your feet and you try to know how big it is. Only you can't because it's bigger than the world. Bigger than anything you can ever understand."

The afternoon was getting along. The shadows of the lodgepole pines had stretched to the full length of the side yard. In the distance, they could hear the Grand Teton Music Festival orchestra tuning up for the out-door concert. "You know what happened last year on July Fourth?" Braden asked. "Mom was worried the out-door concert would scare Brewster, so she put him in the bathroom and turned on the radio so he couldn't hear it. Only the radio station she turned on was broadcasting that same concert she didn't want Brewster to hear."

For however long each of them would live, they would remember this first private conversation in the driveway. This was a moment children explained in great detail during show-and-tell or scribbled down in a diary or whispered about when they were supposed to be quiet in the school lunch line.

*I have a brother.*

*I have a sister.*

*It's the oddest thing.*

"If my dad doesn't—" Braden stopped. "I mean, *our* dad doesn't have enough time for both of us, will you make sure he won't leave me out? I've been thinking some about that."

"You're so lucky," Samantha said. "You're the one who gets to live with him every day."

"Yes, but . . ." Braden frowned. He scuffled his feet again as they crossed the pavement, sending a rock skit-tering into the grass. "I don't know. Do you think a dad can love two kids as much as he can love *one?*"

"Don't know." She kicked a rock, too. "When I came here, I wasn't thinking about there being anybody else."

A pause. "Well, there is." Then, "Hey, you want to see my favorite bat? I hit two homers with it in the game against Cody."

"Yeah. Sure. I'll come see it."

"It rocks. It's an Easton, with z-core and titanium. You ought to hear the ping it makes whenever you connect up with a fastball."

"Really?"

"Yeah."

"Show me."

So Braden led her to the garage where he displayed his bat to her, and his cleats (which his mom wouldn't let him bring in the house because of their smell), and his Rawlings Heart-Of-The-Hide infield glove, which Brewster had chewed and his dad—their dad—had used a leather thong to stitch and repair.

# Chapter Nineteen

*A*t the Uptergrove's wedding anniversary party, Floyd Uptergrove decided to bring out his potato gun.

"Floyd." Viola stood beside her husband of sixty years today, dressed in a tea-length golden gown that, coupled with her gold dragonfly clasp behind her ear, her sapphire blue eyes, and her white gossamer hair, made her glow like a jewel herself. "Do you have to bring that thing out when you're wearing your tuxedo and a boutonnière?"

"Of course I do, Viola. The grandchildren are here."

All afternoon long, cars had been coming and going from the shady side of Long View Lane. The refreshment table had been refilled three times. Relatives took turns heeding the doorbell, welcoming guests, and telling them to sign the guest book on the table with the white feather pen.

"Thank you so much for coming."

"Nice of you to be here."

"Just shove your way on in. Grandma and Granddad are in the other room."

Around Abby's feet barreled the stampede of barking

Chihuahuas who, once they'd heralded and herded the
next onslaught of well-wishers, settled into a huddle on
the sofa where Floyd was not allowed to put his feet.
Through the scissoring legs of guests, Uptergrove great-
grandchildren and first cousins and nieces and nephews
scampered without supervision. David and Abby had
brought Samantha along. Braden and Sam, although
still awkward with each other, joined in on the wildness
of the other kids without much coaxing at all.

David stood next to Abby in the crowd. The muscles
around his mouth were stiff. All these jostling and hugging happy people, and the Treasures remained about as
animate as two planks of cedar.

He frowned, a sort of slow discomfort in his face.

She tried to smile, but only managed a closed, mul-
ish grimace.

All that had come between them, and here they
were, pretending to rejoice. Here they were, celebrating
someone else's marriage that had lasted sixty years.

Tightly, David said, "Well, we'd better go and min-
gle. Find Viola and Floyd and let them know we're
here." The rest went unspoken between them: *The
sooner they know we're here, the sooner we can leave.*

"Okay," Abby said, taking a breath as if she was on a
springboard about to plunge in. "I'm with you." Because
her mind was set on surviving through this crowd, Abby
absently reached, the way she'd reached for a dozen
years at crowded parties, to find the security of her husband's hand.

It wasn't there.

She jerked her hand to her side, hoping David hadn't
noticed. He was looking over her head, greeting people
he knew from the bank, and several of the Uptergrove

children he'd met in the office who helped Floyd keep his financial affairs in order.

"Have you met my wife, Abby?" he asked. And, this time, it was David's turn to reach for her without thinking. She felt the slight pressure of his arm, the splay of his fingers gathering fabric in the fiddle-bend of her back, searing her skin as he guided her along.

"There's a picture of them over here. Look." Abby flipped open the leather-bound album. "Do you want to see?"

*Would this be enough for you, Lord? If I grit my teeth and made myself accept him touching me? Even if I don't trust him anymore, could I just trust the way his touch makes me feel?* How many times had she counseled women at the shelter about this very thing?

Reality isn't something you can make yourself feel.

And you don't look to find it by your feelings. You have to stand on it, even though you don't feel like it's there.

In the picture, there stood the Uptergroves, as neat and polished as a pair of farmer's Sunday boots. Floyd grinning, Viola with her curled-under hair and her rich, dark lips, brandishing that knife as if she was going off to hand-to-hand combat herself.

"Is that Floyd?" David asked. "And look at Viola!"

"Look. I can prove it to you. It was really me," boomed a voice from behind them, and there stood Floyd in the same dusty old Navy brim hat. "Like Cinderella. See, I can come up with the glass slipper to prove I was there."

"Crazy Grandpa." One of the many children hugged him around his legs. "Grandma's the Cinderella today, not you."

"It fits, too. Head hasn't gotten any bigger in all of sixty years."

"Oh, I don't know about that, Floyd Uptergrove," Viola said from across all the people in the room.

Just that fast, Floyd stole David away. "Come outside for a minute with me, son. I'm looking for somebody to help me fire up my potato gun."

"I haven't shot one of those things off for years."

Floyd bent his lips toward his teeth and nodded once, a sign of pure confidence. "Handmade by my brother. The good old-fashioned way. Viola, do we still have potatoes?"

"There's a whole sack in the pantry."

Braden, Samantha, and a throng of other distantly related children strung along past them just then. David grabbed Samantha and Braden's hands.

"Come see this, you two. You aren't going to believe what you're about to observe."

"What?"

They were out of the play and intrigued by their father's plan faster than a mayfly gets gulped by a trout. The three of them tumbled out into the yard, both children with their chins lifted in adoration toward David. David's limber length bent low so he could hear what they had to say, while Abby stood at the Uptergroves' window, clutching a curtain, watching them go.

Abby struggled with an unwanted pinch of melancholy. This was the first time, in all the years she could remember, that David hadn't turned and said, "Abby, come on. Don't you want to go with us, too?"

*Well, she would miss some things. But she would have her own special times with Braden. She would see to that.*

In the front yard, while revelers gathered, Floyd

brought around his esteemed and prized toy. While the others watched, Floyd polished up the span of black PVC pipe on his arm. Abby watched him say something to the kids, who began pawing with both hands through the sack of potatoes with the zeal of treasure hunters, obviously searching for the perfect size.

The satisfactory potato was inserted, the end of the pipe was unscrewed and, out of his tuxedo pocket, Floyd pulled a can of Final Net aerosol hairspray. He shot one squirt of the stuff into the PVC, rescrewed the end, and, ready to go, stood like Arnold Schwartzenegger in a movie, his legs straddled, his shoulders thrown back in his tuxedo, his eyes searching the rooftops for possible targets.

He waited as long as anybody would let him. The children began to vault up and down beside his knees and David wasn't much better. At last Floyd hitched up his pants legs and aimed the gun at an appropriate angle. He found the handle on the attached charcoal lighter and he pulled the trigger.

With a rewarding *pop*, the potato launched. Up, up it sailed, high over the rooftops, high against the backdrop of the mountain, and higher still. If it hadn't been a fat potato, they would have lost sight of it all together.

Hard to tell the moment the potato began to come down. One moment they were watching it grow smaller, and the next it started getting big again. Down it came while the children clapped and cheered. Down, past the telephone poles, toward the rooftops. It came straight at them so they scattered and ran.

The potato hit Viola's bird feeder and pulverized it. Thistle and wood splinters flew like a small explosion.

Chickadees and finches fluttered away in a state of shocked confusion.

All that remained was the metal hook extending from the eaves and half of a shingle that had been its roof, still swaying from the force of the blow.

The potato shattered on the ground.

"Well," Floyd said, sounding a little dejected. "I just built that birdhouse for Viola. I guess I can build her another one."

Outside the window, everyone jostled in line for a turn. David went next and shot a potato to the north over two condominium buildings. Braden went next. Then Samantha, very proud and careful, got to do the same.

Inside the window, Abby clung to the curtain, peering into a life that had once been hers, halfway smiling. Because, no matter the reality between her and David, it seemed impossible not to smile at this.

Viola and her walker, which had been twisted and tied with silver and gold streamers for this grand occasion, sauntered up behind Abby as if she could feel her being left out. "Come help me spread this new quilt on the bed," she suggested. "The kids gave it to us for our sixtieth. Did you see what Floyd just did to my bird feeder?"

"I did."

"He builds it, he breaks it, he builds it again. Sounds like a sign you'd see in a china shop."

Grateful, Abby followed her, flopped the quilt lengthwise upon the mattress, and admired its stitching and colors.

"It's pretty, isn't it? But a new quilt? After sixty years? What on earth am I going to do with the old one?"

A daughter poked her head in the room as she passed in the hall. "Give it away, Mother. That thing is ratty and as old as the hills."

"But it was a wedding gift."

Abby smoothed out the new one while Viola watched. After a long moment, in spite of the walker, it seemed as if Viola couldn't stand to keep her hands off the pattern. She touched with her fingertips the cool, plump edges of the fabric, the tiny perfect embossing of the thread. "You know," she said in a girlish, confiding voice without ever looking up at Abby. "I *have* kissed another boy in my lifetime besides Floyd."

"You have?"

"Yes."

Abby couldn't keep the incredulity from her voice. "Only one?"

"Only one."

Abby's considered her hands where they lay on the hand-patched cotton. She stared hard at the new-moons of her own fingernails. Goodness, but Viola was sharing the secret of her soul!

"He had the prettiest curls I'd ever seen whenever he took off that straw hat." Viola looked past Abby's left shoulder, as if she could see something far away. "Clifton Bates, that was his name. We'd been out for a drive and then he brought me home to the porch swing. Sitting right there, where I could see the top of my father's bald head through the front bay window, Clifton says, 'Miss Viola Lynn, do you mind if I give you a kiss?' "

"Oh, my." Abby leaned on her hands, surveying quilt stitches intently in an effort to hide her smile. "What did you do then?"

"I said no. Any girl in her right mind, when asked for

a kiss, should say no. Then I sat there looking at him thinking, Laws of mercy, Clifton, why do you have to be such a gentleman? Why don't you just kiss me without asking and not put me in a spot like this?"

"But, I thought you said—"

"I *did*. But that's it. Because there's times that what you're thinking you ought to do and what you want to do are two entirely different things."

"So?"

"So I grabbed Clifton Bates by the hat brim and *I* kissed *him*."

Abby hollered right out loud, "Viola!" Even now, Viola blushed.

They smoothed the quilt together a third and fourth time even though there wasn't a wrinkle or lump to be had. Every few seconds or so, one cast an amused Victorian glance at the other, across the movement of their hands. Abby's gentle laughter mounted from deep within her, a place both protected and vulnerable, that she didn't know still lived.

Viola laughed, too. She shoved the gilded walker away and watched it roll. She plopped into a threadbare wing chair and chortled like a meadowlark, kicking her swollen feet up onto the ottoman and leaning back hard like she was in a porch swing just this minute.

"S-shame on you, Viola," Abby said, giggling, her mirth bubbling from a free fountain. Nothing on earth could make it stop. "Talking about old boyfriends at your wedding party."

"Oh, pshaw!" Viola waved the whole thing away with her hand. "That's one reason you do it, don't you see? I think of all the things I might have had, and then

I look at what I *do* have, and . . . and it's okay. It's very good."

Abby's giggling toned down a notch. "You really think so, Viola? That it's okay to measure what you do have with what you might have had?"

"I think so." Viola kicked her feet sideways off the ottoman and leaned forward. "When you look back, you count all the times you've broken faith with each other. And you count all the times of truth. Because, if you're being really honest with each other, every marriage has plenty of both."

"Yes," Abby said. "But some marriages are worse than others."

"During sixty years of marriage, Abby, do you want to know what was the hardest thing of all for me?"

"What?" Abby asked, yearning for some answer, yearning for a way to survive these next days. "What was it?"

Viola said, "Being kind to each other. That was sometimes the most difficult thing. Just being kind."

"Presents! Picture show!" a family chorus went up from the next room. "Grandma, can you get him in here for this? If you don't, he'll be out there with the potatoes all day."

Abby stood by the bed, her palm across three hand-sewn squares, looking like she'd been taunted—as if that hadn't been much of an answer at all. Viola turned back to her. "Can I ask you a question, Abby?"

"What?"

"It's a question about David."

Silence. Then finally, "I guess so."

"It's this. How calm does water have to be before you walk on it?"

"What? What does that have to do with David?"

"If you walk on water during a storm or during calm, you're still walking on water. Do you measure the journey by the wind and the waves around you? Or do you measure the journey by knowing you're walking somewhere that's impossible to walk in the first place?"

The squares of the quilt, so many shapes and sizes and colors stitched together. Abby said, "But I thought I knew the man who would be reaching for me when I went under. Now I don't know the man who's holding out his hand."

"Look at the ten commandments in the Bible, Abby. Look at every one of them that starts with 'don't' or 'stop.' All those rules, and God was telling people that they ought to stop walking away from love."

Abby said, "Maybe I don't even know what love is anymore."

"Mother!" a good number of people bellowed at them from the other room.

"I wanted to be achingly in love with my husband," Abby said. "I didn't want to be afraid."

"Oh, honest to John." Viola fumbled up onto her walker and pulled it into her grasp. "Someone else is going to have to get Grandpa. I can't move that fast. Besides, he'll never give up the potato gun for *me*."

She turned back to Abby one last time.

"When he comes in, just look at how handsome Floyd Uptergrove is in that tuxedo. And wearing that flower to please his children. Sometimes I wonder what Clifton Bates looks like right about now. I'll bet Clifton Bates is . . . Clifton Bates is . . . well, I'll bet Clifton Bates is *dead*."

David and Abby Treasure, who had once been so anxious to leave this party the moment they arrived, had gotten crowded in with the other party guests to watch the opening of the gifts.

David and Abby Treasure, whose differences seemed irreconcilable and whose future together would be bleak, sat hipbone to hipbone on the cold stone hearth. He sat with his elbows propped on his knees and his hands dangling between them in a knot. She sat with her fingers aligned perfectly, pointing downward, pushed hard between clamped thighs as if she was hiding a prayer.

Abby's son curled like a kitten on the rug beside their feet.

David's daughter sat as close as she could without bumping into his arm.

Abby could feel the warmth of David's leg through the linen of her skirt. She scooted a half-inch to the right so their thighs wouldn't touch anymore.

The tilt of David's spine was severe, lunging forward, as if he had to force himself to be still beside his wife. Once, when his eyes met Abby's, they moved indifferently away. How unimportant gifts seemed to David and Abby Treasure right then. After all these years of housekeeping, Floyd and Viola didn't need a thing. But Viola sat with her hand proudly on Floyd's shoulder while he said, "You grandchildren, slow down. You're opening too fast. Can't we wait?"

"Here. Hand me that card, Floyd. I want to read the letter."

One by one, Floyd and Viola exclaimed, thanked,

hugged, and passed the loot around. More things to fill up the already overburdened storage spaces, David thought. A golden bell with their name and wedding date inscribed. A set of coasters with hummingbirds. A glass hummingbird to hang in the kitchen window. Matching polo shirts that read "Sixty Years Together" and a plaque that said "Each New Day Is A Gift From God."

After the gifts had been unwrapped, someone extinguished the lights, someone drew the curtains, and a proud son showed huge black-and-white pictures on a screen.

All the talk of years-gone-by could not suffice for the sepia-tinted photographs that confirmed it. There were pictures of the wedding gifts, not so different from the ones their grandchildren had opened moments ago. There was an assortment of houses and cars and communities and friends. There were baby pictures and Christmases and Easters where the children sat with curved bonnet brims holding baskets aloft with eggs the color of a sunrise.

There was Viola stretched out full tilt on the hood of the old bullet Chevrolet, a sight that made several men in the crowd wolf-whistle.

There was Floyd dressed to the nines in his new white Navy uniform, which made one of the women say, "So *that's* what you fell for!"

"You gonna be one of those tugboat boys like your great-grandpa?" An uncle touseled the hair of a little boy as they all stared up at the Navy cross on Floyd's proud, young chest, his impressive chiseled face overshadowed by the regalia.

Faster and faster the images came, as everyone in the

room forgot themselves and began shouting out comments.

"What were they doing, Viola? Saving material for the war effort?"

"Oh, those bobby socks and those shoes. Weren't they something?"

"Which one is the Welsh Corgi who rode in the baby carriage, Floyd? Was that Paddlefoot?"

"Have you seen Mom's pictures when she was a blonde?" More wolf-whistles. And someone's laughter. "Hey, she was blonde for a long time! And red-headed, too."

On and on they went, through the growing children and the flashier cars. "Look at those two! Out for a date in the fifties."

Viola's gentle, reminiscent voice. "Remember? We didn't even have heat in that car."

Something entirely different, almost lecherous, in Floyd's voice. They all saw him poke Viola in the ribs with his elbow. "We didn't need heat back then, did we?"

"Daddy!" someone hollered, sounding scandalized.

Everyone burst into laughter. Everyone, that is, except for Abby Treasure, who stared at the ceiling and worked her throat against the ache. Everyone, that is, except for David Treasure, who scrubbed the back of his neck with his hand and looked like he wanted to be anywhere but here.

# Chapter Twenty

Abby watched her husband fall in love with his daughter from a remote distance, from a far-flung space that left her separate. She watched David moving with purpose on an outlying horizon, and she felt totally, completely alone.

They had only hours before Susan arrived. David made the best of them. Like a Santa Claus, he showered Samantha and Braden with fun. As the mid-summer day progressed, Abby watched as the three of them played, running in and out of the house to change or to get something.

First, he had taken Sam for a ride on the candy-apple stagecoach through the square, where people perched on the top or hung out of windows and doors like hedgehog spines and waved at friends and family, and at people they didn't know.

Next, they took a jaunt to see Menor's Ferry, where wagons had crossed the Snake River before there was any bridge. They followed the trails, dust adhering to their tennis shoes, through the once-bustling town of Moose, Wyoming, viewing the carriage house and the log Episcopalian chapel, where David took turns holding them both high so they could yank the chain and ring the chapel bell. Once David decided that the bell had been clanged enough to give everyone within a ten-mile radius a headache, he took them to the Moose General Store and bought them spearmint candies from a jar.

Abby heard the details while she spread mayonnaise onto their sandwiches for lunch. She held a piece of Country Farm loaf flat in her palm, wiping it first with one side of the blade and then with the other. She kept spreading long after the thick, creamy dressing had soaked into the bread.

"I know what we'll do," David said around the edges of his sandwich. "How about a float down Flat Creek this afternoon?"

"On inner tubes?" Braden was already standing, fists lifted in victory in the air. "Sam, you'll love this. It's the best thing you'll ever do!"

"It's your favorite thing, huh?" Samantha's fingers were working, happily braiding the fringe of Abby's placemat.

"Yeah. It is."

As much as she begrudged it, Abby had to give David credit. Whenever he talked for long minutes with Braden, he would turn and give Samantha a wink. Whenever he went rapt with awareness of Samantha, he would clap his hand heavily on Braden's right shoulder, squeezing hard on his son's bones.

David moved, in Samantha's presence, like a man entranced. His eyes followed her with delight and reverence when she bounded across the room. Whenever Samantha came near him, the whole stature of David's

body went gentle. He became a knight ready to do battle for her. With every movement, every glance and
smile, he paid homage to this new daughter. He was so
proud of her, his movements were excruciating. And
Abby felt like she was a foreigner to them, living on the
opposite side of some impenetrable boundary, looking
inside a store window when she didn't dare to walk into
the shop.

After lunch, David, Braden, and Samantha loaded
the Suburban, tossing towels and mud shoes and dry
T-shirts into a pile on the backseat. Inner tubes, inflated
as large as they could inflate, lay perfectly aligned in the
cargo hold like donuts in a box. The engine was already
running when David turned to Abby as if he'd forgotten
something.

Well, this would be a surprise. Maybe he was going to
ask her to join them on the creek. She loved floating
Flat Creek. There was one spot she especially liked,
where the banks twisted back on themselves, where
forget-me-nots and wild violets grew in miniature
nosegays, hidden on the banks beneath the fierce protection of the willows. Hikers who explored the riverbank would never see them. But from the low water,
moving at the level of the current, tiny blue-purple
flowers peeked out everywhere.

In another spot, downstream, the creek slowed, to
where it moved just faster than a mirror. Abby had
learned that, if you held your limbs motionless and let
yourself bob along with the stream in that place, finger-
ling trout would rise beside the inner tubes to snap at
mayflies.

This, she could show Samantha. She could gather
her towel and her dry clothes and her Teva sandals fast,

if David wanted. She *could*. She waited, her hand frozen in mid-air, her breath in her throat.

But David didn't invite her. He watched her for a moment with his head slightly turned, as if he knew they had no other choice but this one. He didn't tell her good-bye. She remembered the first morning when he'd left, when he hadn't kissed her. How many of their partings had been like this since then, with him leaving, or turning away? As if it didn't matter to him what she did at all?

⌒

That afternoon while the children were gone floating Flat Creek, it began to rain at the house.

Heavy drops began to pelt the dust and the metal roof; water ran in rivulets down the window. Abby looked out the front door and worried. Storms could be spotty in this valley, one square mile doused with rain, another never out of the sun at all. David had a bad way of being caught in the wrong place during storms.

Outside the front window, ominous gray clouds hung like scalloped, thready valances over the mountains, obliterating any view of the Tetons. Town would be busy today. Campers from Yellowstone would drive all the way into civilization just to get warm and dry. They'd wait in line for hours at Bubba's for a hot plateful of ribs and, since they'd been forced out from the wilderness, they would do laundry at the Soap Opera Laundromat and make use of the time.

Abby was scrubbing the condensation off the front glass when she heard the sound of a car. That's how it came to be that Abby was watching when Susan Roche parked far away on the road, as if she didn't know whether or not she was allowed to drive close. She didn't get out of her car.

Abby opened the front door and held Brewster back by the collar. For long moments she waited, while Brewster barked low and hard, warning her of danger. For long moments, Abby didn't move, issuing a challenge, making herself visible to the woman parked on the street. Beside her feet on the walkway by the steps, the handprints they'd joyously smashed into the cement when they'd first built this house—David's big hand, Abby's medium one, Braden's tiny splayed fingers—sparkled with rain.

*I have a right to confront her in anger. Lord, I have a right to accuse her of sleeping with my husband.*

A figure in a white cotton sweater and a pair of jeans finally unfolded from the driver's side and came moving up the driveway in the mist. The woman's blonde hair was streaming, a magazine unfolded, crooked to keep the rain off, over her head.

Abby shoved Brewster back inside the front door and shut him away to make him be quiet. Through the heavy wooden door, she heard him still going at it, his deep voice frantic.

The word came from someplace deep inside her, somewhere unguarded and surprising, an entire thought unformulated and unbidden.

*When you ask for My love, beloved one, you ask to set more of yourself aside.*

*I'm angry, Father. I'm hurt.*

*You aren't asking not to be angry, are you? You're asking Me to take charge.*

Here the woman came, and the two of them stood

face to face in the rain. "Is David Treasure here? Is this his house?"

"Yes."

"Is he inside?" A step forward that Susan Roche had no right to take.

"You're looking for Samantha?"

"Yes."

"They'll be back in a little while."

"They? Who's they?"

"My son," Abby said. "My husband." A hesitation in which they each held the world in their eyes. "And your daughter."

Susan still held the magazine, a current issue of Better Homes and Gardens, high over her head. She laughed self-consciously, brought it down, and folded it wetly beneath her arm. "Abigail? Is it you?"

"Yes."

"Well, hello."

Neither of them knew what to say. So Abby did the only thing she knew to do: she brought Susan in out of the rain.

While the woman took time drying off in the bathroom and Brewster prowled suspiciously through the house, Abby opened the freezer door and stared inside. She thought, she's here, and surely I can't be expected to cook for her. Of course, there was that frozen Stouffer's lasagna. David hated frozen lasagna. That would be the perfect thing.

Abby zipped open the box and read the instructions, which proved indecipherable in her state of mind. Remove film cover from tray. Bake on cookie sheet in center of oven. Let sit for five minutes for best flavor.

She leaned her head against the cabinet. No. No.

And turned to find Susan standing behind her, watching.

*I choose to give this to you, Lord. I do. I choose. Take it.*

"I could ask you to forgive me," Susan said defensively, "but it wouldn't matter. What's done is done."

For a long time, Abby stood silent, her teeth biting into her lower lip.

"I've gotten my daughter out of it. I don't regret one moment."

Abby pressed her knuckle against her mouth.

"The prayer was nice," Susan said. "And you probably expect me to ask for forgiveness, but I'm not going to. I've raised a wonderful daughter."

For a long time Abby stood waiting, not trusting herself to speak. *That's beside the point*, she wanted to say. Then words, from somewhere other than herself, began to pour forth.

"I don't expect anything from you, Susan," she said quietly. "I know you feel like you need to say something or explain, but I want you to know that you don't have to."

"You don't—? I don't have to?"

"No."

Those two sentences, and it seemed as if some dam inside Susan had come crashing open. Her face crumpled. She stopped trying to make herself clear. Instead, "I was so young then," she said, crying, free to react from her heart. "Oh, Abigail. That was when I thought everything in the world belonged to me."

"I see," Abby said. "I see."

That's exactly where they were standing when Abby's husband entered the house with his children, and looked from one woman to the other.

～

David took off an hour early from the bank the next afternoon to cut firewood for the church. He stopped by the house, where he knew Abby wouldn't be, loaded up a dented can of gasoline, and set out to tune up his cherished Husqvarna chainsaw.

He removed the bar guard, found his sharpening file, and ran it with smooth precision over each blade along the bar. He worked the choke and adjusted the throttle, hit the Smart Start feature, and tested the chainsaw's center of gravity.

He couldn't stop thinking about his daughter, how much he loved her already, how sick she was.

He couldn't stop thinking of Abby and Susan in the room together, a portrait of his infidelity, a divided house.

He gave the engine a test run. As the chainsaw rumbled, David searched for reprieve in all 6.1 horsepower of the engine in his hands, the way it revved to the speed of 12,000 rpms. He pointed the bar at a two-o'clock-angle and closed his eyes, enjoying the smooth, powerful vibration before he switched it off. He set the throttle lock, replaced the bar guard, loaded it into the back of the SUV along with the little pouch of sharpening tools, and started on his way.

He and the kids had come back to the house yesterday, never having seen a lick of rain, as boisterous as blackbirds, as wet as otters, with Wyoming mud splattered all over their legs, ready to tell Abby stories.

And there had stood Susan Roche, as if she belonged in their living room, talking to Braden, hugging Samantha, wagging that little girl back and forth in her arms, while Abby stood to one side, looking stricken.

He didn't begrudge anything Susan had done, except not telling the truth sooner.

He was grateful to her for raising Samantha.

But she'd told him she was staying at the Elk Country Inn. He'd never pictured what it would feel like to walk into his home and find Abby playing hostess to her. These were the rooms where they had built their lives together. This house had long been their place of joy and safety. Good things and bad things both, *he* was the husband. He was the one who had unlocked the door and let everything in.

Mosquito Creek Road was bumpy as a washboard and filled with ruts. The farther David bounced along on it, the more distressed he became. Seeing Susan sitting with Abby was like seeing every transgression he'd ever committed. Seeing the two women standing together, each with her own child, was like seeing his mistakes magnified and projected on a screen bigger than the one at the Spud Drive-In. Much bigger.

David found a spot with deadfall trees and parked. He revved up the chainsaw. With every winter-kill tree he found and felled, with every length of pine and spruce he severed and shoved into the cargo bay of his Suburban, he worked to absolve himself of his wrongdoing. With every log he lugged and every woodchip he scrubbed out of his eyes with his knuckles, he fought to release himself from the horrible tug-of-war in his spirit.

David staggered, bearing a massive log that he lugged over and pitched into the SUV. The shock-absorbers gave way an inch or so beneath the weight of it. His muscles burned. He stood back and gauged the space.

He might cram three more small sections in, then he'd head down to the Christian Center to unload before he came up for a second installment.

And maybe a third.

Two cords he could take credit for, if he could get that much in before dark.

But, all that measuring, and David didn't make a move toward the next piece of wood. He stood with his feet straddled wide and his solemn gaze directed toward the bare branches in a dead-standing tree. No matter how hard he worked, no matter how many pounds of firewood he hauled in, he couldn't make the sick regret and the longing go away.

*I didn't have any right to be defensive with Abby. Every criticism she's heaped on me, I've deserved.*

Deadfall trunks lay in haphazard disarray around David's feet. He picked his way through them until he came to one he had hewn, one that looked like it would fit perfectly into the space left for it. He lugged it over and began to shove it into place.

*How many years have to go by—*

The log barely budged. He put his shoulder to it and heaved.

*—before a man is forgiven?*

David pushed with everything he could muster.

*Lord, why did you wait this long—*

The log slid in.

*—to let me be proven guilty?*

The back filled, David hammered the forest-service permit into one log, slammed the gate, and brushed sawdust off his palms. He headed down the jarring road, keeping his foot off the brake as much as possible, gearing down because he conveyed a heavy load. After he arrived at the church and parked in the Hulls' driveway, he began pitching everything onto the grass, hurrying so he wouldn't get caught before he could make another run. But here came Nelson across the yard.

"Need a hand?"

"Naw. I got this. You've probably got plenty of other things to do."

"Sure. I've got plenty of other things. But nothing else I'd *rather* do." Nelson stepped up to help him and, for a long time, the two friends labored side by side, the flying chunks of wood hitting the ground with hollow, splintery thuds. For a long time David waited before he said what was forcing itself out from him, everything that was on his mind.

"You think she's going to die because of my sin?" David asked.

Nelson curled his arms around a huge section of wood and *thunked* it on top of the others.

"You think God's doing it this way to make me pay?" David didn't stack two logs in his arms this time. He stacked three. "Christians get forgiven for what they did before they got saved." His muscles strained. He let the logs roll off onto the pile, *thunk thunk thunk*, by themselves. "But what about this? I did it after." Nelson paused and measured the width of the sky with his eyes. David straightened and crossed his arms. He stood with his legs wide apart and his face turned up toward the pale summer sky and the clouds that drifted across it like cotton wadding.

"Maybe," Nelson said to the air above them, "he wants you to stop struggling. Maybe he just wants you to *be*."

"I'm a man, Nelson. I can't just *be*." David turned to

the cargo bay and started pitching logs again. "And what about Sam, Nelson? What about all this awful darkness in her life?"

"What about it, David?" Nelson propped a foot on a stump and hesitated. "You don't think Christ dying for you was *enough?*"

*Ridiculous.* "Of course it was enough. What's that supposed to mean?"

"A sin as devastating as adultery, David. Thinking your mistakes are different from everybody else's, that they're somehow bigger. That, because they're yours, they're unpardonable."

More logs hefted, more logs thrown. Nelson kept up, right beside David, chunks of rotten bark covering his yellow shirt.

"He's bringing you to yourself, David." Nelson scrubbed sawdust from his eye with one finger. "Humans love us because of what we are. God loves us because He knows our full potential. Because Jesus Christ died for us, the Father looks at us and doesn't see us as we are. He looks and sees everything he created us to be."

"Oh," David said. "Oh." And felt the tears coming to his eyes.

"For God is light," Nelson said, "and in him there is no darkness at all."

⌒

Sunday morning at the Jackson Hole Christian Center and two children sat side by side in the chairs, nibbling on peanut-butter cups that their father snuck them, each of them busily drawing their own separate sketches on a church bulletin.

Braden drew a soldier crouched in a warrior's stance, with a huge belt, a sword drawn for battle, and an up-held shield.

A little boy's picture.

Samantha drew little creatures, round and cute, with antennas. Some of them were happy, some were mad, and some were dancing.

Not the type of picture either Abby or David had expected a little girl to draw at all.

Abby did not stand at her chair for the praise music. She sat with her head lowered, her hands curved over the seat in front of her, as if lifting her eyes to the Lord would have revealed something inside her that she herself didn't want to see. Something scraped raw, bruised, broken.

David sat with his knees crossed, his chin propped on a thumb, his pointer finger curved in a cee beneath his nose.

Nelson Hull took the pulpit when the music ended. While everyone waited, he attached a small, cordless microphone to his lapel. His auburn hair never looked quite as ragged on Sunday mornings. He smiled at everyone with his entire face.

Just when he did, Braden touched his mother's arm. "Mom," he said, louder than a whisper. "There's something I have to do. I have to find out if it's okay."

"Sh-h-hhh." She narrowed her brows at him. "Not right now. Later."

"No, Mom." He shook his head. "Sam and I have to do this. This is the chance."

"The chance for what?"

Their conversation was disturbing others. Several people glanced in their direction. Abby leaned in close so he could whisper in her ear. And when he did, her fingers draped loosely over the pew in distrust.

During the past three days, they had all begun to know Samantha. If they had tried not to, she would not have given them that chance. "Do you want to know about me?" she'd asked Abby as they walked along the bank of Fish Creek looking for muskrats. "I just finished reading a book about Squanto. I like to French braid my hair, but only when my mom has time to help me. If I do it myself, it gets too messy."

"It's fun hearing about girl stuff," Abby had said. "Your hair."

"My favorite drink is Dr. Pepper and my favorite food is cotton candy. My favorite movie is *The Great Outdoors*. My mom bought me the video."

"What else?" Abby had asked. "Tell me."

"I always wanted a dog but, instead, I have a cat that's mellow."

"Mellow? Is he a calm cat?"

"No. That's his color. You know it. Kind of orange with stripes, and white yellow. Mellow." Then, a pause. "Do you ever wonder what heaven's like?"

"Yes," Abby said.

"Well," Samantha said. "Maybe I'm going to get to see it before you do."

*No.* Abby had faltered right then. She realized how tired this was making Sam, just walking along the creekside with them, searching for forget-me-nots and water animals. The little girl had gone pale from exhaustion and there were deep circles beneath her eyes. "Hey," Abby said. "We'll go back to the house. Call your mother to come over from the motel."

And now, this. We haven't arranged it. Nelson is already in the pulpit.

*Lord, is it you who wants this? Does this family have to be so . . . so transparent together?*

"Mom," Braden whispered again, his voice growing frantic. This time, he gripped Samantha's hand. "We want to do this."

*Oh Lord Oh Lord Oh Lord.*

If Abby searched for one spark of peace inside, she couldn't find it. She felt shaky, with nothing solid, nothing stable, to hold on to. Her heart ached with panic. Across the heads of the children, she sought David, even though they hadn't talked in weeks.

*If I could catch David's eye.*

But David was staring straight ahead, as lockjawed and undistractable as a soldier standing at attention.

"It might make a difference." Samantha, who was always braiding the fringe on things, was now braiding the straps on Abby's purse. "If you don't mind him doing it."

Abby stepped forward onto something that she didn't know would hold her. "Of course we'll do it. Of course it will make a difference. Wait here."

Loving in secret was one thing. Loving in public was another. As Abby sidled the length of the pew and came out into the aisle in front of a settled congregation, her fear did not dissipate. As she walked forward toward the altar and motioned for Nelson to hear her, Abby knew what she had to do to be right.

*This is what you're asking me for, isn't it? I've been hiding in a glass box all this time. I haven't wanted to let anybody else inside.*

Nelson Hull's voice came just a tad softer than usual when he said, "We're going to change the schedule around a little bit today. Something has come up. We've decided it would be appropriate to share this with the congregation."

Abby had just gone back to her seat. Everyone peered around to see who might be standing up next. Seconds passed. Congregants scrunched lower in their seats as if they were concerned Pastor Hull might call on them. Only Viola Uptergrove rose higher, pushing herself up on her walker as if she needed to take stock of every head.

For a moment, everyone thought Viola was the one going to say something. But she sat back down, too.

Nelson extended his hand. "Braden Treasure, will you come to the altar, please?"

Braden stood up and laid his picture of the warrior on his seat. Samantha rose beside him. Braden smiled and took Sam's hand, then led her sidelong into the aisle.

They got to the front of the church, climbed up the steps to the altar, and didn't know where to stand. Together, they sidestepped one way, and then the other. Nelson stooped low, murmured something, and braced Braden with a broad, firm hand behind the shoulders.

The pastor retrieved the microphone from its stand, checked to make sure it was on, and positioned the children to one side of the pulpit so their faces could be seen.

"Hi," Braden said into the microphone. His voice rang out loud. "I'm Braden Treasure."

An undertone moved through the audience. David sat back hard in his chair. Beside him, his wife's shoulders rose and fell. When she turned to meet his face, their look was long.

"Hi," Braden said again as he adjusted his weight from his left foot to his right one. "Lots of people just thought we had a friend visiting, but this is my sister, Samantha."

The whispering grew louder.

"I've just met her because she came to find us. She has leukemia."

Well, *that* made everybody hush.

Braden shifted the microphone from one hand to the other. "There's this place called a bone-marrow register and they know where people are all over the world. If somebody needs the kind you have, they find you and take it out of you and they fly it to the person who needs it in a plane. There isn't anybody registered who matches my sister, not even me."

While her son talked, Abby plopped her elbows on the pew in front of her and laid her forehead on her stacked hands. *Oh, Father*, she finally admitted, *it's been so dangerous to let myself care about Samantha. But I do. Oh, Lord, I do.*

"Samantha's mom tried all the places like that before she ever called our family. My dad doesn't match Sam, either, even though he's her dad, too. I've talked to everybody on my baseball team. But then I started thinking, well, this is *church*. I started thinking that, if you all will go to the hospital and get that test like I did, we'll be able to find somebody." Braden found his mom and dad in the rows on the left side of the sanctuary and looked directly at them. "We're all really sad, but things are better because we're together—"

David moved his hand from below his nose to his eye

sockets and, with his thumb and his forefinger, pinched hard.

Abby lifted her face and stared at the wooden cross at the front of the sanctuary.

"Do you want to say something, Sam?" Braden held out the microphone to his sister in front of them all. Samantha shook her head no.

"Come on. It's okay. You take it." He'd whispered, but the sound came over the loudspeakers.

That didn't leave her much choice. She *did* take it. She shot everyone a shy smile. "Hi," she said, and her own voice rang so loudly it made her jump. She regained her composure before she went on. "I'd just like to say that I'm glad I found this place."

⌒

Many people in the congregation that day began praying for them. Many people made decisions that moment to drive to St. John's and have a test. But only one person in the rows of seats prayed from a place of complete devotion. Only one prayed from a place where a wall had been broken down. She prayed as if her own life depended on what she gave that moment to the Lord.

And maybe, maybe, it did.

# Chapter Twenty-One

On Monday afternoon at the shelter, Sophie Henderson lugged her blue plastic trashcan toward the office, hugging it possessively against her chest. Her Dodge truck keys swung to and fro from her pinky finger on her favorite key chain, the skeletal-link fish. She paused in the middle of the courtyard and took one last look around.

She would miss Abby, but she honestly hoped she would never have to see this place again.

Sophie set the trashcan by the stoop. Before she went inside she bent to give the cat one last, long rub. Phoebe the cat curved low, dipping her vertebrae beneath Sophie's hand, curling her tail and pushing it as high as it would go.

That taken care of, Sophie gave the door handle a twist and bumped the door open with her hip.

She found Abby sitting at her desk, her fingers splayed on a stack of forms she must have been processing for a new client. She was staring sightlessly at a line of self-help books, the ones Sophie knew she trusted for a quick reference. Sophie watched her studying the spines of the books, the colors of the jackets, the embossed titles, before she began to thumb through forms again.

"Hey," Sophie whispered.

"You ready?" Abby asked, without pivoting in her chair.

"As ready as I'll ever be."

Abby tamped the papers on her desktop, aligning them in one perfect rectangle. Sophie touched her friend's arm with sadness.

Abby said, "It's not going to be the same without you, you know."

"Let's hope not."

"You know what I mean."

Sophie took a deep breath, deep enough to move her shoulders and sink all the way to her diaphragm. "Talking about going is a whole lot easier than really doing it."

"I checked out your truck. It's full of gas."

"Thank you."

"I had to put air in one of the tires. There are a couple quarts of oil in the back in case you need to top it off."

"I probably will."

They stood square and looked at each other, neither of them wanting this to be quite the last they said. "Oh, Soph—"

"Wish me luck."

"Luck. Prayers. Send me your address when you get settled. Or your e-mail so we can stay in touch."

"You'll have to give it to me."

Another quick scramble while Abby jotted it down. "There." And then, another hug.

"Thank you for everything. Words won't do this."

"Don't try."

"I mean it, Abby."

"It's okay, Soph. I know."

Sophie hurried down the steps and turned one last time to wave. The phone rang inside and Abby stepped back, shutting the front door so she could answer the call. Sophie bent, brandished the truck key to unlock the door, and found a scrap of paper stuck inside the truck handle. She unrolled it, and read.

*Oh, dear.* Not what she needed right now.

You are the apple of my eye,
the blue in every sky,
the—

Sophie wadded Mike's poem and shoved it inside her pocket. She wrestled with the key, opened the lock, and had just opened the truck door and pushed her belongings across the front seat when a rough hand clenched her arm.

"What's wrong?" Mike had come from nowhere. He must have been hiding in the bushes behind her. "Don't you like what I wrote?" His hand clamped around her elbow like a vice.

"S-sure," she said, hating herself because she stammered. "Sure I do. I'm just not in the mood—"

"You're going away, aren't you? I *knew* you were going somewhere. I saw the truck at the gas station a few hours ago."

"I'm just—"

"Just what? Leaving town?" His lip curled against his teeth. "I know you aren't going to Elaine's."

"No, I'm not going to Elaine's. I haven't even talked to her."

"She thinks you're wrong. I've got your sister on my side."

"What are you doing, Mike?" She wrenched her arm free. "Writing me poetry? Sending me flowers? Bringing me a wild *pheasant?*"

"You can't do this to us. I'm letting you know how I feel. That's what I'm doing."

"Mike, we can't ever have an argument of equals. You start out ahead every time because I know what you're going to do at the end. In the end, you always hit me."

She tried to climb up into the truck but he held her down by the arm. "How do you know what I do at the end? You're running away. You aren't even staying until the end."

"If you'd stop to count, you'd realize how many endings I've stayed around for." She tried to step up again, struggling against his grip. Mike's fingers tightened against her biceps. Her arm had gotten past the point of throbbing. She didn't feel the pain anymore.

"I have to go, Mike. It was a bad poem," she said. "It wasn't even any good."

She felt him go stiff beside her. She wrenched around and found him staring at her the way he always did when she knew she was in trouble. The wind had changed, and Sophie felt danger.

"Oh, Sophie Darling," he said, shaking his head and chiding. "Sophie . . . Sophie . . . Sophie."

"I'm leaving because I never can catch my breath with you. You keep me off guard." She kept on talking and talking, pressing it beyond her better judgment, beyond the point of caring. "I never know which one of you is coming in the door next."

"Well, why don't we try it and see?" This time, instead of yanking her down from the truck, he began to shove her up inside. "Get in," he ordered. "You're the one who wanted to drive away so badly. Just get in."

"Not with you." She felt herself being bodily lifted. "Not—"

But it was too late. He forced her across and climbed in beside her. The trashcan fell over. All her belongings toppled out onto the floor.

"Where's the keys?"

She bit her lip and shook her head, tears streaming down her face. "I don't want to."

"Sophie, give me the keys." He grabbed her and tried to wrench them out of her hand. She dug into him with her fingernails.

At that moment the front door to the shelter slammed open. Abby ran toward them across the yard, her cell phone in hand. "Sophie!" Mike saw her coming and banged the truck door shut.

"Mike, c'mon." Sophie pleaded with him. "Don't make this worse than it is."

"You can't abandon me, Soph. I won't let you."

Abby grabbed the door handle on the passenger's side and groped to open it. Like a mallet, Mike slapped the lock button down. "Let me have the keys."

It was a brave thing for Sophie to do. She hadn't denied her husband anything but herself in a long time. She'd been too smart. "No."

*Crack.* Mike slapped her hard with one huge, wide-open hand. Her head snapped against the window behind her.

Enormous pain, and things went black for a minute. She struggled upright again. Sophie curled the back of her hand against her mouth.

She circled the sides of her mouth with her tongue, probing for damage, feeling the raw cuts her own teeth had made in her gums. She tasted blood. With the flat of her other hand, she touched her eye. She'd probably have another black one.

Mike cursed in frustration. "Why do you make me do this?"

"Sophie," Abby called through the window, her voice a mixed tone of command and strength. "Open the door. Climb out."

"Leave us alone," Mike said.

"Come on, Sophie. You don't have to be here. Come with me."

Mike throttled Sophie's wrist and yanked her hair.

She cried out in pain. Through a dim fog of shock, she saw Abby moving around the truck's front fender, racing for Mike's door. He let Sophie go long enough to swivel in his seat and lock his door.

Sophie felt with blind hands, sorting through the belongings that had fallen to the floor. What was down here? Everything she'd brought with her, the day she'd run away. She tried to remember, and couldn't.

From the shadow beside her feet, she seized a canister and remembered her hair spray. With more courage than she'd ever summoned before, Sophie brandished the silver canister against him. EIGHTEEN-HOUR PROTECTION AND HOLD, the label read.

Mike pivoted toward her. Before he had a chance to yank the can away, Sophie sprayed the toxic aerosol fumes straight into his eyes.

He bellowed, clawing at his face.

Sophie launched herself past Mike's shoulder and unlocked the door.

Abby jerked open the door and jammed her cell phone against the back of Mike's neck. "Put your hands on the wheel," she growled. "Both of them. Let her go."

"What's back there?" he asked, panicking at the feel of something cold and blunt on his skin.

"Let her go," Abby said without missing a beat, "or I'll hurt you."

"All right. All right." How easily he gave in. Mike folded his hands over the steering wheel and laid his head atop his knuckles, as the two City-of-Jackson police cars rounded the corner, their blue-and-red lights swinging arcs against windowpanes and tree limbs. The sound of their sirens crescendoed, then abruptly cut, decrescendoing again to silence.

For a long time, Abby would remember the snapshot views of these next moments, these next hours.

Sophie staggering down from the truck, her face bruised and swollen, her upper lip dripping blood. Mike leaning his forehead against the truck beside the gas cap, his eyes downcast, his bangs sticking stiffly up from the coating of hairspray, wrists cuffed behind his hipbones, his jean legs straddled wide. The officers consulting among themselves as they loaded him up, congratulating one another on a completed mission.

Their last view as the police had driven off while she and Sophie waited hipbone to hipbone on the plank steps, their arms encircling their shins and their chins on their knees, had been a view of Mike's face through the squad car's rear window. There he sat secured behind some sort of a metal cage, his eyes wide and following Sophie as he passed, devoid of any emotion.

"He's going to have to wear one of those outfits," Sophie said after the cars and that haunting last view had gone. "One of those bright yellow ones that will make him look like a yield sign."

Abby waited a while, unwilling to leave Sophie alone, before she went into the shelter kitchen to get some ice. She dropped the cubes into a Ziploc baggie and folded it inside a washcloth. "Here." She handed it to Sophie. "This'll help with the swelling."

For a long time after Mike had gone, they heard only the sounds of siskins chittering in the pines above their heads and the click of ice in its little bag and the pounding of bass notes in the one car that went past. As Sophie stared out into the street where she'd run with Mike's roses, she began to quiver.

Abby touched her. "What's up? You okay?"

Sophie nodded and clamped her knees tighter together.

"I'll get you some water. You're shaking. Maybe that will help."

"No, don't leave." Sophie laid a hand on top of hers. "Stay with me. Everything's fine. I just get scared sometimes, feeling this much *relief*."

Abby reached for the cloth in Sophie's hand, refolded it around the ice. "You don't have to leave tonight. If you're too shook up after what he's done, you can wait until tomorrow."

Sophie gingerly reapplied the cold pack. "I'm doing it tonight. If I don't take the next step while I'm feeling this courageous, I might not take it at all."

Abby stared at an ant as it scurried past a crack on the sidewalk, and said nothing.

A second ant scurried along the cement, a third, a fourth, before Sophie spoke again. "Will you . . . Well, you know how you've been telling me about God's love and what it's done for Braden and Sam? How you said, 'God's love never fails'?"

Abby nodded.

"Well, what about me and Mike, Abby? How can you say God's love never failed for us? When I've waited so long for him to stop hitting me? And now, I'm leaving?"

*Oh, Lord. I can't answer that.* When Abby reached to enfold Sophie inside her arms, Sophie bent against her like someone starving. The top of her head pressed against Abby's chest as Abby spread her hand wide across the dip of her spine. They rocked to and fro, to and fro.

"Maybe God's perfect will would be to have two people seeking him together. But when there's one who doesn't . . ."

Abby struggled to find her own answers as she stopped the hug and took over the icepack to dab it against her friend's damaged face.

"All I know is this." She shrugged. "When you're the one who allows God to love the other person through you, you haven't any regrets when you look back. I think you can trust that with God. When you let him work through you, you are changed for the good even if the other person isn't."

*You were never wrong to trust Me, Abby. Even when you couldn't trust in people, you were right to trust in My love.*

*Oh, Father. If I understood your ways, I would tell her.*

*If I understood everything you wanted from me, maybe I could tell Sophie, too.*

"Oh, Soph. I don't know. I don't know." They hugged, rocked again. "Right now, I'm just learning to let people see my own heart."

# Chapter Twenty-Two

Susan had agreed to remain in the valley for one week to allow Samantha time to get to know her new family. After that, she would travel home to Oregon, to the care of her oncologist. For three days, the Treasures had kept David's daughter before her mother arrived. For six days more, Susan had stayed at the Elk Country Inn while Sam camped on the Treasures' floor in Braden's sleeping bag. A length of days that had changed everything in some respects and, in some respects, had changed nothing at all.

Many friends and church members had heard Braden's speech. They were quick to offer Abby a hug whenever they saw her. "This must be hard," they'd say. "But seeing Samantha and Braden the way they are, it's got to be worth it. And you and David still *together*."

"I just want to be real," Abby repeated every time. "I just want to stop pretending."

On Tuesday morning, Abby's mother phoned. "You need to know that Frank has heart arrhythmia," she said. "They did tests at the hospital and they're giving him medicine. He's going to be fine, but it really shook him up."

"Mom, I'm sorry."

"When you get the chance, would you send him a card or something? You know how he likes to get mail. He's blue. And he's always seen you as a daughter."

"I know that, Mom. I'll do something."

On Tuesday night, Samantha put ice cubes in Braden's baseball cleats, and Braden put ice cubes in Samantha's sleeping bag.

On Wednesday morning, they packed Braden up for the team trip to Newcastle and the Little League Wyoming Shoot-Out Baseball Tournament. Samantha stood with them in the Kmart parking lot at six A.M., teary-eyed because she didn't know when she'd next see her brother again, waving off the caravans of SUVs and cars, shoe polish words emblazoned across rear windows:

"Go Jackson All-Stars!"

"Baseball Rocks!"

"Win the Shoot-Out!"

Braden peered through the back window, through all those white words written on the Hubner's Landcruiser, waving, too.

On Wednesday night, two nights before Samantha and Susan would leave, Abby dreamed of Sophie. "What would you take if you had to leave your house and didn't have any time to plan?" Sophie kept asking over and over again until Abby wanted to shove her away. What would you take? What would you take? What would you take?

In the dream, Abby searched from room to room. She gathered her most precious possessions, piling one thing on top of another, until everything toppled out of her arms. Everything was too heavy, too large, too cumbersome to carry. Everyplace she tried to go, a dangerous presence preceded her.

She couldn't open the front door. Her feet wouldn't budge. Not until the door flung wide of its own accord and she stepped out into the moonlight did she realize what it was she'd managed to save.

The two most precious things in her possession.

Braden's Little League baseball trophy. And the comforter from their king-sized bed.

Abby's eyes popped open, her heart pounding, her pajamas rumpled high around her,.wet with sweat. She lay flat, wide-eyed, clutching the comforter to her neck. Night, as black as velvet, draped around her, in a room that felt vacant and strange. The only thing she could see, three tiny pools of light—the same phosphorescent green as a firefly—from the digital clock. Three-forty A.M.

The first thing she thought to reach for was David. But his side of the bed was empty, the way it had been empty for so many nights before. The pillow lay cold and unspoiled, the sheets unsullied, as creased and flawless as they'd been when she'd climbed in alone hours ago.

Unable to fall back asleep, she turned back the covers and padded to the window.

Out in the driveway, moonlight fell like finely powdered dust over the Suburban and the roof planes of the garage. A glitter-streak of pale white spilled through the tree limbs and lay like lace doilies on the grass. At the edge of the yard, the buck-railing and the little wooden sign that read: "The Treasures, 3475 Peaks View Drive," bulged with the shape of the logs, catching the illumination, a pencil drawing of shadow and light along the fence.

Abby squinted her eyes shut, then opened them again. She saw what she thought she'd seen in the shadows, a gentle, sad discovery. Two people stood together in the darkness of their driveway. Her husband, David. And Susan Roche.

Susan's jacket was draped over a lower rung of the fence. Abby could see the zipper, its ties and snaps etched in the meager starlight. She could just make out Susan's blonde hair, light enough to show blue in the midnight radiance.

The view of them together in the dark, as they must have stood so many years before, two figures tempting fate. Abby put her fingers to the bridge of her nose and pinched out the sight of them. When she pulled her hand away, they were still in the driveway, Susan's face upturned.

Abby watched as Susan reached toward him in the darkness and gripped his forearm.

Abby felt as empty as the mountains. This was *her* house, *her* territory, *her* child, *her* husband. Of course, there would be some explanation. Probably just papers to be signed or plans to be made, something a mother and father needed to do together for their child.

Probably just . . .

Probably just . . .

With all the uncertainty Abby might have felt at that moment, all the broken questions she might have asked, all the accusations she might have flung—What more do I have to do? Why do we keep returning to this? If you wanted to talk to her before she left, why couldn't you do it in the house?—were not what sat foremost in her mind.

Foremost in her mind, a memory. Two figures standing in a driveway in the dark, at a different house, thirty-five years ago.

*"Mom? Why were you and Dad in the driveway in the middle of the night?"*

*"What?"*

*"You were doing something out there. I saw you."*

*"The question is, why were you looking out the window at four in the morning, Abigail? You should have been asleep."*

*"I couldn't. I had a dream."*

*"What were you dreaming, sweet? Was it something that scared you?"*

*"Yes."*

*"What?"*

*"I heard you and Dad yelling at each other again. I didn't like it. It scared me."*

*"Maybe you weren't dreaming, Abigail. Maybe that yelling really did happen."*

Now, Abby dressed soundlessly, tugging on a pair of jeans and a turtleneck, closing the bedroom door with two hands against the jamb so it wouldn't click and awaken Sam. She carried her shoes to the front door.

*"He wouldn't leave us, would he, Mom? Yesterday I saw him packing his socks."*

*"Yesterday? You saw him packing things yesterday?"*

*"Yes."*

*"He must have planned this all week long."*

*"Planned what?"*

A thin, pursed line on her mother's lips. *"Leaving. Yes,*

*he's gone. Now you know. He doesn't want to live with us anymore."*

"Why?"

*The dishrag, going round and round in circles on the counter. "Who's to say?"*

Abby opened the front door with a squeak of hinges.

David saw her first, and turned. He gripped Susan's shoulder as if he wanted to protect her from this. "Abby—"

"What are you doing out here, David? What are you doing with *her*?"

Susan's forehead shone full and sallow in the unearthly light. She stepped away from David, even though he tried to hold her there. "We were talking—"

"Don't explain," David said to Susan. "We don't have anything to hide from Abby."

"We were talking about Sam's birth certificate," Susan said in their defense anyway. "I never put his name there. I wanted to find out if he wanted me to change that."

Abby said, her voice uncommonly steady, "She was touching you. What am I supposed to think?"

"Aren't we past this?" David asked. "Past the point of what you're supposed to think?" *We are past it. That's what Nelson's tried to show me.*

"I should go." Susan glanced from Abby to David, then back to Abby again. "I'm sorry."

"No, we aren't past this," Abby said. "That's something you owe me, David. We'll never pass the point where I won't be thinking."

Susan retrieved her jacket off the fence. "It's late. I'll see you both in the morning."

"We'll never be past the point where we're both here in spite of ourselves."

Susan's car had been parked behind the trees in the street. She left them and drove away, not turning the headlights on until she'd driven past the neighbor's yard. They both watched her go, the low beams two pin-points in the darkness, sweeping through the bottom limbs of the trees. Then, only starlight again, but David didn't move toward the house. The heavy stare of his eyes through the darkness showed that he resented her, that he'd hardened himself against her for interrupting them. The moment Abby saw his reaction, *she* resented *him*.

She asked, "You're out in the middle of the night, in the driveway, with a woman who used to be your mistress. How did you expect me to respond?"

"I didn't want her in the house again. You don't know what it does to me, seeing the two of you together. You should have trusted me, Abby."

"I'm trying to trust you. But I can't just . . . pull it out of a hat. You have to earn it."

"I've been trying to earn it for eight years, Abby."

"For yourself, maybe. Not for me."

"I have an entire lifetime of my little girl to catch up on. I don't know how else I'm supposed to do this."

She didn't turn to him. She hugged herself instead, tears coursing down her cheeks, while she saw a ghostly moonlight reflection of his face from behind her in the Suburban window.

"Ab." He reached for her, but she drew back. "You're a lot better than I am, Abby. Do you know that?"

"Don't say that."

"You think I don't know what I've put you through? Or that I don't care?"

"David, you broke something between us. I'm just trying to get by."

In confusion and sorrow, Abby saw a little girl's face suddenly peer through the front window, a hand drawing back the curtain, solemnly watching their exchange from behind a sidelong wash of light. Her breath caught. *Samantha.* A girl's face in the window that, once-upon-a-time, had been Abby's face.

"I can't do this," she said. "I just need to get away. So many people depending on you."

"Abby." Just as he took one step toward his wife, Samantha backed away from the window, disappearing into the vast, empty darkness of their house. In the moonlight, Abby watched his face go grim. "What did she see?" he asked. "What did she see? Did she see us fighting?"

*It's endless*, Abby thought. *Look what I've done.*

"You go in there," she said to David. "You go in to her and tell her it doesn't matter what she saw. That it wasn't what it looked like."

With one sad, solemn look, David went into the house, leaving Abby broken, clenching her fists at her sides, unclenching them, the chasm of helpless guilt growing broad inside of her.

~

The Treasure's house had many hiding places large enough to conceal a small girl and her sleeping bag. David checked the kitchen cabinet beside the massive sack of Brewster's dog food. He checked beneath the dining-room table where the chairs made a forest of wooden legs. In the family room, he checked behind the sofa and beneath the black Mendenhall grand piano where Braden used to play.

It wasn't until David heard a choked sob from the rear of the mudroom and followed the sound that he found the humped figure leaning against the wall, hidden behind the wicker basket where Braden kept his staggering collection of baseball mitts.

"Sam."

She sat folded like a fishhook inside the sleeping bag, with her hair hanging in clumps across her face. Beside her, the hot-water heater clicked on and seemed to sob with her. She stared at a baseball in the basket with a timer in it, a radar ball that gave a speed readout to indicate how fast it had been thrown. "She doesn't want me, does she?"

"No, Sam," he said. "It's *me* she doesn't want."

Sam's guileless face shone with her willingness to take the blame. "But, if I hadn't come . . ."

"I'm the one. I've made her hurt like this. It's my fault." He was being forced to face his own pride like layers of an onion being peeled away. How much of his apologizing had been acting, doing what he'd needed so he could get his own way with Abby?

At that moment, he heard the Suburban roaring to life.

"Dad, where's she going?"

"I don't know." How bittersweet, the first time Sam had actually called him the name he'd longed to hear for a week. *Dad.* He scooped his daughter, sleeping bag and all, into his arms. "We'll stop her. She ought not to be driving when she's this upset."

It took David precious seconds to punch the button and open the garage door. More precious seconds to load up, get seatbelts on, and fumble for the keys. He could see Abby's headlights turning out onto the highway by the time he backed out of the driveway.

*Come on, Abby. Don't endanger yourself. It doesn't matter what happens between us.*

By the time he turned onto the highway, she had disappeared around the broad curve, the cutaway bank above the South Park elk feed grounds. He pressed the accelerator to the floor, but by the time he had passed the feed grounds, she had disappeared completely across the Snake River Bridge, behind a stand of cottonwood trees that rose like plumes into the sky.

David checked the speedometer. Seventy already.

"How fast is she going?" Sam asked.

"Too fast."

*It's my pride that's done this. It's been so easy to take offense at her offense. I've even been proud that I haven't been proud.*

His speedometer had inched up past seventy-five on this winding two-lane highway and still he couldn't see her. When he crossed the bridge, the road became a straightaway and he caught a glimpse of her a good half mile ahead. *Abby, slow down. Slow down.* It was the time of night when the animals could be out—elk, deer, moose, even coyotes. In the direction they were headed, an entire herd of big-horned sheep grazed on a hill just above Highway 89. Just as he thought it, he saw her brake lights come on. He saw her swerve. He'd made her promise once that she'd never swerve on that road. And there she was. He'd seen her.

If he sped up to eighty, he could catch up. Wild-eyed,

Samantha clutched the door handle on the passenger side. As David pressed the accelerator to the floor, the panic started somewhere deep inside his own chest, smothering him.

*If she gets away now, I'm never going to see her again.*

The panic edged even higher. Where would she go? What would she do, on this road?

*If she gets away now,* he thought, panicking, *I'll lose her forever.*

The gentle nudging came inside of him, the quiet, surprising wisdom he had come to rely on during these past weeks.

Beloved, let her go.

The thought came with such clarity, David knew God whispered in his heart. *But if she gets away now, Father . . .*

Slow down. Let her get away.

The hum began in his ears, the pounding in his chest. How could he do this? What would he say to Abby, if she ever asked him why?

With sorrowful resignation, he eased his foot off the accelerator, and his breathing slowed. Okay. Okay. So, I let her go.

David steered the Suburban onto the shoulder and cut the engine.

~

The sun was just beginning to come up when Abby turned in off the highway to Horse Creek Station. She hid the car in a parking space behind a row of A-frame rental cabins. With one glance behind her, she scrabbled up the pathway between two rusty barrels where

the restaurant burned its trash, through a narrow vee between two boulders, out into a grove of aspen, tree
trunks silver-blue in the waxing light.

A fox crossed the forest floor in front of her, stopped,
and peered suspiciously in her direction. Abby leaned
her head against a tree trunk, staring at the colors of the
sunrise as they began to mount into the sky and stain
the hilltops. Only then did she sink to the ground, wrap
her arms around her middle, and finally let loose.

*Oh, Father. What is this? What is this awful thing in me?*

She held herself so tightly that her ribcage and her
shoulder blades ached, and she stared up into the leaf-
framed shapes of sky. She had expected David behind
her, but he hadn't come. For some reason, a weight fell
off her chest. This moment, this moment, she didn't
have to answer to him. She felt an odd sense of peace
with that.

*Why does blame get cast everywhere except where it be-
longs?*

In this place, where she was separate and alone and
alive, the leaves on the trees, the silence of the rocks,
seemed to whisper of what she had to do and why she'd
come here. Abby stood, brushed off the seat of her
pants, took a breath that expanded her stomach like a
balloon.

Yes. *Yes.*

Later, she would go back and find Samantha. They
would lower the steps to the attic together and climb up.
She would go to the unsealed cardboard box containing
a papier-mâché piggy bank with rhinestone nostrils, spi-
ral notebooks with pictures doodled in ink, old scribbled
notes that had been handed desk-to-desk during school
days, and a pink cardboard jewelry box. She'd lift the

jewelry box and run her palm over the top of it, brushing off a thick layer of dust. She would wink at Sam, find the little key on the back, and wind it up.

When she lifted the lid, there would be a dilapidated ballerina there, still leaning sideways from her long incarceration beneath the lid on her rusty spring. Even though her tiny tulle skirt had been eaten away by a moth years ago, the ballerina would begin to spin with one hand held high over her head. Ever so slowly, the old music box would begin to play "The Waltz of the Blue Danube."

"You have to understand why this has been so hard for me," she would say to Samantha. "You have to understand how I want you to have your dad because, after awhile, I didn't have mine."

She would pull the cotton out of the jewelry box and find the rabbit's foot that she'd hidden there, the black-and-white fur worn off the toes from too much rubbing. "A Souvenir of Yellowstone," the little tag would read. When Sam asked, "What is that?" Abby would say, "This is the last thing my dad ever gave me before he left my mom. It's really important that I give it to you. It's time I started giving things away instead of counting the cost."

Maybe later in the afternoon, she and Samantha could drive up to Moose, to the entrance to Grand Teton National Park and the little log Chapel of the Transfiguration. Maybe they could stand in the front gateway of the church and they could yank the chain on the bell and, after the sound clanged across the river and echoed back from the Cathedral Mountains and across Jenny Lake, she would say to Sam, "I heard once that forgiveness is like a bell. God's the one who makes the bell ring. But it doesn't stand a chance of making a sound if we're not willing to pull the rope."

Abby picked her way back down the trail, shivering. Even though it was mid-July, the temperature hovered around freezing this early in the day. She opened the Suburban door, checked the seat for the cell phone, and realized she hadn't pitched it in. Well, she'd have to do it the old-fashioned way and use the pay phone. She gathered up all the loose coins she could find in the cup holder, walked to the front porch of Horse Creek Station, and began to feed in coins. She stopped short once to check the sun. It would be okay. Baltimore was two hours ahead. It wouldn't be too early to call.

She dialed information for the 410 area code and asked for a listing for Charles Higgins. When the operator announced the number, Abby foraged through her purse for a paper and pen.

She found a pen in time to jot down the number on her arm. She hung up and stared at her hand for a long time before she fed in more quarters.

"Y-ullo?"

"Is . . . is . . ." She hated herself for her voice sounding so small. She cleared her throat and tried one more time. "Is Charlie Higgins there?"

"Who's this?" asked a male voice she didn't recognize.

"It's . . . well, it's Abigail Treasure."

"Who?"

"Could you . . . could you just get him? Please?"

A long wait in which she plunked down more money. Then, "Y'ullo?"

"Charlie?" she asked. A pause. "Dad?"

A drop in tone. "Who's this?" But of course, of course, he already had to know.

"It's Abigail."

Silence.

"I just . . . wanted to talk."

"Abigail?"

She clutched the receiver with both hands, hoping. "Yeah, it's me."

"Well, sheesh. It's been years."

"Yeah."

What could she say? She had never been a part of his life again, not really, after he'd gone away. He'd gotten married again, had a batch of kids she hardly knew, and for years she'd been the outsider.

"Well, what do you want?"

"I'm calling to apologize, Dad. To ask you to forgive me."

"What?"

"I'm calling to tell you how sorry I am."

"What for?"

"Maybe you weren't a very good father. Maybe you really hurt us. But I wasn't a very good daughter, either. I held a lot against you."

"Abigail."

"I should have done something. I should have phoned way before now."

"Well," he said quietly. "Isn't this something? Isn't this just something? You still got that crazy rabbit's foot I bought you that time?"

"I do," she said, the hollow in her heart growing to the size of the Bighorn Basin. "I've kept it a long time. I have somebody I've decided to give it to."

"Well, isn't that just something? Can't believe you've kept that thing all these years."

For the time being, there seemed nothing more to say. Abby waited. And, on the other end of the line, Charlie Higgins waited, too.

"Dad?" she asked just before she hung up. "Can we talk again sometime?"

"Sure we can," he said. "You want to give me a number?"

"You'll call me?"

"Sure."

"I'd like that."

She gave him the number. Then, just before she told him good-bye, she added one more thing. "I'm not out to prove I'm right with this. I just . . . well, I think it's worth working toward something. Not deciding who's right and wrong. Just . . . finding out who we still are with each other."

"Yes," Charlie Higgins said. "Yes."

She hung up and saw that the sun had topped the trees. A beautiful thought came to mind as she turned the key in the Suburban and then inched out onto the road toward Hoback Junction.

You've been going through a desert, beloved one. I've been watching you journey for a long time. It won't be much longer before you get to the water.

*Will I? Father, it hurts so much to even hope.*

She signaled to the right, turned toward home.

# Chapter Twenty-Three

"Oh, David." He could tell she was self-conscious when she walked back inside their door. If she hadn't been, she would have dropped her purse on the couch and knuckled away those first tears.

"Ab. You're back." David's words held the weight of the world in them.

"Yeah, I'm back." Then, "You won't believe it. After seventeen years, I called my dad."

He stared at her, thinking how something subtle was changing, something he didn't understand. "Ab, are you nuts? When?"

"At Horse Creek. I stayed there for a while."

"I know."

"I'm sorry."

"It's okay."

"Where's Sam?"

"Asleep. Last night was a little rough on her." He took a step forward. "Maybe a little rough on you, too."

"It's been seventeen years since I've talked to him," Abby said again.

"I know that."

"We're going to talk some more later. I gave him the number."

"You think he'll use it?"

"Maybe. Maybe it'll be a start."

"Are you going to tell your mother?"

"I don't know."

David stood across the room from her, the sunlight streaming in the window. Across the living room, it dusted the folds of the afghan strewn across the ottoman and lay in a rectangle upon the floor.

"I think . . . I—I mean . . . I don't . . ."

"Abby, what is it? What's wrong?"

She stared at him as if she was seeing him for the first time. "David, when we first got married, I didn't trust anything. I said I did. I wanted to. But wanting to do it and doing it are two very different things."

"I'm sorry about your dad, Ab."

"What I'm trying to say . . . what I'm trying to say . . . I think I closed you out when I was preg- . . . pregnant. Because, with what happened with Dad, and all the responsibility of a baby, I was just so scared."

"I know that's been really tough."

"What I'm trying to say is . . . when you started reaching out to Susan, I think that happened because of me."

"Look," he said, wanting to shake her. "Look. It wasn't you."

Her shoulders shuddered with her gasping breath. He watched her fight her own grieving down in silence. She turned fully toward him, shivering even though it wasn't cold. Her face, her entire silhouette, was nothing more than shadow to him against the sun. "I don't know why, but I'm not seeing what *you* did anymore, David. God's showing me things in *myself*."

⌒

Braden Treasure began praying for his sister, Samantha, on the day that the Jackson Hole All-Star Little Leaguers brought home the state championship trophy. He prayed the day his mother came home with an X of white medical tape crisscrossing a cotton-ball in the crook of her arm.

"What'd you do, Mom?" he'd asked, readjusting his Elk's baseball cap to one side of his head.

"You know what I did, Brade," she told him. "Something I should have done at the same time you did yours."

He touched the bandage. "Did it hurt?"

"Only for a second. That's all."

Braden kept praying. And this morning, while Braden watched his dad hold the telephone receiver against his ear with both hands, sounding concerned, he prayed the hardest of all.

"Yes? *Yes* . . . I see . . . A week. Not much time, then? . . . We'll be there. She would *want* us to be there. We'll get a motel in Portland."

Braden stood holding his mom's hand with his heart poised in his throat. David hung up the phone and turned to them. "We've got to pack our bags," he said somberly. "We're making a trip to Oregon."

"David. Tell us."

"Dad, what is it? Is she okay?"

Braden's dad smiled. With one hand, he clamped down hard on Braden's shoulder. "It's good news, sport.

They've found a transplant. Almost an identical match."

"What?!" Abby shrieked. Braden couldn't keep from leaping up and down. Brewster barked the way he always did when his family got this rowdy. Braden saw his dad staring gratefully out the window, up toward the summit of the mountain.

———

"Will it work, Dad?" Braden must have asked a hundred times while they drove west on the highway, through American Falls and Meridian, the four-lane winding down deep, curvy plateau edges as they headed toward Pendleton. "Do they know it's going to help?"

"They think it'll help. They can't be sure," David answered. Braden didn't know what to do to make the time go faster. He counted mile markers as they disappeared along the pavement.

Road-worn and travel-weary, they all helped read the maps and point out the street signs to help David find the way in Portland. They got stuck on the wrong interstate going the wrong direction at least two different times.

When they got to Sam's room in the hospital, they had to put on masks. "Can you believe it?" she asked. In her hand, she was holding the old dusty rabbit's foot his mother had given her. When she hugged their father, Braden noticed she had tears in her eyes.

During the entire process, things changed and got harder every day. Braden stayed with his sister, talking and waiting, finding things to do with Sam for as long as they would let him. He brought her a Slinky and some Silly Putty.

He got into trouble for the Silly Putty because it stuck to the bed.

On the opposite wall from Sam's pillow, Dr. Riniker hung a chalkboard where nurses wrote down numbers after the doctor tested her blood. "You're doing a good job," Braden heard him say to Sam one day after she'd stopped feeling very good. "I know the chemo's tough, little one."

"It's okay," she said. "My brother's here."

While Sam lay there, her brown hair, which he'd liked so much in her pictures, fell out in big clumps.

For a few days after they arrived in Portland, Sam's room seemed like a party. Friends stopped in to visit. Get-Well cards lined an entire wall. Flowers topped every surface and bouquets of balloons bobbed beside the bed. But then, as time passed, things had gotten quiet. The green, pink, and purple lines on the Hewlett Packard monitor moved in mesmerizing waves. Occasionally, when a beeper went off, a nurse would rush in and adjust a setting on Sam's oxygen.

Braden knew, without anybody telling him, that this had become very frightening and serious.

Dr. Riniker measured Sam's blood early on Tuesday morning. He scribbled figures on the chart, and the nurse erased the numbers on the chalkboard and wrote, "Red-.01. White-.01."

His sister didn't wake up that morning to play tic-tac-toe with him or to make the funny, bare rabbit's foot of his mother's scamper without its body across the blanket. She kept sleeping all day.

"She's almost down to zero," Braden overheard a

nurse say to Sam's mother. "What's done is done now. There's nothing left to do. Only time will tell."

And Braden kept praying.

—

As the hours progressed for Samantha, Abby watched Susan forget that anyone else was in the room. She only left when she needed to remove her mask. Sam's immunities were so low from the chemo, the doctor made those who entered keep their faces covered.

Abby watched Susan go without meals because she didn't want to leave her child.

She listened as Susan sat close beside her daughter's head against the pillow, not knowing whether she could hear or not, while she sang "Day O" through her mask just like Harry Belafonte.

Abby watched while Susan swept her hand across the dome of her daughter's head as gently as if she was rearranging downy fuzz on a baby's head, making herself remember, as if she had sculpted the smooth shape of it herself.

As days passed, Susan stood at her daughter's bedside, more isolated and friendless than anybody Abby had ever seen. "It was an anonymous donor," she said aloud once, even though she'd never glanced in their direction. "We don't even know where it came from. Maybe Jackson Hole."

"You'll never know, will you?"

"Probably not." Another stroke on Sam's head. Another, while she read Sam's sleeping face. "We'll always be so grateful." Then, with eyes raised to David, "What if she doesn't survive this?"

"I don't know. I just keep praying—"

"It's an awful thing to watch her body go through," Susan said, her voice twisting with pain.

When Abby turned toward David, his entire stature registered the same shock and sadness as Susan's.

Abby watched him glancing at Samantha's still face whenever he thought nobody saw him.

She watched him sit down and stand up, sit down and stand up, desperate to do something that no one could do.

Whenever a nurse or an orderly entered the room, Abby saw David hoping someone might be able to tell him something.

"Hey," he said to Abby as she brushed against him, reaching for the water pitcher on the nightstand beside the bed. "Those pants make you look like Julia Roberts."

Abby straightened, the pitcher in her hand. "You like these?"

"Yeah, I do."

Across the room, Susan lifted one of the slats on the window blinds and bent to peer out. Abby and David's gazes locked. She remembered something Viola Uptergrove had told her once. Hardest thing you'll ever do, being a Christian, Viola had said, is to keep believing in believing. You've got to expect things from Jesus, and then start looking for them.

Abby followed David's gaze across the hospital room, saw him watching Susan, and felt a sense of rightness. She wrapped both hands around her husband's arm so he'd know she was sure. "If you want to hold her during some of this, I'll understand," she whispered. "She's so alone. I think she needs you."

"Ab?" he whispered a question.

"I know what we're working toward, David," she said without a doubt in her voice. "I know I'm your wife. I also know that Susan will always be Samantha's mother."

"Abby," he said with the depths of his soul in his eyes. "Thank you."

⌒

The bag of marrow for Samantha was brought in almost as unceremoniously as a rack of ribs into a smokehouse. "Here it is." Dr. Riniker hitched it up on an IV stand and let it swing there, a long narrow baggie with rich, red thickness inside. He attached it to a port that had been in Sam's chest since they arrived. "The gift. It drips in like this. And it's amazing; this stuff finds its own way into the depth of the bones."

"How long will it take before we know anything?" David asked.

"A few days," the doctor said. "It'll take hours for this to drip in. Tomorrow we'll start with the blood markers again. If those numbers go up, we'll count it a success."

Braden stood by his sister's bedside for the next few days and watched Samantha struggle. There were good days and bad days, victories and defeats. There were days when Sam was smiling even though she was too weak to raise her head. There was a day of fever, when nurses brought ice in and put it on her and her mother, Susan, cried.

Always, always there was the chalkboard. Every day

Dr. Riniker would check Sam's blood and the nurses would write the numbers on the board. It got to where Braden couldn't understand their words anymore; he could only understand the numbers. Every day, the nurse would write "Red-0. White-0." and he would know that nothing had changed. Every day, he would wait for the board to be erased, and he would try to guess at the numbers before she wrote them down.

But it was always the same. Zero. Always zero. Until, one day, when Dr. Riniker smiled. He gave the nurse his papers and she picked up the chalk for the board.

*Our Father, who art in heaven*, Braden prayed. *Please. Take care of my sister.*

The nurse wrote, "Red-.03. White-1."

For a long time, everybody stared at what she'd written. Another nurse said, "Well, that's interesting. The markers have started to climb."

Dr. Riniker stood back and crossed his arms over his chest with pleasure. "That's progress," he said. "That's certainly progress."

Samantha's mother wiped away tears. Braden's dad scrubbed his eyes with his fingers. Braden's mom sat down hard in a plastic chair beside the bed.

"I'm pleased," Dr. Riniker said. "She's moving in the right direction."

Braden stood beside the bed where he thought nobody could see him. He wanted to cry and laugh all at the same time.

"Hey, sport. Come over here with me." His dad gestured and slapped his knee.

Braden climbed into his father's lap with pleasure, and they held on to each other for a while. "I love you, son," his dad whispered.

Then, unable to contain their emotion, they started wrestling and knuckling each other's hair until they couldn't stop laughing, and both of their heads looked like Don King.

# Chapter Twenty-Four

Samantha Roche, standing four-feet-four with her toes curled deep into the sand, and healthier than she'd been in eighteen months, gave her brother Braden—who hadn't seen the ocean during his entire life—a tour of her favorite place. Even though jewel-sun mornings can be rare on the Oregon coast, today the light glittered on the swells and dips of the water. The sky was crisp and broad and glorious with blue, a gift from a heavenly Father who delighted in the treasure of his children, both the young ones and the grownups, who had sought him even though it hadn't always been easy or felt right, and were letting him prove himself faithful.

Gray gulls sailed overhead, dipping deep into the air as if they were attached to riggings, their bowed broad wings bearing them aloft like kites. Gulls began to zoom in for a landing beside Sam and Braden. One came, then another, a dozen, maybe two, screeching with greed and beating hard at the air as they alighted, side-stepping, their alert eyes on the little sack beside Sam's leg.

A MORNING LIKE THIS

"No fair," Braden whispered to her. "You're baiting them with fries."

"Sh-hhh," Sam whispered back. "I know what works. McDonald's."

"You're bribing the birds."

"Yep, I am. This is how it's done. You ready?" Sam asked.

"Yeah," Braden whispered.

The two children raised themselves on their haunches, then sat as still as driftwood while seagulls continued to descend. Birds landed beside their knees and behind their backs and upon gnarled roots that protruded from beach sand like bent elbows. They landed on rocks and limbs and water-glossed sand. They didn't stop touching down until Sam and Braden launched themselves in unspoken agreement, springing from their places like they were springing from a starting block, sand flying from their feet. They parted that huge gathering of seabirds like Moses, with God's help, parting the Red Sea.

Braden flapped his arms at them. "Go! Go! Fly! Fly!"

Samantha leaned her head back, her hair streaming in the wind, her mouth wide with joy.

An unfathomable number of birds took flight, emitting screeches of terror and complaint, wheeling away, circling over the breakers, rising higher.

"Ah! You're killing me." Braden held his ears against his sister's screams.

Of course no beach scene like this one can be complete without a sandcastle. So, while the children were occupied chasing birds, Abigail Treasure took it upon herself to scoop a trough out of wet sand beside the weathered log where she sat. She worked a good while, digging deep, using a McDonald's soda cup to shape and stack turrets one upon another. So absorbed was she by her task that she only stopped once to tuck a strand of stray hair behind her ear.

Little by little, the surf inched closer to her creation. Little by little, water encroached. When Abby least expected it, a shallow, gentle wave dashed itself over the edge of the moat she'd built, and filled the hollow. The castle settled into the moat, its foundation receding. The next wave would take it down.

David, who'd been running along the beach in his Nikes, stopped behind his wife, silently surveying her handiwork. "It's going to fall in," he said, sounding tentative, as if he still didn't know how he ought to approach this woman sometimes. "Let me move it."

"You can't move sand," Abby said. "It siphons through your fingers and then it's gone."

"Okay," he said. "But it's a shame to lose all you're building."

"Yeah." Abby stared at it as another wave washed in. "It's tough."

David knelt and began to dig the same shape in a different place. "Look. We'll do it here. This is better. It's solid ground."

She hung back a moment, saying nothing, staring at his digging hands. Then, "Okay." She whispered it again, with emphasis. "*Okay.*"

The only sound as they worked, for the longest time, was the froth of the waves, the cries of the gulls, Braden and Sam laughing down the way. With seashells, Abby created a tiny fence around the edges, scalloped with the soft pinks and purples and peaches of the sea. David laid out a tiny slab of driftwood, worn smooth, for a bridge.

The children joined them once, bringing over a collection of seagull feathers to jab into the tops of the towers and use as flags. Then as quickly as they had come, they disappeared again.

Abby focused on her fingers and the trails she was carving in the sand, suddenly realizing that her breath wouldn't sink deep enough into her lungs. Did she want this man beside her? Her hands froze with awkwardness. Doubt and hope, all Abby knew, rolled in on her like waves from opposite directions, slapping together on the shore. She sat so close to him that his sandy elbows and his sandy knees brushed hers when they moved, and Abby became keenly conscious of that slight contact.

David straightened, picked up the hand on which he had been bracing himself, and pitched a stone from his digging into the surf. "Abby." She began to scrub a hole in the sand with a seashell. When he leaned forward to see her face, her eyes were full of hope. Brief and questioning, his gaze touched hers and then went far out over the ocean. "We've got a lot of work ahead of us, don't we?"

She kept scrubbing, scrubbing. "If I had to pick," she spoke at last to the sea, "I'd fall in love with the man you are now, David. Not with the man you used to be."

"We go *forward*," he said, "instead of backward."

"I think so."

"To have and to hold," David recited. "From this day forward."

"From this day forward," she echoed. "I like that. From this *morning* forward."

"It's a beautiful morning, isn't it?"

"Yes."

Abby remembered the gift Sophie had once said she'd give. *If I could, I'd give you a morning. I think it's the morning times that change our lives, Abby. The times we give ourselves permission to start fresh.*

"I'm willing, Abby, if you are."

"When would we start?"

"Maybe we already have."

It was a fragile beginning. They had hope, but no guarantees. They had the goodness of the Lord, but that didn't mean they'd always be comfortable.

A long-billed curlew came stalking past on tiny knobby knees, piercing the sand like a needle with its beak. Four brown pelicans skimmed the waves in formation, inches above the water. Abby whispered, her voice breaking, "I miss you, David. I've missed you for a long time."

He turned to her; he barely swiped her nose with his thumb. "I've missed you, too."

They sat together through one long silence. Today, beside the ocean, they wouldn't hold hands. But sometime in the not-too-distant future, they'd be willing to touch and to need and to depend on each other. Today, as the Treasures watched, a brother and sister raced the width of the ocean, still discovering, waves splashing in and sliding out, gilding the beach with silver.

# Author's Note

My husband and I met each other after I had moved into his room. Not one to rest long on square footage that can be used as an asset, Jack's mother had turned his apartment into a rental property within three months after Jack joined the U.S. Coast Guard.

So, I moved in. And then Jack returned.

We both give the cat full credit for our romance. When I was gone, Jack would come downstairs and take my cat so I had to come get her when I came home from the newspaper office. When I was in my apartment, I would turn the cat loose so Jack would have a reason to bring it down. The poor cat, Puffin, lived to be over thirteen years old. It's a surprise she had any legs left when she finally departed from us.

Every marriage starts with fun stories like this one, and with a lot of hope.

*A Morning Like This* is a composite story of one friend's very real, very difficult, marriage. As Christians we often make the human commitment to grit our teeth in a relationship and get by. This story began as a simple cry from a friend's heart after an hour of walking by the river. "I don't want to just survive in my marriage," she said. "I wanted to be in love. I wanted to feel passionate towards my husband. Don't I have a right to ever expect that?" And so began, in my own heart, the story of David and Abby Treasure, Braden and Samantha. This story became a journey, a responsibility, a burden, and a joy. It became, in the end, about much more than God's healing a marriage. It became a story about understanding the depth and the truth and the character of God's love.

I believe the mistake we make as we walk with Christ is that we forget to expect the full goodness, the full miracle, of what a loving God, handed our trusting heart and our greatest sacrifices, can do with our marriages and with our lives. There is, I believe, a beautiful straight-arrow place that exists when we both trust our Father with the reality and the expectation of our lives.

We need to shout to the world that we don't settle for second-best when we settle for God. Trusting him *can* mean waiting and watching when we're stuck in a place where we think we'll never find enthusiasm or ardor again. But what he gives us, when we'll only trust him with frank and transparent hearts, far surpasses anything we could ever have imagined for ourselves.

May God's love bring its sunrise of passion into your life!

Deborah Bedford
www.deborahbedfordbooks.com
P.O. Box 9175
Jackson Hole, Wyoming 83001

# Suggested Reading

The author recommends these books to couples seeking
help in restoring their marriages:

*Why Should I Be First To Change?*
Nancy Missler
Koinonia House Publishers

*Reconcilable Differences*
Andrew Christensen, Ph.D., and Neil S. Jacobsen,
Ph.D.
Guilford Press

*Getting The Love You Want, A Guide For Couples*
Harville Hendrix, Ph.D.
Harper Perennial

*Boundaries For Marriage*
Dr. Henry Cloud and Dr. John Townsend
Zondervan Publishing House

*Men Are From Mars, Women Are From Venus, a Practical Guide for Improving Communication and Getting What You Want in Your Relationships*
John Gray, Ph.D.
HarperCollins Publishers

*The Language of Love*
Gary Smalley and John Trent, Ph.D.
Focus on the Family Publishing

# DON'T MISS . . .
## *A ROSE BY THE DOOR*
### by Deborah Bedford

Every summer visitors come to Bea Bartling's home in Ash Hollow, Nebraska, to see the historic yellow rosebush that served as a famous trail marker for wagons on their way out West. And every night Bea prays she will find a special face among those at her door. Then Bea gets the crushing news that the son who ran away years before has been killed. Overwhelmed by grief—and a bitterness as hard as steel—she has no welcome in her heart for the woman and child who soon show up at her door . . . and no room for them in her life. Yet their arrival changes everything. Now, as old secrets are revealed, a lonely woman discovers a prodigal son may still come home if she accepts a precious gift of grace—and if she dares to believe in the miraculous power of love.

ও

"This emotionally intense story of a mother's heartbreak will inspire readers with its message of hope and healing through the power of love."

*—CBA Marketplace*